I0586820

The Pursuit
of the
Unicorn

Book Four

Of the

Renaissance Sojourner Series

Kristin Gleeson

An Tig Beag Press

Other works by Kristin Gleeson:

In Praise of the Bees
CELTIC KNOT SERIES
Along the Far Shores
Raven Brought the Light
Selkie Dreams
A Treasure Beyond Worth (novelette)

RENAISSANCE SOJOURNER SERIES

A Trick of Fate (novelette)
The Imp of Eye (With Moonyeen Blakey)
The Sea of Travail
The Quest of Hope

HIGHLAND BALLAD SERIES
The Hostage of Glenorchy
The Mists of Glen Strae
The Braes of Huntly

NON FICTION
Anahareo: A Wilderness Spirit
Listen to the music inspiring the work:
www.kristingleeson.com/music

Sign up to my mailing list and get
FREE *A Treasure Beyond Worth* and *Along the Far Shores*
www.kristingleeson.com.

ISBN:
978-0-9956281-3-7

To my wonderful Alpha Team

CHAPTER ONE
VENICE, WINTER 1447
BARNABAS

A tense hush fell over the inn where moments ago shouts had filled the air. Candles sputtered in the draughts from the ill-fitting windows and doors, adding more smoke to the fug of the room. Carefully, Tomaso the monkey crept up on the empty chair provided and placed the small brimful cup of wine on Pietro's head. It wobbled a moment, eliciting a few gasps from the crowd, but Tomaso steadied it and it settled in place. Tomaso looked over at me. I grinned and nodded and he gave a pleased squeal and clambered down from the chair and onto my lap.

A roaring cheer went up and Pietro, laughing hard, pulled the wine cup from his head, spilling nearly all of its contents on his long, dark curls. Niccolo, Marco, Antonio as well as Vito and Polo, my other friends from my early days of Venice, all clapped each other on the back.

"Pay up," I said. I stroked Tomaso underneath his small red collar and set him down.

"Oh, but Giacomo, no," said Pietro. He scraped back curls from his face and gave a mock pout. "You never mentioned that it was the best Venetian wine in the cup. No living being would dare spill a drop of that!"

I pretended a hearty laugh to answer his jibe. It still felt strange to be called Giacomo after the return journey from Africa, when the only three who knew me were those who knew my true name, Barnabas. Now, back in Venice, I had taken up my old disguise. I was Giacomo the scholar, the trader and sometime lothario who would seize any opportunity for adventure and profit. It was a guise that didn't always sit well with me and seemed far from the truth, but now I must play it to its full.

"You seemed to have little enough care when you took it off of your head, Pietro," I said. I held out my hand, my manner good natured. "Now, stop prevaricating."

"Oh, and now we have the big words. I guess there is no choice, then." Pietro gave a dramatic sigh, reached inside his doublet and pulled out a small purse and threw it on the table.

"*Mille grazi, amico,*" I said. I scooped up the bag and threw it from hand to hand. "An admirable weight. I think such a weight can stand my good friends another round of drinks."

Shouts of approval sounded and I gestured to the owner. It wasn't long before the cups were refilled and the drinking resumed.

Beside me, bold and brash as always, Niccolo nudged my arm and nodded to Pietro. "That is the best way to get him to pay for a drink. Well done, Giacomo. Your monkey is as clever as you."

I gave a mock bow of thanks. "Ah, but it is I who taught Tomaso."

"Does he play cards too?" asked Marco.

"Ah surely not," says Pietro. "Haven't I lost enough of my money to the other Tomaso?"

I suppressed the tension that surged in me at the mention of Tomaso's name. It was what I had come for, what I had hoped I might hear, beside the welcome opportunity to acquire some money.

"He's still gaming? I asked casually.

Niccolo and the others all looked at Pietro, who shrugged his shoulders. "I know not."

Marco glanced nervously at me. I felt the tension of the others. "Did I hear that he went off with Alessandra?" he said in a doubtful whisper.

I forced an offhand laugh. I knew this already, but I hoped to learn more. "Those two have gone off together? Can you imagine Tomaso keeping Alessandra entertained? Why, he wouldn't last past Rome before she would send him packing."

The group laughed, perhaps a little too long, but the tension had evaporated. They all knew Alessandra had gone and they wondered about the circumstances. None heard that she'd taken all the money the two of us had earned through trading before my trip to Africa. Taken that and my life with it. And even more importantly, Alys's child. I corrected myself. Our child.

"Nay, not Rome, I hear, but a sea voyage somewhere eastward," said Polo.

"In that case, she will dump him in the sea!" I declared and raised my cup. "To Tomaso, may he learn to swim with the fish."

The others raised their cups and banged them against one another, the metallic clank ringing through the room. We were silent for a moment, allowing for a deep drink and then we slammed the cups down on the table in satisfaction.

"What ventures will she get up to in the East? Surely she knows courtesans wouldn't be welcomed in that direction. The customs are different."

"Perhaps she means to trade something else," said Pietro. "I think I heard she might have taken some cloth and possibly some spices with her."

"Spices? But surely she would be better served to go north with spices. There would be many trading their spices eastward."

Pietro shrugged. "It probably isn't true. She's probably gone north with spices, or eastward with some other goods."

"Women! She's gone with women," said Vito.

"She's gone to join a harem. Then she wouldn't have to worry about wearing veils," said Polo. He nudged his brother Vito and guffawed.

Marco laughed nervously and the others joined in.

I forced a grin. "Such wit as I have seen here would stun the best minds of Padua."

The door opened and a figure came in with a gust of wind. I strained to see who it was and recognised the broad frame. Hal, Alys's brother.

Hal raised his hand. "Jacko."

I waved him over and he approached the table, greeting the men gathered there. They returned the greeting with nods and raised cups.

"Come, join us," I said and searched his face for clues to his sudden appearance here. Hal had known what I was about at the inn and wouldn't have bothered me unless it was important.

He bowed briefly. "Ah, but I can't, Jacko" he said in his awkward Italian. "I've come to fetch you. There's a visitor back at the rooms who seeks word with you about some goods. He says he cannot wait."

I looked around at my companions and raised my hands as if to acknowledge a defeat. "I'm afraid my pleasure must end, *amicos*. Business calls now."

I rose amid strong protests, straightened my doublet and looked down at Tomaso. Seeing the little nod, he leaped up into my arm and then perched on my shoulder. I bade my companions farewell and made my way out of the inn, Hal following.

The light was fading and the damp air drifting off the canal made us tug our cloaks closer. Along the street, people huddled and walked quickly. There were few enough barchettas on the water and the gondolas were even fewer in number. A misty rain was beginning to fall and everyone knew it would soon turn heavier. The grey light combined with the damp made the worn, older buildings that clustered closely in this crowded area of the city loom overhead, the mould and stains at their foundations only adding to it. It wasn't the best area of Venice, being too close to the Arsenale, but I'd had no choice, given that my companions favoured such inns of questionable reputation.

When we had walked sufficient distance that I was certain we wouldn't be overheard I turned to Hal. "What trader is this that's looking for me?"

Hal sighed and gave me a pitiful look. "'T'is not a trader," he said in English. "'T'is Alys. She's terrible distraught. She says she can't wait any longer. She'll go to the Doge and demand that 'e send soldiers after Alessandra. I thought it best to fetch you. The Lord knows I can't reason with her, though she be my sister."

I patted Hal on the back and gave a rueful laugh. "You were right to do so. I can imagine what it was like for you to try." I sighed and pushed on ahead back to our quarters, with the reassuring weight of the small purse at my side. It was something to start with. But to start where? East or north?

❦

I walked up the stairs to the rooms we'd hired only a few weeks before in one of the newly built homes on the old foundry site of the city. I tapped on the door once, and finding it unlocked, I opened it and went in. Alys sat pale-faced in a chair, gazing out of the window, searching the street below. Joanie, her childhood friend and staunch companion through all that she'd endured, stood beside her, a hand on Alys's shoulder.

Alys's russet gold hair, burnished by the light that shone through the window, hung loose, unattended. Her gown, sun faded and salt stained, draped her frame looser than I would have liked. Though she had only the gowns she'd taken to Africa, and those now much the worse for the trials of the journey, I wondered if she would have bothered to change her gown even if there was a sumptuous one to hand.

"Alys," I said softly.

She turned at her name and I saw that her eyes, at one moment dull and lacklustre, suddenly sparked fire. On a silent signal Hal and Joanie slipped from the room.

"So, you are back from your foolish carousing. I am glad, sir, that you have been able to amuse yourself, for I have not. There has not been a moment's amusement for me since my arrival."

I winced at the bitter tone and let Tomaso down to the floor. His cage stood to one corner, but I left him free and he scampered to Alys and leapt into her lap. Her angry expression eased and I moved forward and placed a hand on her shoulder.

"It's not for amusement that I haunt the inns and seek companions for gaming," I said gently.

She looked up at me and her eyes grew hard. "Perhaps not, but nothing has come of any of your attempts to find information. What precious funds we have are wasted and poor Tomaso is made to caper in a manner that will teach him bad habits."

"Nay, I'm very careful about Tomaso." At least I tried to be. My efforts couldn't always account for Tomaso's inclination to devilry.

"Well, have your efforts borne fruit this time?" she said. She couldn't keep the hint of optimism from her voice.

I forced a smile and tried for a light tone. "I have discovered that my old friends are, if nothing, more given to drink, women and gaming than before."

"So, in other words, nothing. You have discovered nothing of help to find Eleanor."

"That's not entirely true." I toyed with putting some hope into the scant bit of information I had gleaned.

Alys stared at me intently. "What? What have you learned?"

My smile faltered. "Something. A little. A clue, perhaps."

She narrowed her eyes, the brief light in them already gone. "What clue?"

"Well, they think Alessandra had spices with her to sell. And she might have gone north or east. Now if it's spices she had, that could only mean she went north."

Alys raised her brows. "Is that it? Your precious clue is that she *may* have had spices with her and therefore she *may* have gone north? What are we waiting for? We must leave at once for somewhere north of here."

Her tone was mocking and bitter and I tried not to wince at it. I knew behind the tone was an immeasurable despair. "There are few enough places north that she would trade such things and she would be remarked upon. It wouldn't be difficult to find her."

Alys snorted. "So easy that we've had no real information on her direction these past weeks. Nothing." She studied her hands. "We should write to the Doge. He can inquire and send soldiers to retrieve Eleanor." Her voice was thin, the words forced out.

I bent down before her and took her hands in mine. "Alys, beloved. There are a thousand and one reasons why we cannot write to the Doge. In his eyes it would seem to be a dispute between two courtesans."

"But all of Venice thinks the child is Cosimo Fabriano's."

"But he didn't officially recognise Eleanor," I said. I took a deep breath. "And I would prefer the world to know the truth, in that respect."

She looked up at me. "But not if it helps to get Eleanor back," she said sharply

I shook my head. "There are other reasons we cannot involve the Doge. Both of us are not Venetian. We've presented ourselves to be something other than who we really are. Me as Giacomo Bonavillagio, son of a Venetian merchant, and you a courtesan, not to mention your secret life as a painter."

I'd said the last bit in an attempt to make her smile, but she heard the truth of my words and her expression dulled. While it probably mattered less that a courtesan took it upon herself to paint religious scenes, it might matter more to the prudish Venetian nobility that she sold them. It would offend a Venetian nobleman's sensibility and preference for order that anyone from the underbelly of Venice might create something for religious minded families and churches to hang on their walls.

Alys clutched my hands tightly, taking me from my musings. "Barnabas," she said softly, her eyes suddenly pleading.

I looked at her, knowing deep in my heart what she was going to ask. It had hung between us, unspoken, ever since we'd discovered Alessandra had taken Eleanor and vanished. I'd ignored it, assuming initially that it would be no trouble to unearth Alessandra's whereabouts, that someone in this seething crowded city, where it was nigh impossible to sneeze without someone making a note of it, would know where Alessandra had gone. When the impossible became fact, and I could find nothing out, ignoring it had become difficult, the voice in my head had become louder and louder until it nearly deafened me with its noise. And it was made even more difficult knowing that it was my own voice in my head, drowning out anything Alys might be screaming silently. *Use your gift.*

It was no gift, in my mind. It had become a curse. One that had cost me more than my body or mind could say. One that I acknowledged had led to an education and position in the world beyond my wildest dreams, but it had made me hunted for treason and witchcraft in England, forcing me to flee with al Qali – who appeared to be a mentor and saviour, only to have him groom me to be sold to the Grand Vizier of the Turks for his pleasure and my talent and ultimately to try to force me to murder a Sultan. If not for a lucky escape aided by Hal I would have most certainly been dead. After chasing al Qali across Africa and witnessing his death, I'd sworn I would never use that talent again.

I looked away and shook my head. "I can't," I said in a whisper.

"Why not?" she demanded.

I turned back and looked at her again. Her face was a mixture of rage and despair.

"I vowed I wouldn't." I pleaded with my eyes.

"You vowed?" Her voice was all anger now. "You vowed! Are you saying that it's of no bother to use the showstone for al Qali, or that Vizier, people that you hate, yet you cannot set aside your vow for our daughter, your own flesh and blood?"

I put my hands on her shoulders to draw her in for some comfort, but she shrugged them off.

"Know this, Barnabas," she said, spitting my name. "I will never forgive you if you don't make an effort to scry to find our daughter."

I tried to take her hand, but she put it behind her and shook her head. "It's not just the vow," I said. "I-I'm not certain I can anymore."

She scowled. "What do you mean? Is this some feeble excuse?"

I shook my head. "No excuse. I haven't tried in earnest for a long time, now. And, and before there was always something I could feel, some inner instinct that I had." I stumbled, trying to find the words to explain to Alys. "It was a feeling I had when I saw things in a certain manner. An inquisitive manner." I looked away again, fighting the emotion that was inside. "I don't have it any more."

"But have you tried?" asked Alys.

I nodded and spoke softly. "I promise, when I first knew that Eleanor was gone. I looked at Alessandra's place. I looked at you, but I could see nothing." I studied my hands. "I am sorry, Alys. More sorry than you can ever know."

"But you haven't tried with a showstone."

"No. But I have no showstone."

"Then something else. A bowl of water—anything. Didn't you say that you scried with a bowl of water in the past?"

I nodded slowly. "But it may not work again. I don't know."

She touched my arm. "Then you will try?"

I sighed and nodded again. "Yes. But I can promise nothing. Even if I manage to scry, there is nothing to say I will see anything that can help."

"You will. You will. You must. After all, it's our child that's missing. Surely if you can scry to find anything, you can scry to find Eleanor."

The desperation was plain to see in her face. I could only hope she was right.

CHAPTER TWO
VENICE, WINTER 1447
BARNABAS

The room was dark except for a lone candle that flickered beside me. I'd waited two days, until an evening when the feeble winter light had been swallowed whole and no trace of stars were evident. Those days were filled with tension as I prepared and Alys watched me wordlessly, for the most part, her face saying all that she felt. Alys's brother Hal and Joanie, her companion, had tried to fill the silences with aimless chatter or hearty observations, until I was forced to send them on errands that took them away.

Now, I sat in the smaller of the rooms, alone, as I'd requested, but the weight of their expectations hung over me, as heavy as if they were sitting on my shoulders and not waiting anxiously in the next room. I sighed and reached for the silver bowl. It was chased with mythical designs on the outside, but inside it was smooth and polished to a high shine. It had taken me a while to find something suitable. I'd scoured the Rialto market and the backstreets of the Jeweller's area, finally locating it in a remote room of a shop run by a shrivelled old Jew. It was a place of many wonders, but this was the wonder that seemed to meet my requirements and I hoped it would fulfil its promise.

I picked up the ewer and poured the water it contained into the bowl. The water had come from a well that was as pure as I could hope for in Venice. I had sent Joanie to fetch it from a small private well near Piazza San Marco, one of the oldest wells in the city. I'd told Joanie it was needed to scry properly, but it was really just an excuse to stop her chattering and get her away. Now it seemed important the water was from that well, some instinct in me had known I would need it. A well from before the time of Christ.

The candle flickered again, driven by the small draught that came from the window. The bed beneath it was the one Alys and I shared nominally, for I'd spent little enough time in it since we'd taken these rooms on our return from Africa. I'd spent most nights out with friends and acquaintances to garner information, returning only in the early hours of dawn, my vigilance, I only now admitted, due mostly to avoiding this very thing that I was about to do now.

I stuffed the gap in the window with a cloth and the candle flame steadied. I closed my eyes for a moment and slowed my breath, slowly opening my eyes when I felt the calm of the water before me. I focused my attention in the water, on its surface and yet not on the surface, a sort of middle area between. The water remained still, its surface smooth as silk, not a ripple or stirring. I continued to stare, willing, asking with my heart, my mind, to give me some kind of image or indication where my daughter might be. Where Alessandra, might be. Anything.

My eyes strained for a vision, and for a moment I thought there might be something. I closed my eyes and opened them again, hoping it would crystallise into something meaningful, but it was just a trick of the candle flame. I snorted in frustration, closed my eyes and breathed deeply, working hard to clear my thoughts. This time the water rippled slightly. Perhaps it was my breath, for I was bent so close to the water my nose was nearly touching the surface. The candle wavered and the bowl's silvered bottom reflected the flame in a gleaming flash. A pale shadow glided across the water and for a moment I thought it might take shape, become my old friend, Limping Sam. An instant later the shadow vanished and the bottom of the bowl was as before.

I sighed and rubbed my hand across the stubble that had grown these past days nearly towards a beard and then pressed my fingers into my eyes, trying to erase the tiredness. I stared again, feeling each agonising moment pass with no sign of any image appearing.

I don't know how long it was before I couldn't stand the strain on my eyes and I shut them. It seemed as if a thousand years had passed, and it might have well have, for I knew that my life would be ending in some part of me. And Alys's too. I lifted my head, easing the crick that had formed from my intense staring. I realised the leaden feeling inside me was resignation.

I sighed and rose. The bowl stood on the small table, the water inside it clear and smooth, the grinning mythical figures chased on it seemed to mock me. In a fit of anger I swiped the bowl off the table. The water spilled everywhere and the bowl landed upside down on the floor with a clang.

A moment later the door opened and Alys entered, Joanie and Hal close behind her.

"What happened?" Alys said, alarm in her voice. "Are you all right?"

The three looked at me, their bodies tense, waiting to hear what I'd seen. Bitterness, rage and the futility of all that I'd tried to do in the past weeks surged up and before I could stop myself, I snatched my sheathed dagger from the table, strapped it to my side and heaved past them without a word and left, eventually exiting out into the wintery rain.

～

I walked through the streets alongside canals, down small alleys and crossed bridges, barely taking in my surroundings or the heavy rain that pelted my head. Eventually I became aware that I was near the Rialto, my hair was plastered to my head and my clothes were soaked. I took refuge in the Sturgeon Inn. It was crowded and candles struggled to cut the smoky air. I found Pietro and Niccolo by the wall nearest the entrance, downing wine and talking with some man I didn't recognise. Pietro saw me at once and gestured for me to join them. Suddenly it seemed like a good notion, in fact the only one to suit my mood. I sat down beside Pietro and nodded to Niccolo and the man who stood beside him.

"Giacomo, my friend, it is good to see you," said Pietro. "But you look so glum. Come, we must remedy that."

Niccolo grinned and nodded. "Yes, and so we must." He shouted to one of the servants for another flagon of wine and a cup for me. He indicated the man standing. "Let me introduce you to Antonio, here. I was just trying to persuade him to join us too." He nodded to Antonio. "Our friend here is Giacomo Bonavillagio, a merchant of sorts as well as a sometime friend and carousing companion of ours. Antonio is the Doge's nephew."

Antonio, dark tall and slender with long curling dark hair, was as perfumed and beringed as any young noble Venetian man who aspired to fashion and dissipation, but there was an undercurrent of something more that told me not to take him at surface value. He considered me carefully, his eyes slightly narrowed, a careless smile on his face. I stood and gave a slight bow. He took the seat next to Pietro.

"Signor Antonio," I said and affected a wide, genial smile. I turned to Niccolo. "I am surely not sometime, but always your companion, when I can manage."

"Ah," said Pietro. "It is the management of it that is so poor. These past few years we've hardly seen you at all."

I shrugged. "It couldn't be helped. I was away."

"Trading, I suppose." He gave a bored yawn. "Isn't that what all newcomers to Venice desire and weave into all conversation? All so very tedious. In fact all of Venice seems tedious right now."

"I'm afraid I will bore you then."

"What goods?" Antonio's eyes lazily surveyed the room, seemingly only half paying attention.

"Oh, various sorts. Some pepper, spices, cloth, things of that nature."

He nodded dully. "Various, as you say."

"Giacomo knows cloth well," said Niccolo. "He has partnered with Alessandra and they've done well together."

"Alessandra, the former courtesan?" He turned to study me again.

"The very same," said Niccolo.

I had an urge to kick Niccolo under the table to shut his mouth. I preferred this man to know as little about me as possible and now wished I could take back the bit of information I had given.

"You know Alessandra?" I said, adopting a mild tone.

"Who doesn't know the famed Alessandra," he said, his tone even. "It's a pity she was compelled to retire after she was burnt. Though the young delicacy she took on to replace her showed much promise." He smiled and his eyes glittered for a moment at a memory and then they darkened. "But alas, though few could fault her beauty, she was not what she seemed and showed little of the …energy and versatility of Alessandra."

Niccolo and Pietro glanced at me. I managed a neutral smile.

"Did you meet her at Alessandra's?" asked Pietro.

I shrugged. "I think perhaps I met her once or twice." I had no wish for any of them to know that Alys was the woman they spoke about, or how she was connected to me. That way led to danger.

Antonio gave me a quizzical look. "If you'd met her, you wouldn't forget her. In fact I have tried to seek her out recently, thinking that she might have matured. Grown wiser and better able to manage her lifestyle. But Alessandra has left Venice, it seems."

I bristled at his remarks about Alys, but kept my eyes down, in the hopes he wouldn't notice. "Yes, she was striking, I believe. But Alessandra and I had a strong connection and I limited my time at her place to business discussions."

"Then perhaps you'll know where she's gone?" asked Antonio.

"Giacomo himself would love to know," said Niccolo.

"You are partnered together in business and yet she didn't tell you where she was going?" said Antonio, disbelief in his tone.

I shrugged. "The partnership had finished by the time she'd left. She was under no obligation to tell me. Though

I wouldn't mind knowing where she went so that I might write to her with another business proposal."

"And what business proposal is that?" said Antonio. "Only, I might find it of interest."

I shook my head. "I'm sure it's a proposal few would find worthy other than Alessandra."

"You intrigue me more," said Antonio. He took a deep draught from his cup and sat back on his bench, leaning against the wall. "I have heard that Alessandra has an older sister who though didn't possess Alessandra's beauty and conversation, possessed the dowry necessary to make a marriage. Some would say it was fortunate for the two sisters that the oldest was less able to fend for herself and had the dowry to secure her a place in the world and Alessandra had her wit and beauty to do the same."

"Alessandra has a sister?" I said, stunned. "She never mentioned her."

"No," said Antonio. "I don't suppose she would, given that her sister got all and Alessandra was sold to the world of the courtesan."

I knew he meant that Alessandra's mother, with little choice, had sold her daughter's virtue after training her to be a courtesan. The funds ensured Alessandra's future was secure – a practical arrangement, so much so that Alessandra had done the same for Alys, thinking that Alys's income as a courtesan would fund Alessandra as well.

"Do you know the sister's name and where she is?"

Antonio cocked his head and smiled. "I might be able to discover this. If you enlighten men about your proposal."

I forced a grin. "Ah, but signor, I'm afraid it would profit you not at all, so there's no point in spending time on it."

"Alas, then I'm afraid I must keep it to myself."

I nodded. There was little I could do except invent a proposal and make it interesting as well as feasible. "I'm sorry, but I cannot divulge it until I consult an associate."

"You have another associate in this venture?"

"Yes, but I will need time to contact them. I will have an answer for you, if I can, in two days' time."

"*Bene.* I will look for you then. And should it not be possible to reveal your proposal, I can say only that should your proposal not prove the right distraction I can at least thank you for reminding me of Alessandra's little morsel, Maria. I believe I will take her up again, show her how she should behave."

I smiled weakly and nodded. Now I had yet another reason to come up with a proposal that would intrigue this man. I couldn't afford to have him make an effort to discover that the little morsel he wanted back was under my very own roof. I'd kill him first.

The rain was still falling by the time I'd left and I had enough drink in me to be oblivious to my wet clothes. I made my way back along the Grand Canal, heading towards our rooms. Once I left the canal, the way was dark enough, only a few torches from passing gondolas or groups making their way to their next pleasure shedding any extra light. I carried a small torch, taken by Antonio from the inn wall in a moment of whimsy. I was glad for it, but nevertheless I was dispirited and miserable, reluctant to face Alys and the others to tell them of the danger I had put Alys in once again. What use was a sister when Alessandra clearly hated her and had no contact with her for years? Yet now I must come up with some fake scheme to intrigue the Doge's nephew for a chance that this sister might be found. I cursed my own stupidity at allowing myself to be drawn into this fiasco.

A group of drunken young men jostled me as they passed by in the small piazza and I stumbled and struggled for my balance. I flailed a little, but my efforts were in vain and I landed with a crunch on the ground. Searing pain went through my side and I felt something sharp pierce my flesh. The men walked on, seemingly too drunk to notice me fall. The torch dropped from my hand and I lay there, stunned, the breath knocked from me, preventing me from shouting for help. The torch was still lit, but it had rolled away from me during my fall so even had I been able to move a little in order to see the damage or signal for help, I couldn't.

Moments passed and blood poured out, pooling beside me. I reached for my left side carefully and felt wetness there. The dagger was nowhere I could see. My own, carefully hidden in my doublet, remained in its useless position. I cursed myself for a fool for the second time that night at such carelessness.

With a long groan I struggled to sit up and eased myself to my knees. I squinted at the pool of blood, trying to decide how much I'd lost. Dazed and hardly aware of my actions, I reached for the torch and brought it close to the blood. It was more like a small puddle I decided. I stared at it, trying to interpret the meaning of its size. The torch light reflected back, and I marvelled at its yellow brightness against the dark burgundy of the blood. I laughed and shivered, aware it was the sudden attack that made me do so. The rain had nearly stopped, leaving only a fine mist that clung to my eyelashes and added a refractive quality to the mirrored torchlight. The refraction splintered and cleared. Suddenly an image of a woman appeared, swathed in white cloth except for her eyes. I knew those eyes. Alessandra.

I gasped. The woman turned to stare at me. Behind her rose a dome tiled in brilliant colours amid an azure sky. She stared hard, her hatred plain to see.

"Alessandra!" I shouted. But the image had gone. I held the torch closer, straining to see her again in the blood, but only the reflected light of the torch and a vague image of my despairing face were visible.

I struggled to my feet, clutching my side. Somehow I would get back to the rooms. Try to scry again. Surely I could do it again. I could discover more. That dome. It was no dome I had ever seen. But it was too distinctive to be unremarkable. Surely someone would know where it was if I described it to them.

CHAPTER THREE
VENICE, WINTER 1447
BARNABAS

"Barnabas!" cried Alys. "You're bleeding."

She'd been sitting in her night shift in the little reception room, a shawl wrapped tightly around her and had risen when I entered. Her cries startled me when I walked weakly into our rooms. I had heaved myself feverishly along the streets and up the stairs to our rooms, my mind consumed by what I had just seen, and what I was determined to do.

I looked down distractedly at my clothes. "Oh," I said. "It's nothing."

She came to me, her face filled with concern. "That's not nothing. Your doublet is soaked." She touched my side and her hand came away covered in blood. "Sit there." She indicated the chair she'd been seated on.

Once she was satisfied I was seated she fetched the pitcher and bowl from the table by the wall, placed it on the floor beside me and went in search of a cloth. I poured the water in the bowl and took a branch of candles from the table and placed it on the floor beside the bowl. I blinked slowly, trying to clear my vision and stared in.

"What are you doing?" Alys whispered loudly.

I held up my hand for silence and stared into the water. As before in the other room, the water only reflected the flames. I tried to relax, distract my concentration in the hope that the vision would return, but there was nothing.

"Let me tend your wound before you bleed to death," Alys said in a low voice. "You can do that afterwards."

She bent over and tried to pull me up but I pushed her away. On a whim I touched my side and then dipped my blood-covered fingers into the water and watched as it seeped into the liquid and swirled around into shapes. I followed the pattern carefully, hoping for some kind of image or sign that would help me further. After a few moments Alys tugged at my doublet.

"What is it? Have you seen something this time?" she asked, hope and fear in her voice.

I remained silent for a moment, still studying the water. I heaved a sigh and got up, knowing it was useless. She saw my face and her own sagged for a moment, then she became efficient and brisk, pushing me back into the chair and starting to remove the doublet.

"Where have you been that you should come by such a wound?" she asked sharply.

"I was on my way back from the Sturgeon Inn. Someone stabbed me with their knife. I don't know who, or why, but it was someone in a group of youths."

"But why?" she said. My doublet was shed and she was busy removing my shirt.

I shrugged. "It might not have been anything more than a malicious random incident. Or it might be someone acting on Alessandra and Tomaso's behalf."

I winced as she pressed the wound gingerly, causing more blood to seep out. It had slowed from a steady flow and my light headedness told me that was probably due to the amount I'd lost rather than the superficiality of the wound.

"It's deep. It will have to be stitched," Alys said, clucking her tongue in concern. "And you've lost a lot of blood already."

She dabbed at it with a cloth, wiping away the concealed mess that had formed. "At least it hadn't dried to your doublet or shirt."

"It's too wet out for that," I said wryly.

She continued to tend the wound, muttering to herself, until finally, her task done, she could contain herself no longer. She looked up. "You know this must stop."

"What must stop?"

"Fumbling around, asking questions of everyone who will listen. Clearly, you're stirring up trouble. Someone is offended."

I thought of Antonio. Had he told me all? Was there more than coincidence he was talking to Niccolo and Pietro when I came in? A quick word and a message could be sent after I'd left the inn.

"In my fumbling, as you call it, I did discover that Alessandra has a sister," I said.

"A sister?" Her face lit up in sudden hope.

"A sister who she never mentioned and has every reason to hate," I said in a flat voice.

"But still, it is worth trying to find her. Do you know where she lives?"

I shook my head. "She could be anywhere."

"But it is only a matter of asking the right people, surely, and you will discover."

I raised my brow. "Fumbling around some more? Didn't you just ask that I stop that?"

She flushed. "But now you have a specific question. You can be discreet, ask quietly of only those who might know."

I shook my head. "She didn't go to her sister's."

She looked at him curiously, a hint of anger in her face. "How do you know? Why didn't you say this first?"

"I know because her sister doesn't live in the East, in a desert area. That's where Alessandra is." I tried to keep my voice firm and convincing.

"The desert?" She stared at me, attempting to take it in. "What desert? What is she doing there? Do you know if she has Eleanor there with her?"

"I don't know." I looked away.

She pressed her hand to my face and turned it toward her, staring at me intently. "How do you know this, Barnabas?"

"I saw it. In a pool of my blood."

She blinked. "Your blood? Where?"

"Where I fell after I was stabbed. I leaned over to get up and in the torchlight I saw her, wrapped in white cloths, a great tiled dome behind her."

She looked at me, a confused expression on her face. "That's all you saw? And you think that means she is in the desert?" She shook her head. "It's so little. You cannot be certain."

"I know she's in the East. I'm sure of it." I held her gaze, working to convince her.

"And based on that we should go east? East where? To some desert without a name, a location, except that it's east of here?"

I sighed. "We know more than that. The clothes, the dome, all point to a specific area. Somewhere along the great trade road to the silk country." I was more certain of it than anything I'd learned since we'd arrived back in Venice. The dome, I knew I'd heard about it somewhere. The blue tiles, dazzling in the sun.

She groaned. "Don't you see how foolish that is? The risk of our lives, and Eleanor's, on what might have been a vision. We can't."

"Only a few hours ago you were pleading with me to attempt scrying and now, suddenly you have nothing but disdain for it?"

"No, no," she wailed. "It's just so tenuous, fleeting. It didn't come in a manner that seems...trustworthy. Barnabas, you'd just been stabbed, you were bleeding, in shock and light headed. "

"Are you saying I was imagining it?"

She hesitated. "Perhaps. But is it a risk we can take?"

I frowned. "I wasn't imagining it." I pronounced the words slowly, firmly.

"But her sister. Don't you see? We know she has a sister. That's certain. And what would it take to find her? Going on a wild goose chase along some trade road could take months and months. Even years."

"Alys, we both want to find Eleanor as soon as possible, but chasing after her sister could take a long time and lead nowhere. In fact it probably would. She wanted nothing to do with that sister."

"She's her sister, and if she was desperate, she would go there." Alys's tone was just as stubborn as mine.

"Alessandra wasn't desperate. And besides, she had Tomaso with her. She would hardly take her paramour with her to her sister."

"Perhaps they married."

I burst out laughing. "Perhaps, but I doubt it very much. I don't think Alessandra would tolerate Tomaso in that role." I took her hand and kissed it. "You must trust me on this. I will do what I can to find exactly where this dome is located. I think I have some idea. But eastward I must go."

"If you go, I'm going with you." She glared at me. "But how will you pay for such a journey?"

I sighed. "Yes, I think you must come with me. I don't want to leave you behind. Too many people know how dear you are to me and might harm you because of that. As for the finances, let me worry about them."

I took her in my arms, careful of my wound and kissed her slowly. "I can't bear the thought of losing you again, *amore*."

She returned my kiss and it became tender and yearning at the same time. There was something else there too. Sorrow. I could only hope my statement about Alessandra's location was right and not the wild guessing my saner self said it was. Then I could turn that sorrow into joy.

࿎

Hal and I pretended to talk animatedly, seemingly deep in discussion as we made our way along Corte da Ponte, while out of the corner of my eye I scanned passers-by. Suddenly, I veered off into a smaller street, leaving Hal to continue straight. I proceeded along, turning again at the next calle, eventually winding to Ramo al Ponte Santo Francesco when I was certain we weren't being followed. I rejoined Hal at the designated point, outside the Chiesa

San Francesco della Vigna. He clasped my hand as if we were just meeting for the first time that day and with his arm around my shoulders we made our way inside.

It took some while for my eyes to adjust to the dark interior, but it appeared empty, as I hoped it would be. It was a moderate sized, triple-naved church founded by the Franciscans. I slipped into a small chapel dedicated to Ste Claire. After a brief genuflection, I went to the prie dieu, knelt, and held my hands up, clasping them as if to pray. Hal did the same. I turned my head a fraction and scanned the area behind me, checking again that there was no one in view. I listened hard and could hear nothing of the street noise or anything else. The walls were thick, as were the doors.

"You know it's still there?" asked Hal softly.

"I'm not certain, but there is no reason it shouldn't be," I said. "Wait here and keep watch."

Hal nodded and I rose and quietly made my way to the rear of the altar. It was hollow, with only three sides of marble and a wooden back. I withdrew my dagger and began to pry away the board. It came away smoothly. I breathed a sigh of relief at the sight of the small black bag and gave a brief prayer of thanks to the saint for looking after my little treasure. Carefully, I stuffed the bag inside my doublet and replaced the board. There was no sense in removing it, for it may be that I would need it again in the future.

I'd created the hiding place shortly after I'd arranged to go into business with Alessandra and placed a small portion of my earnings there. Experience had made me cautious in the case of money and I'd seen no need to change when it came to Alessandra, when I knew how much she feared poverty, or any kind of limitation on the life she enjoyed. On this occasion, the wisdom of my actions could now enable me to at least attempt a journey that would doubtless be costly in so many ways.

I nodded to Hal and walked past him. He rose and followed me. It wasn't until we were out in the street that he spoke.

"You got it then?"

"Yes." I grinned, for it was the first piece of good fortune that we'd had in a long time. We walked along a short while until, spotting a tavern, I ducked in and Hal followed. When we were seated with our drinks, he finally spoke.

"So you mean to go east? Along the trading route?"

I frowned at him. Joanie's and his reluctance had persisted since I'd told them of our plans that morning.

"I don't like it," he said. "I don't like it one bit."

"So you keep saying," I replied drily.

"Yes, but you don't listen, do you? Nor to Joanie, either."

I turned to him and sighed. "I know you have objections, Hal, but I don't see any other course of action that will get Eleanor back."

He shook his head, speaking softly in English. "No, you don't see, do you? But Alys does. And she makes sense. We should look for the sister, Barnabas. It's a good possibility."

"And I'm telling you it isn't. I know with what venom Alessandra spoke of her family. She wouldn't go to her sister, trust me."

Hal gave me a doubtful look. "I know you knew her well, especially before she was burnt. But much 'as 'appened since then and you've only seen her for a few days 'ere and there, after you went with al Qali to the land of the Turks."

"While what you say is true, there are some core aspects of Alessandra's personality and that's one I'm certain wouldn't change. She would have nothing to do with her family." I put my hand on his shoulder. "I know you have doubts about this journey, but can I count on you nonetheless?"

Hal sighed and nodded. "You can. Not only for your sake, but most especially for the sake of my sister. I'll not desert her. Nor will Joanie."

I smiled. "She's fortunate to have such a loyal brother and friend. No one could ask for more."

Hal frowned. "I am your loyal friend, Jacko, you know that. It's just my sister comes first and her objections made sense when she told me of them."

"Yes, it was only fair that you should ask her why she objected after I told you and Joanie of our plans. But I hope you understand there is much about this journey that makes sense and has a good chance for success."

Hal raised his brows. "If you say so. I know that your visions were good and keen in the past, but you 'ave to admit this one is a little different."

I waved his statement away with a gesture. "Every vision is different and can come by any number of means."

Hal just looked at me. "Do you have enough now to pay for the journey?"

His tone was neutral, but I could tell he hadn't been convinced about my vision. I decided to drop it and began to consider his question. "Well with a bit of luck and selling a few of my pieces I think we should have enough to get us a good ways on the journey."

He gave me a puzzled look. "A good ways on the journey? What do you mean by that? Do we 'ave enough or don't we?"

I cocked my head and tried for a light hearted tone. "It depends on what you mean. There's certainly enough to pay our passage on the sea journey. And if I can get what I hope when I sell a few of my things we should be able to buy a few goods that should see us through to at least Samarkand."

"Samarkand? I've not 'eard of that place. How far is that?" There was deep scepticism in his voice.

"It's a jewel of a place, from all I've heard. You'll find it full of wonders."

"Why would we want to go there? What's in Samarkand?" He pronounced the name of the place carefully.

"A dome, Hal. A blue tiled dome. At least I think so, from what I've been able to discover."

"A dome," he repeated dumbly and shook his head.

I pulled the black bag from inside my doublet and withdrew a handful of gold coins. I gave them to Hal. "Here, that should be enough to book us passage."

He took the coins and gave a reluctant nod. "Where shall we be sailing to then?"

"Tyre."

Hal raised his brows. "Is that ruled by your Arab friends?"

I bristled. Hal referred to the Ottoman's Grand Vizier who had held me captive in Hüdavendigar. "No, it's the Mamluks that hold Tyre. They are a different sort to the Turks who rule where I was."

"I see," said Hal. "Then you 'ave no fear there."

"I have no fear, in any case. I doubt there would be any interest in me now." I could only hope it was true, but any doubts I had I wanted to keep to myself.

"Fine. We go to Tyre. And after Tyre?"

"We'll hire donkeys or horses, if we can and go on to Damascus and then Palmyra. From there we'll go on to Doura-Europos, head south and then east into Persia."

"And eventually to Samarkand?"

I nodded. "Yes."

"And who will take us there, show us the way?"

"Don't worry, Hal. We can find a caravan and join them, I'm certain."

"Aren't we travelling through lands ruled by your Vizier fella and his sultan?"

I shook my head.

I gave a reassuring smile, trying to convey all the confidence I didn't feel. My source for the dome's location was a speculative guess by a wizened old bookseller fond of tales, but I wasn't about to tell Hal that. The man had said some part of the route was called the Royal Road, possibly because it was said a princess from Cathay hid quantities of silkworms in her extravagant coiffure when she travelled to her future husband in the land of Turks. The route wasn't as well used as it had been in the past. Truth be told, the old merchants I'd spoken to who knew of the route said there was not just one route, but many, though several led to Samarkand. I hoped I had picked the right one, the one that Alessandra and Tomaso had followed, if they had really done so. It was difficult to maintain my own certainty in the cold light of day, that what I had seen was a vision and not something born of a serious wound and too much drink.

CHAPTER FOUR
MEDITERRANEAN SEA, WINTER 1447
ALYS

The sea rolled in angry winter fits, choppy and disagreeable to all merchants who dared to travel on her in this season. Alys couldn't help but agree, her stomach roiling along with the ship. After days of finding herself confined to a small box of a cabin with only a chamber pot to spew into and Joanie to rub her back in between her own bouts of sickness, she finally felt able to come above deck and take some air.

Alys had lost count of the number of days they'd been at sea. All she knew was that it was too many. She raised her hand to her cheek, feeling it burn at the touch. The wind was strong and already her face felt chafed by it. But after the fetid air of the chamber she had to admit it was an improvement to be up here. There were others beside the crew on board, taking passage to Tyre. Another merchant and a merchant's representative, but it was still a small group so it was difficult to avoid Barnabas when above decks.

Her woollen cloak blew in the wind, revealing the dark wool gown beneath it. Her thoughts drifted to her daughter. What would Eleanor look like now? When she'd last seen the child she'd been no more than three months old, but even then her golden curls, her eyes, her mouth, they were a reflection of Barnabas's. Would she know her own daughter? Would her daughter know her? The thought tugged at her hard, causing her pain. She reached for the memory of Eleanor lying in her lap while Carlo Crivelli painted them, Eleanor gazing up at her, blowing bubbles and waggling her legs. Eleanor had looked at her then, knew Alys as her mother. She'd latched onto Alys's finger, holding it tightly as if she never wanted to let go. A sob rose up and nearly choked Alys. She would kill Alessandra, she swore it to herself.

Another gust caught her hood and blew it back and tugged a great lock of her hair from its tangled and hastily made braid. She glanced up at Barnabas, standing on the quarter deck and staring ahead, as if willing land to appear. She frowned at him, angry and worried. Since boarding the vessel her emotions had been in as much turmoil as her stomach, but now though her stomach had calmed, her emotions had not. In her mind this journey was a wasted one and the time it was taking would be better spent elsewhere. Not to mention the cost of it. Once again she marvelled at Barnabas's ability to conjure up funds and goods for trade, an instinct she couldn't deny was his from birth. But he was just as capable of losing it to misfortune and plain foolishness, she knew that through bitter experience. To her mind this was one such occasion.

Alys walked over to Tomaso's cage, conscious of the limp that made her balance more precarious against the rolling of the ship. She bent down to talk to him. She'd had him out of the cage as much as she'd dared, but looks from the crew and from Barnabas had told her it was wise to keep him locked up for the most part.

She reached in her hand which contained small bits of fruit she'd managed to keep back from her own meal and offered the morsels to him. He snatched them from her fingers and chittered his thanks. She clasped one of his fingers and played with it, smiling. He was a comfort amid a very comfortless and distressful time.

"There, Tomaso. Hopefully the journey will end soon and we can get off this godforsaken ship. Though the saints alone know what Tyre will be like. Full of pirates and scoundrels, no doubt."

"Tyre is an ancient port, rich in history."

Alys rose and turned. Barnabas stood there, a smile on his face. His eyes, wary and hopeful at the same time, searched hers. Alys stiffened. The sight of his smile, the determined lightness and good humour she'd encountered the few times she'd come into contact with him since they boarded, put her out of countenance. She tried to find some lightness herself, or at least a calmness, but none would come.

"Pirates and scoundrels disdain ancient ports rich in history?"

"No," he said carefully. "I just meant that it was no barbaric place teeming with ruffians. There is much to recommend Tyre. Merchants and men of repute have travelled there through many centuries."

She scoffed sceptically. "I care nothing for the centuries past, or the masses that might travel there now. I only care about one such traveller."

"I'm sure there will be some news of Alessandra. She is distinctive, to say the least, and to add the fact she has a child accompanying her and Tomaso, makes her doubly noticeable."

"I think you're being overly optimistic," said Alys. "Recall that I have travelled to areas where those of the Muslim faith live. The women are veiled in varying degrees. No one would think it remarkable that a heavily veiled woman with a child pass through in the company of yet another unremarkable merchant."

Barnabas looked away. "While what you say may be true, Alessandra is clearly not an Arab. She has no familiarity with their ways and will soon reveal herself as such. As for Tomaso, he has no notion of a merchant's role or habits. Mark my words, someone will have noticed them. Trust me."

That was the problem. She trusted that he wanted it to be true, that he might even be convinced it was true, but she couldn't believe it. She knew he was clutching at straws. There would be no evidence at Tyre of Alessandra's presence. And then what? Continue on to the next place and the next place, hoping that each time someone would have remembered seeing Alessandra or Tomaso? A fool's game, that's what it was, and she was the greater fool because she knew it to be so.

∿

"It's a bit late to be thinking these thoughts," said Joanie.

Joanie worked patiently at Alys's hair, lacing her fingers through the knots and snarls that had formed over the past few days when Alys's churning stomach had usurped any other concern for her appearance. Alys had hoped the usual calming influence of Joanie's sure hands working on her hair would alleviate some of the anxiety and frustration she'd felt since her encounter with Barnabas above deck, but it hadn't. Instead, she had found herself replaying in her mind her conversation with

Barnabas and her criticism of his statements and assurances as worthless. "Is it too late? Can't we turn back at Tyre?"

"To what?" said Joanie.

"To Venice of course. We can inquire about the sister."

Joanie sighed. "I thought Barnabas had convinced you there was no point."

"You know he hadn't really convinced me. It was more a matter of I couldn't convince him that it was a better course of action than this." She waved her hand around the small cabin.

"I suppose I did. But we're 'ere now, so I suppose we must make the best of it."

"Perhaps in Tyre we could try again to convince him to abandon this…," she paused. "This foolhardy venture," she finished, in a sharp tone. "For I'm certain there is nothing to be found there, except thieves of all kinds and sailors, despite it being 'an ancient port, rich in history'," she finished in a mocking tone.

"Well, let's 'ope not. For I'd much rather that it be full of fine trade goods and friendly people who are more than ready to welcome a stranger at the very least. And God willing, we shall also find Eleanor 'ere too, safe and well."

"I can only hope so," Alys said, suddenly bone weary and sad. "But I fear that won't be the case. Even if she was here, do you think Alessandra would surrender her without a fight?"

"Ah, Alys, you mustn't fret. I'm sure it will turn out well in the end. Your daughter will be found."

Alys fought the tears that suddenly appeared in her eyes. She was tired and out of sorts, which didn't help the urge to suddenly weep with all her heart. Overhead, she heard a shout.

"What's that?" she said.

Joanie smiled at her. "Land is sighted. We must be nearing Tyre. See? All will be well, my dearie. Once we get ashore with firm land under your feet, you'll feel much better."

Alys nodded. She could only hope so. She sighed and rose to go above once more so that she could see what this ancient city rich in history looked like.

It stood out boldly into the sea, imposing with its ruined pillars from ancient times to set the backdrop against myriad buildings, old and new rising up from the shoreline. Behind Tyre was fertile countryside full of meadows and tilled fields and the mountains of Lebanon. In the course of its ancient history it had been part of many different empires, including the Assyrian, the Babylonian, Alexander the Great, the Romans and the Egyptians, and for a brief time, the Crusaders, under Frederick Barbarossa, until the Bahri Sultanate claimed it. It was the Burjī Sultanate who ruled it now.

As they drew closer, Alys could see merchant ships, small and large, lining the docks. A trading port, clearly and one, as Barnabas explained to Alys, famous for its purple dye extracted from a special type of sea snail.

No sooner had they docked when a number of harbour officials, dressed in black silk robes boarded the ship with three soldiers. Barnabas made his way to them along with the captain and exchanged greetings easily, speaking the language with an effortlessness and grace that Alys sensed was hard won. It was the tightening in his jaw and his stance that hinted at his unease. This was perhaps too close for him to his ordeal with the Grand

Vizier. He'd told her little about it, but that in itself spoke volumes of the pain and emotion it had caused him. And to see his discomfort just from speaking the language with those who were not directly connected to the Grand Vizier and the Turks reinforced her conclusion.

Greetings dispensed with, the two officials gave orders to the three accompanying soldiers who moved to the sails and hauled them down, the crew and the rest of those assembled watching from the deck. They were officious in a manner that spoke of a rule that was harsh enough, and it made Alys uneasy, a feeling that was in no way lessened when, once the sails were secure, the harbour officials proceeded to write down the names of everyone on board.

Barnabas acted as interpreter and though he was polite, there were none of his usual quips and jovial mannerisms Alys was used to seeing. Even in Alexandria, when they were returning from the long journey from the Nile, he'd seemed more at ease. Barnabas gave his own details in clipped tones and then gestured one by one to the group. When it came to Alys, he drew her to his side. At his instruction she had donned the loose robes and head covering from that journey beyond the Nile. Even so, the harbour official averted his eyes, talking only to Barnabas. Alys smiled to herself. She could only imagine the disapproving looks and comments her revealing attire at one of Alessandra's little parties would have elicited.

The crew and passengers duly noted, the officials requested the goods to be hauled up from below, the crates and chests stacked on the decks. They proceeded to examine all the goods on the ship, making a careful note of everything, despite being shown the documents stating the items the ship contained. Clearly a list wouldn't satisfy them. Or was it an opportunity for a bribe? Or something worse? Had they reason to be suspicious of the cargo on this ship? Or the people? Alys looked over to Barnabas and was suddenly anxious. His behaviour could provide her with no real clue since past memories were obviously influencing his reactions and behaviour.

Suddenly, one official tapped a chest and gestured to a soldier. The soldier stepped forward and without further ado, prised open the chest with his dagger and a wooden stave he had with him and spilled out the contents onto the decks. It was a chest filled with pepper, the sack placed carefully inside the chest, but during the opening the dagger had pierced the sack, splitting it wide. Alys prayed the pepper wasn't one of the few precious goods that Barnabas had brought to trade in the east. She regretted now that her anger and frustration in Venice had been such that she hadn't asked Barnabas about his cargo.

The captain, a Portugee, stepped forward and uttered some words of protest in his own language. Barnabas stepped up beside him and added his own in Arabic. The shorter official turned and frowned at Barnabas. He scanned the assembly and the deck and suddenly pointed, firing off some questions. Alys looked where he indicated and her heart stopped. Tomaso.

As if he knew he was under scrutiny, Tomaso suddenly started jumping up and down, screeching his own protest. Alys tried to step forward, to go to Tomaso, but one of the soldiers held up an arm, preventing her from moving past. With a nod from the short official one of the other soldiers went over to Tomaso, lifted his cage and carried him to the official.

Barnabas spoke up again, but the official shook his head and uttered a terse reply. He looked at the other official, they exchanged a few words and after a brief moment gave a nod. Without further word the two officials left the ship, the soldiers following in their wake, including the one carrying Tomaso.

"Tomaso!" Alys shouted.

The monkey screeched and chittered at her call. She hurried to the side of the ship, leaning over as far as she could, her hand stretched out, though she knew it was useless. Barnabas came up beside her and rested a hand on her shoulder. Alys turned to him.

"Why didn't you do something?" she demanded.

"I tried," he said, his brow knotted.

His tone was stiff and she knew there was anger beneath it, but she wasn't certain about its source. "What happened? What did he say?" she asked.

Barnabas frowned. "He said that our permits to carry such cargo were not in order."

"Not in order? What did he mean?"

Barnabas sighed. "He said there was an extra crate of pepper and that Tomaso was not accounted for."

"But he's not cargo!" she said.

"I tried to tell them that, but they wouldn't accept my explanation."

"But where will they take him? What will happen to him? We can't lose him." It was just too much. She wouldn't permit it. She allowed the anger to rise up within her, rounded on Barnabas and gave him a small push. "You have to do something. Now. That monkey saved your life, don't forget." Her voice was low, filled with a deadly, dark tone that came from a place somewhere deep within her. "Because if you don't do anything soon, I will, even if I have to hire someone to kidnap Tomaso."

He took her hands and held them up tightly in front of her. "I know he saved my life," he said, in a studied tone.

"How could I forget that? And it's not just that. He means much to me. And I know he means much to you." He paused and stared into her eyes. "I promise, I will get him back."

"How?" she said, her voice filled with scepticism and doubt.

"I'll make inquiries. Find out if this is a usual procedure and requires a bribe of some sort."

"But we don't have the money for a bribe, and besides, the captain's reaction certainly didn't give the impression it was the usual course of things."

Barnabas shrugged. "You don't know. It could be part of the bargaining. A strong protest, dramatic gestures and threats. Different ideas of how a merchant proceeds when arriving in a port. To ensure the authorities give the cargo suitable protection while it is in the port warehouses."

Alys frowned and shook her head. "Surely this would never be the case in London."

Barnabas laughed, but there was no real humour in it. "Ask your brother, Alys. I'm sure he can enlighten you about the behaviour and customs in London ports." He sighed heavily. "You have my assurances that as soon as we get ashore I will do everything I can to get Tomaso back."

Alys nodded, but found little comfort in his words. These days she found it difficult to believe anything but the worst. But she was certain about one thing. She would find some way to get Tomaso back, if Barnabas didn't. She wasn't leaving until that happened. She frowned. Her doubts about this journey were growing all the time.

CHAPTER FIVE
TYRE, WINTER 1448
ALYS

"I found Tomaso," said Barnabas. He was standing in the door, Hal behind him, his head down, avoiding Alys's glance.

Alys put aside her sewing. The light was poor, even by the window, for the room of the house where they were staying was in shadow, unlike the houses opposite where the raking sun beat in the windows. Sewing had been something to occupy her hands, if not her mind, as she and Joanie waited in their cramped quarters near the port while Barnabas and Hal had tried to retrieve Tomaso and resolve their problem with the port authorities. Meanwhile, their cargo remained on the ship, guarded by a few of the Mamluk soldiers.

She brushed her hair away from her face. "Where is he? Can you get him?"

Barnabas shook his head. "I can't. At least not yet. The situation is complicated."

Alys frowned. "What do you mean?"

Barnabas sighed and took a seat on the small cot against the wall that she and Joanie shared. With little remaining choice, Hal and Barnabas had opted for the floor. It had been an uncomfortable night for all of them.

"The official who took Tomaso, Shafik ibn Taghri, was seen taking him to his home. When I approached him he claimed it wasn't so, that, as he put it, 'the animal had been disposed of, according to regulations'."

"So he has Tomaso at his 'ome?" asked Joanie.

Alys rose in agitation. "Have you gone there? Have you seen him?"

"I've gone to the house, just to see where it is and decide how to approach it. It's possible that I could bribe one of the servants to find out where in the house Tomaso might be."

"Why don't you just bribe them to bring out Tomaso?" said Alys impatiently.

She bit her lip. Would they indeed 'dispose' of Tomaso? Perhaps he only took Tomaso home to give to his cook to kill so they could eat him. Who knows what these people thought was acceptable to eat? She fought to keep her mind from spinning off in hysterical directions. Joanie touched her arm in comfort.

"Let's see what Barnabas can find out first. There might be an easy way yet, once we know where and why 'e's there. Maybe it's to amuse the man's children."

Alys nodded and tried to derive comfort from the suggestion. "Yes, perhaps that's the case."

"I must go now," said Barnabas. "I only returned to tell you what I discovered." He gestured to Hal. "It's best you stay here and keep an eye on Joanie and Alys. It was risky enough this morning for a few hours. Until I know why I was singled out and by whom, it's best not to take risks and leave them unattended."

"But I should go with you. For those exact reasons," said Hal.

Barnabas shook his head and gestured to the plain white robe and turban with its piece hanging ready to cover his face. "Few would know me in this garb."

"They would see your eyes," said Alys. "Take Hal with you."

"But they would know me more with Hal accompanying me," said Barnabas. "No, you'll stay behind. If I am to wait to talk to a servant, it's best that I am alone and unnoticed for the most part."

Alys nodded reluctantly. She saw the sense in his words, but she felt unease about what he might face should anyone discover his intent. She was worried for him, but knew nothing more than that. She rubbed her eyes against the strain she'd felt for so long, it was difficult to separate it from herself. Her emotions were so mixed and confused with anger, longing, grief that she had no idea what she felt for anyone and most especially Barnabas. The anger had sustained her, and to a degree it still did, but her tiredness and exhaustion were in the forefront now, and she could only sit and fiddle with the tear she'd been mending in her undershift. She remained sitting there a few moments later after Barnabas had taken his leave of them.

By the time he'd returned in the evening, his drawn face and pallor indicating that he'd had no success at all, Alys was pacing and checking the small window for signs of him, convinced that he'd know something. Frustration gave way to anger in a moment and she barely waited for him to enter before she rounded on him.

"This afternoon has been a waste of time. We must find our opportunity, go in there and get Tomaso. Before something happens to him."

Barnabas held up a hand, frowning. "No. That's the worst thing we could do. We insult Taghri, his family and the port's hospitality if we do that."

"Hospitality? What hospitality?" said Alys. "It's they who have acted outrageously. Tomaso is ours. They have no right to him whatsoever."

"I know. It's true, but just because it is doesn't mean they can't decide that we have infringed on their city's regulations and customs and we won't suffer consequences. Severe consequences."

She felt the tears prick her eyes. Frustration, tiredness and sheer anger at the injustice of all of it were behind the tears, but they were still unhelpful. She brushed them away.

"What do you suggest? More vigils by the house in the hope that some servant might come out that you could talk to?"

"No. I think tomorrow I will go to the bazaar and speak to the servants buying goods and food for the day. Someone there will know Taghri's servants and which ones would be open to questioning and bribes."

"I'll come with you," said Alys. "If there are women they will be more likely to talk to me."

"No, it's not safe, nor is it customary," said Barnabas. "Only slave and servant women go to the market, or anywhere in the open. You know that."

"Let me go with you, then," said Joanie. She rose from the other stool. "I can be your servant."

Barnabas looked at her kindly. "That's good of you Joanie, but it wouldn't work, I'm afraid. You don't speak their language, or any language they might understand." He looked her up and down, taking in her plain dark blue wool gown, the cloth head covering of a lighter blue.

"And I'm afraid that your dress as well as your manner marks you out as a foreigner."

"I'll change clothes with Alys," said Joanie stoutly.

"No, Joanie," said Hal. "Listen to Barnabas. You're best to remain 'ere."

"As Hal says, It's better if I go on my own. I've said it before and I haven't changed my mind. Hal will stay with both of you."

Hal made no objections and Alys remained silent. She had made her own decision about the matter and she thought it prudent to appear to agree with Barnabas and hold her tongue.

⚬⚬

The door was barely closed behind Barnabas when Alys picked up her cloth head-covering and wrapped it closely around her head and across most of her face.

"What are you doing?" said Hal. He rose from the floor where he'd perched after Barnabas had departed. "You're not stepping outside of this room, if that's your plan."

Joanie got up from the stool where the small pile of mending still lay from the day before. After a brief meal of dates, cheese and flatbread they had all gone to bed, exhausted, but Alys knew that, like herself, the others had found little sleep. She could see it in Joanie's tired eyes and drawn face. Hal looked little better.

"You're coming with me, brother," said Alys. "I need you to guide me to the official's house."

He narrowed his eyes. "You're mistaken, if you think I'll do that."

Alys took up his hand. "You must. Listen to me. If we go now, it's likely I can catch their servants coming back from the bazaar, and I can talk to them, find a way in and get Tomaso back."

He shook his head. "You heard Barnabas."

Joanie rose and came beside Alys, "You can't do it. You mustn't. Barnabas said it was too dangerous."

Alys waved her hand. "He's overly cautious because of what happened to him in the past. With my head covering and you escorting me, no one will think anything is amiss."

"Barnabas said your manner and clothes are too fine. You wouldn't be taken for a servant."

"I know how to behave. I'll keep my head down," said Alys. She looked around the room and, on impulse took the long threadbare covering from across the bed. "I'll put this on, as well. No one could think me other than a servant wearing this."

Hal gave her a sceptical look. "But you don't know the language."

She lifted her head. "I can speak Latin well enough. Someone will know that. And if not, I will manage, you can count on it."

Hal shook his head, still uncertain.

Alys took his arm and led him to the door. "We must go, now. There's no time to waste."

Hal sighed and took up his own length of cloth and wrapped it around his head. He opened the door and looked back at Joanie. "You'll explain to Barnabas, if he gets back before us?"

Joanie pursed her lips. "I'll explain, but I'll make it clear that I didn't agree. But God go with you both and be careful. This is a drear place that leaves me very uneasy."

Alys leaned over and gave Joanie a quick kiss on the cheek. "We will have a care. But all will be well, you'll see."

A moment later Hal and Alys were making their way down the narrow street and turning down the next. She followed him silently, her eyes cast down, trying to minimise her limp. The noise and bustle of the bazaar reached her from the next road and it gave her some reassurance and some element of calm. Her sturdy leather shoes skidded on the cobble from something slimy and rotten. She felt a jar in the hip of her bad leg. The smell of fish, meat and fruit in various stages of ripeness mixed with the pungent odour of spices made her head spin a little.

Men jostled her as they passed by, intent on their destination or just plain uncaring of her, dressed as she was as some poor servant. She smiled, glad suddenly that the slime that had caused her to slip had also stained her obviously expensive and well-made shoes.

Gradually, the narrow streets widened and became more airy and a few palm trees dotted the ends and enclosed gardens peeked out behind lattice carved stone walls. At the end of one such wall Hal stopped and she nearly collided into him.

"This is it," he said quietly. "But you can't wait 'ere, in plain view. It would look too suspicious."

Alys looked around and then pointed. "I'll wait over there, in the shadow of that gateway. No one will see me from there, but I still have a good view of the house."

Hal studied the gateway and eventually nodded. "Fine. We'll stand there."

They made their way to the opening and Hal positioned himself in front, his broad frame blocking her so she wasn't visible from the street.

"I can't see," she said.

"I can see," said Hal curtly. "And that's all that matters."

She decided against any retort and prepared to settle herself for a while. A servant might take up most of her morning getting everything that was needed to feed a household this size, she realised, and it was even possible that they might have more than one. Though the grain and other bulk goods might be delivered, vegetables and whatever else fresh they might buy would certainly be purchased on a daily basis, she reasoned.

She studied the house. It was a fair size, made of adobe, with three floors and a large courtyard. Overlooking the courtyard was a *mashrabiya*, a type of projecting oriel window enclosed with carved wood latticework, lined with stained glass.

The sun gradually shifted and their small, shaded area in the gateway began to be exposed. Though it was wintertime, in this part of the world there was still heat in the sun. Hal muttered a few complaints periodically until, eventually, he told Alys they should leave.

"Barnabas will be back by now, and perhaps have Tomaso with him," he said.

She wiped the sweat gathering on her brow and the back of her neck, beneath the head covering. "Just a little longer, please," she said.

Hal mumbled a grudging assent and shifted against her. She could feel the heat coming from him and knew that he was feeling the sun's strength too. His reddened face showed as much.

She wiped her own brow again and heard the sound of someone approaching. She peered out and felt Hal straighten beside her. It was a woman, covered from head to toe, carried two heavily laden baskets and behind her an older boy carried another basket. They approached the door to the courtyard of the house where Tomaso was and stopped. The woman placed the baskets at her feet and reached for the latch. Alys took a deep breath, gently pushed Hal aside and made her way over to the woman.

"Please," she said in Latin. "Can I speak with you a moment?"

The woman gave her a puzzled look.

Alys tried again, this time in Italian. Perhaps with all the traders from all the Italian ports the woman might know a few words. She spoke slowly, gesturing.

"Can you tell if there is a monkey inside?" she asked.

The woman stared at her a moment then glanced at the boy beside her. He eyed Alys suspiciously. The woman spoke to him rapidly. She handed him one of the baskets and, reluctantly, he opened the gate and went inside. The woman held the gate open and gestured to her. Alys hesitated. She looked at Hal who crossed over to her, but the woman held up a hand and shook her head.

Hal put a restraining hand on Alys's arm. "You can't go in there. Not alone. It's not safe."

"It's fine, Hal," Alys said. "I won't be long. I'll just check and see if I can find out if Tomaso is there and if so, where he's being kept."

"No. I can't let you do it."

Alys shook off his hand and pushed him away, irritated. "I'll be fine," she said in a firm ton. "I told you. Just stay here and wait. I won't be long."

He gave her a mulish look but said nothing more. A moment later he stepped back to the gateway, still frowning. He put a hand at his waist where she knew he had a dagger hidden in the sash that was wrapped around him. "If I see anything suspicious, I'm coming in."

She gave him an encouraging smile and wondered how much use the dagger would be inside the official's house. But she was determined to go through with it and with a nod to the woman she followed her through the gate and to the house. Once inside, the woman motioned for Alys to remain where she was. The woman disappeared through a door, leaving Alys alone in the small entrance room.

The room was lined with tiles painted with intricate designs in blues and dark reds. Alys studied them carefully, liking their pattern and wondering how she might incorporate such a design in a painting. Her contemplation ended a few moments later when the woman returned. She put her finger to her lips and took Alys's hand, leading her out of the small entrance room, down a dark tile-lined corridor to a staircase. She climbed after the woman, making a conscious effort to disguise the difficulty the stairs caused with her limp. At the top of the staircase was a small landing and a door. The woman tapped on it and spoke a few words. The door opened and a pale face appeared.

Though the light was dim, Alys could see fair hair under the blue sheer cotton veil that wrapped the woman's head and draped her shoulders. Her light brown eyes were rimmed with kohl. The fair haired woman looked at Alys curiously and stepped out onto the landing. Her hair was braided in one long plait down her back, and her gown hung loosely to the floor. She exchanged a few words with the other woman who nodded and disappeared inside, shutting the door behind her.

"Abila tells me you stopped her outside and tried to ask her something but she couldn't understand you. She thought I might help you." she said in Italian. Her tone was even, with a hint of caution.

Alys felt the tension that had wound her tightly for the past several hours release. "You speak Italian. That's more than I expected. But what are you doing here?" Alys said, her relief at being understood causing a flood of words to pour out. "In the home of a harbour official? In his ...." She stopped herself, but she knew it was too late. The damage was done.

The woman raised her brow and gave a slight smile.

"I'm sorry," said Alys. "I'm not here to pry into your affairs. I'm here only to make a brief inquiry about someone." She took a deep breath and began again. "I'm Alys. I've only lately come from Venice. When we arrived in the harbour I'm afraid an unfortunate mistake was made."

"A mistake?" said the woman. "What does a mistake at the harbour have to do with this household?"

Alys paused a moment, phrasing her explanation carefully. "It's a matter of a misunderstanding about our cargo. I think your ....the harbour official who I understand lives here, mistakenly thought my monkey was part of the cargo and confiscated him."

"Your monkey?" the woman asked.

"Yes," Alys said quickly. "Tomaso. He's not part of the cargo, I assure you. He was given as a gift, some time ago and he's very precious to me. I-I wouldn't be without him."

"No," said the woman. She frowned. "You say his name is Tomaso?"

Alys nodded and held her hands apart. "He's about this big, furry and large brown eyes." She gave a feeble laugh. "I suppose that covers any monkey. But he does do some tricks."

The woman nodded. "And you say he was a gift."

Alys nodded again. "A gift, yes. Given to me a few years ago."

"By someone special?"

Alys studied her carefully. The woman seemed to be stalling, but why?

"Do you perhaps know if a monkey was brought here, either by the harbour official or someone else?"

"I—"

The door opened and another woman appeared and stepped out onto the landing in a cloud of perfume. Long dark hair hung loose about her shoulders and waist underneath a velvet cap topped by a sheer saffron coloured silk veil edged with gold. Gold bracelets lined her arms and gold gem-encrusted rings crowded her hands. She wore a skirt embroidered with leafy designs and loose top of matching saffron silk. Like the light haired woman her eyes were kohl rimmed, but her lips were reddened and her nails painted. She spoke with the light-haired woman, her voice authoritative. An exchange ensued and at the end of it the light haired woman bowed and turned to Alys.

"My mistress asks that you enter and enjoy her hospitality."

"Your mistress?"

"Yes, she is the first wife of Shafik ibn Taghri, my master."

"You're not his wife?"

The woman gave a slight laugh and shook her head. "No."

"You're a servant then?"

The woman gave a wry smile. "Of a kind. I'm a concubine."

Alys nodded. "I see." She returned the smile.

The woman bowed to her mistress, opened the door to the room. Her mistress entered, and the fair haired woman gestured Alys to follow. "Come, my mistress awaits you."

"Your name?" asked Alys. "What may I call you?"

"Here I am known as Halifa. But you may call me Caterina."

Alys stepped inside, steeling herself for what would obviously be delicate negotiations. Before she could take in her surroundings she heard a loud screeching. Tomaso.

CHAPTER SIX
TYRE, LEBANON, WINTER 1448
ALYS

Alys balanced the hot glass on her knees, her hands clammy, despite the heat from the small brazier nearby. Across from her, Tomaso sat in his cage, tantalising her with his proximity. Caterina sat on her right, across from Cyla, the harbour official's First Wife, while other women lounged sultrily on cushions scattered around the large room. Thick carpets lined the floor and incense perfumed the air, but mixed with the heavy scents from the women, most especially Cyla, it became stifling and Alys found herself almost wishing for the fetid odours of the harbour.

Cyla spoke to Caterina now, her melodious laugh punctuating her words. Alys watched Cyla's eyes, hoping for a clue as to what was being said, what Cyla thought about her query over Tomaso. So far she was in the dark, having been ushered to this cushion and made to wait while words of hospitality were given and accepted. Some of the women whispered to each other behind their hands, their eyes curious and assessing. It was only after the drink was given to her, a small bowl of figs and sweetmeats placed beside her and a she offered a small explanation of who she was and how she came to be in Tyre, that Caterina had agreed to bring up Tomaso.

The reaction Alys observed and the light tone of her voice made Alys wonder exactly what Caterina had said.

Caterina turned to her. "My mistress wants to know more about the merchant that you travel with. He is your husband?"

Alys gave a casual smile. "No, but we are..."she paused trying to search for the right words, "together," she finally settled on.

Caterina raised her brow and gave a wry smile. "Together? Do you mean you are a concubine of sorts?"

Alys frowned. "No." What made her suddenly so conscious of propriety? Was it because no one had challenged their relationship or required an explanation of who she was for so long that she had begun to believe there was something formal between her and Barnabas? Would admitting to their true relationship harm her goal?

She took a breath and made a quick decision. "No, though I was a courtesan in Venice," she said. "Giacomo Bonavillagio is my patron," she waved her hand delicately, "and something more."

She saw the knowing look in Caterina's face and felt compelled to explain her real relationship with Barnabas, to define it accurately.

"I have known Signor Bonavillagio a long time. Since we were children. We now have a child together."

"Was the monkey for your child?"

Alys glanced over at Tomaso. "You have asked about my monkey?"

Caterina smiled and shook her head. "No, the opportunity hasn't presented itself yet. But I thought if the child were mentioned as longing for the monkey there might be some opportunity to put your dilemma to my mistress."

Alys gave a weak smile. "No, Tomaso was given to me before my daughter was born. But she was taken with him, though she was only an infant."

"Was an infant? Is she no longer alive?"

Alys bit her lip and looked away. It had slipped out naturally to say 'was' and it was only because she was thinking about when she had last seen Eleanor. Was it an omen that she put her daughter in the past tense? Eleanor's blonde head and large eyes flashed in her mind. No. It was impossible to believe that her daughter was dead. She felt a tug – of hope? Certainty?

"She is alive. At least I believe so. She was taken from us some months past."

Caterina's brow creased in concern. She placed a hand over Alys's arm. "I am sorry. That's truly an awful thing for you. I know what it is to lose a child."

Alys looked up at her and saw the compassion written on her face. "Thank you."

Cyla tugged at Caterina's arm and spoke insistently. Alys saw the curiosity and impatience on her young face and heard the soothing tones that Caterina used when she answered. Caterina gestured to Tomaso and Cyla glanced over at the monkey. She fired off some questions to Caterina, who answered them briefly and then turned to Alys.

"My mistress would like to know more about your daughter. She wonders if you would just not try again and this time hope for a son?"

Caterina's expression was neutral, but there was something more in her eyes that told Alys that Caterina didn't support Cyla's sentiments.

"She has no children?" Alys asked.

"No, not yet. But she hopes for a son."

She thought of Eleanor gripping her finger, her weight in her arms, the special milky scent that belonged only to her. "Perhaps you can explain to her that my daughter is as dear to me as any son might be to her."

"Of course," said Caterina. "You must forgive her. She's young, but not without compassion. She has already mentioned that she will consider returning the monkey to you, but she must think what she will say to her husband."

Alys's heart lifted a little at Caterina's words. "Please tell her that it's very kind of her. And let her know also that Eleanor is special to me, that we have been through much already to get her back and hope now, that some trace of her might be found here in Tyre."

"In Tyre?" asked Caterina.

"The woman who took her is said to have come this way. At least we think so."

"Your child was taken by a woman?" said Caterina, concern in her voice. "But that is terrible? How did that come to be?"

Alys studied her hands. "I had to leave my child in her care in order that I could to travel far away to help Signor Bonavillagio, who was himself in extreme difficulty with a man who wished him ill." She waved her hand. "There is much to this tale, but suffice to say that it was resolved, but when we returned we found the woman and our child gone." She took a deep breath and forced herself to carry on. "As far as we could discover she had decided to travel east along the big trading route, towards Samarkand."

Caterina frowned. "But there are many trading routes to Samarkand. Do you know that she came to Tyre?"

Alys shook her head. "No. But we hope to find some trace of her. Do you know if any Venetian woman who came here recently? She is badly scarred from burns and so she is heavily veiled."

Caterina sighed. "No, no one of that description has arrived in Tyre. But most women are veiled to some degree. I will ask my mistress, though." She placed a hand on Alys's arm again and gave her a compassionate look. "It is indeed a difficult task you have undertaken and one that surely must come from a deep love. But I fear I must caution you against journeying on to Samarkand. It isn't safe. The roads are filled with danger from cutthroats and thieves who have no mercy."

Cyla shook Caterina's arm and spoke urgently. Caterina looked apologetic and gave her a long answer while Alys sat back and digested Caterina's words. All the doubt and dread that had filled her about this journey rushed back and set her into turmoil.

Cyla continued to speak, gesturing now to Tomaso over in the cage. Alys followed her gesture, tearing at the sight of Tomaso who peered out and, catching her eye, smacked his lips and made kisses. She gave a weak smile.

"My mistress has said that I must urge you to turn back. The journey onwards is safe only if you are accompanied by many guards and travel in a caravan. Even so, the risks are too great, especially for a woman. She says also that she has heard nothing of that Venetian woman, so there is little reason for you to continue on. She is sorry for the loss of your child, but she says that she will return Tomaso to you and he will bring you comfort until you can have another child."

Alys studied Caterina a moment, taking in her words. She forced herself to nod. "But what of her husband? Will he not wonder what has happened to Tomaso?"

"Ah," said Caterina. "I shouldn't worry over that. My mistress will tell him the monkey tried to bite her so she had him taken away. Her husband will not question that at all. But you must be careful and ensure no one sees Tomaso until you are safely boarded on ship and sailing away."

Alys nodded slowly. "Please convey my deepest gratitude to her for the return of Tomaso. And for her counsel. I will give it my deepest consideration."

Caterina gave her hand a squeeze. "It is hard to turn back from something that seems so compelling. But it will be for the best. I'm certain that this woman will have gone somewhere different. Just as it's not safe to journey to Samarkand for a woman, it is doubly true for a woman and a child."

A thought struck Alys. "She wasn't on her own. She was in the company of a man."

Caterina frowned. "A merchant?"

"No. He was a Venetian who, though knowledgeable about card games and fighting, wasn't a merchant."

Caterina gave a knowing nod. "Ah. Well, I can assure you we have heard nothing of a man of that kind in Tyre."

Alys felt a momentary relief. "But you did say there are other routes leading to Samarkand?"

"Yes. But they are just as dangerous."

Alys spirits sank and her moment of decisiveness vanished. "I see. Thank you for the information. And thank you most especially for everything else. You have been more than kind."

Caterina waved her hand dismissively. "It was nothing, I assure you. I was glad to help you. I found much that was moving in your tale."

Alys nodded, knowing that there was a tale just as moving behind Caterina's eyes.

Cyla spoke to Caterina and then to another of the women, who went over to Tomaso's cage and lifted it gingerly. Tomaso screeched and stuck his hand through the cage, attempting to grab her veil. The woman held the cage away from her and moved quickly towards Alys, shoving the wooden cage into Alys's arms. Alys made some soothing sounds and Tomaso calmed.

"Come, we must go now," said Caterina. "Cyla says her husband will be home soon."

Alys nodded and, with the cage clutched to her chest, she followed Caterina. Her leg was stiff from sitting, but she forced it to behave as she made her way out and down the stairs. In a short while Alys found herself outside the house and opening the gate. She looked carefully along the road, checking for any sign of the harbour official, but could see no one. Not even Hal. She walked quickly to the gateway where she'd left him and stared at the empty space, deciding what to do.

A hand gripped her shoulder and she flung around to see Hal standing there, relief written all over his face.

"There you are, finally. I was beginning to think you'd decided to join their 'arem."

She gave a weak laugh and shook her head. "No, but I did meet a Venetian woman who was part of it. Or at least I think she was Venetian."

Hal glanced up at the windows of the second storey, an incredulous look on his face. "Really? Why would she want to live here, with them?"

Alys shook her head. "I don't know. But she was a great help to me. It was due to her that I was able to get Tomaso back."

Hal grinned and reached through the cage to give Tomaso a pat. "I see. Good to 'ave the little fella returned." He gripped her arm. "But we should get back now. Barnabas will be wondering where we are. 'e'll be glad to know something's been righted. Now we can get back to finding Eleanor and that woman Alessandra. Perhaps Barnabas will have learned something and we can catch up with her soon."

Alys frowned at his last words, for she knew the answer already. And she knew that answer would take her onto a most unpleasant argument with Barnabas. Would she be able to convince him finally that this journey was useless?

❧

"The risk was too great. You shouldn't have gone," said Barnabas.

He looked drawn and tired, and for a moment Alys softened. "I'm sorry, I didn't mean to worry you. I just thought we might have greater success if I approached one of the serving women instead of you."

Barnabas ran a hand across his stubbled chin, and in the light of the late afternoon coming through the small window she could see the shadows under his eyes. He hadn't shaved since they had arrived and had slept little because he'd been too consumed with his need to find proof that Alessandra had been in Tyre. It must stop, Alys could see that. She glanced over at Joanie who herself looked tired and worn out on her stool by the window. Hal stood beside her, his arms crossed. They were both frowning at Barnabas.

Alys took a seat on the small bed. "Well, I did succeed and all is well, so there is no need to dwell on it. Tomaso is back with us, safe and sound, though Cyla did caution us to keep him well hidden until we left." She took a deep breath. "In the process of persuading her to give up Tomaso I explained our reason for being here. She cautioned against continuing along this trade route because it is far too dangerous. And she said it was especially foolish because she had heard nothing of Alessandra's presence here."

Barnabas frowned. "She wouldn't necessarily know if Alessandra had come to Tyre. She is secluded in the harem."

Alys snorted. "She has a whole network of people who give her information about what goes on outside the harem. She probably is more informed than the officials of Tyre. What else can a lively minded woman confined to a few chambers do all day?"

Barnabas studied her and sighed. "Perhaps. But that doesn't mean that Alessandra isn't in Samarkand, or on her way there. There is more than one trade route to Samarkand."

"Yes, Caterina said as much. She also said that all the routes were just as dangerous. Cutthroats, thieves and any other kind of brigand you could name are active there. It's not safe for any man, especially a man not part of a large caravan, let alone women and children. Why would Alessandra take a child along that route?"

"It may be so, but I saw the vision. I know Alessandra. She would be drawn to the thought of the riches she would acquire."

"But with that scoundrel courtier to protect her?" said Joanie, her voice full of scorn. "'e would be no protection. 'e's only good for cards, or a little fancy sword play. They'd cut 'im down in a trice. Alys is right. There is no reason to put ourselves in such danger."

Barnabas frowned. "They could have joined a caravan with soldiers."

"That be only chance. And we've 'eard nothing to say they have been 'ere," said Joanie.

"Barnabas," said Hal, his tone reasonable. "We all know you've done everything to find out if there was sight or sound of 'er and you've found nothing. Don't you think it's time we went back and tried something else?"

"No," said Barnabas emphatically. "I know that I saw in my vision. To do anything other than proceed to Samarkand would be foolish."

"How can you be so foolhardy with our daughter's life?" said Alys incredulously. "We should go back to Venice." She glared at him, her frustration and anger growing.

Barnabas looked at her and shook his head, his face a riot of anguish and sorrow. He sat down beside her on the bed and took her hand. "Alys. My Alys. I know you think this is foolhardy. And you're right, it is fraught with danger. But I must go onward to Samarkand. I know it to be right so deeply, so surely, I can't turn back – and I beg of you to understand that." He squeezed her hand. "But you're right. It is dangerous. Far too dangerous for you and Joanie. So I agree. You must turn back. Hal will accompany you, Tomaso and Joanie to Venice. But I, my dearest Alys, must go to Samarkand."

Alys saw the stubbornness, the determination behind the anguish and sorrow. She could see he believed he was right and there was nothing she could do to convince him otherwise. But it was Eleanor's life that mattered and for her she would go to Venice, because there, reason told her, she could find the way to Alessandra through her sister.

She blinked back tears and straightened, determined not to have him see her cry, but the pain that she felt and the fear that it was the wrong decision threatened to overwhelm her. She stood and he reached out for her. She let him rest his hand on her arm.

"There is no choice. I will return to Venice. And you must do what you feel is best."

She knew he would stay, that there was a chance she would never see him again, but there was no other way. God willing, it wouldn't be permanently. Surely one of them would find Eleanor and they could be a family.

CHAPTER SEVEN
TRADE ROUTE TO SAMARKAND
BARNABAS

I watched the ship become smaller and smaller until it disappeared. The salt air stung my cheeks but I didn't feel it. I was oblivious to the shouts, bustle and clank of men loading and unloading cargo onto boats to take to the ships anchored in the harbour. It was mayhem, created into some kind of order by the harbour officials with their soldiers. I was immune to it all.

I could think only of Alys, Eleanor and Alessandra. Their names were going through my mind on a never ending cycle while I questioned every decision I'd made, every word I'd spoken and everything I saw. Or thought I saw. Now, watching the ship that bore Alys disappear from view, I could only wonder if I was completely foolhardy and driven by my own stubbornness, or just plain mad. I had no money, only the trade goods I had acquired along the way and here in Tyre. I'd given what money I had to Alys for her journey back to Venice.

I tried to conjure up again the vision that had convinced me so thoroughly that Alessandra was in

Samarkand, or heading towards there. The blue tiled mosque. Was that really in Samarkand, or had the man I'd asked been confused?

I tried to recall all the details of that image, noting them carefully. I would do what I could to at least check this part of the vision. Surely I could find someone here who would confirm it for me. That would be my first step. And at the same time I would see if the goods I'd brought might be used to barter more desirable goods to trade on the way and some coin so that I might find a caravan I could join and pay for guards.

I forced myself to turn and head away from the seafront. Already I missed Hal's reassuring company and joking manner. Ahead of me, in a large square, a cluster of merchants waited while their goods were strapped onto the backs of donkeys. The men were swarthy, with the dark hair and beards of the Levant. A large, burly man dressed in robes of tan and white, issued orders to the workers who loaded the donkeys. There were about twenty donkeys in all. I moved closer and listened intently, trying to understand him.

"Not like that, you fool," the man said. "Strap it tighter. Do you want me to lose all my goods along the way?"

"You treat your slaves all too well," said the short, stocky man next to him. His beard was sparse and greying.

The other man just shrugged him off. The few men behind the stocky man stood silently watching. I straightened, smoothed the belt at my waist and approached, a pleasant smile on my face.

"I humbly beg your pardon," I said in Arabic. "But may I ask you gentlemen some questions? You seem as though you are all experienced travellers along these roads."

The men turned and looked at me politely, bowing slightly. "You may ask the questions," said the burly man, his accent thick. "We will do our best to help you."

I swept my gaze around them all and then fixed it on the burly man. "I have a small amount of goods to trade and I was hoping to join a caravan heading towards Samarkand. I had heard it's a place of great wonders." I swept my glance around again and smiled warmly. "Would any of you know Samarkand?"

The men glanced at each other. "While no one here would claim to know Samarkand directly," said the stocky man. "But it is a place of great repute."

I nodded encouragingly. They exchanged more glances. "Forgive me," I said. "I must introduce myself. I am Giacomo Bonavillagio, lately of Venice."

The men nodded and the burly man stepped forward and bowed, introducing himself as Ahmad ibn Allah. The stocky man was Abdel al-Baati. The others were briefly introduced and I bowed to each one.

When the introductions were complete I spoke again. "I should like to hear something of the tales of Samarkand. But I understand that you are engaged in your business. You begin your journey soon?"

"Tomorrow, *inshallah*," said ibn Allah. "That's if the goods are loaded securely." He dubiously eyed the labourers strapping the goods to the donkeys.

"You are travelling far?" I asked in a polite tone.

"We aren't going as far as Samarkand," said ibn Allah. "We travel only as far as Damascus. Even that far brings risks."

He indicated the soldiers who sat on stumps and stools against the wall of the far building. They were oiling their leathers and honing their swords, all the while keeping an eye on the piles of goods being loaded on the donkeys. Clearly, even here in Tyre, something as simple as loading goods on donkeys required a show of force.

"I have heard Damascus provides good trading prospects," I said carefully.

Baati shrugged. "It has some good opportunities. Many years ago, in my grandfather's time, before Timur and his men laid waste to this region there was much more trading." He'd muttered the last bits and glanced sideways at ibn Allah and the rest of his companions.

Ibn Allah reddened. "Timur was a great man. I will not have you disparage his name."

"I only spoke truth," said Baati sourly. "Trading is a more difficult prospect now. The risks are greater, the costs more, and profit less. It is only a matter of time before the silks are made in the West and other trade goods that we obtain from the east, the glass, the ceramics, are routed through less dangerous territory."

"But there is still profit to be made," I said in a warm tone. "We all can share in that until the time comes to find other routes and other trade goods."

"Exactly," said ibn Allah. He turned to me. "And what is it that you trade, my friend?"

"Pepper mainly. I have a small amount of other goods."

Ibn Allah nodded. "And you hope to take it to Samarkand?"

It was my time to shrug. "I'm considering it. I've heard the stories of its wonders so I thought it would be worth journeying there. Gold painted mosques with domes covered in blue tiles, was one story I'd heard. Surely that is a sight to behold."

"And it would be, were you to see it," said ibn Allah.

"You have heard of this story yourself?" I asked.

Ibn Allah gave a speculative frown. "Perhaps. I recall nothing that specific about Samarkand."

I looked at his companions and smiled. "Maybe one of you have?"

The group exchanged glances, some shrugging others shaking their heads.

"You have heard this in Venice?" asked Baati.

"In my travels," I said.

"It could be fabrication," said Baati. "Men enjoy a good tale and that sounds like one."

I shrugged as if it didn't concern me. "It was a woman. With scars from burns. A Venetian woman, who wears a veil covering her head and gloves on her hands all the time. She was full of intriguing tales and mentioned she would go to Samarkand to see for herself. She had a small child and a dark-haired Venetian man with her. Richly dressed they both were."

Baati spat. "Ah, well you would expect nothing but lies from a woman,"

Ibn Allah put a hand on Baati's shoulder and grinned. "My companion here has had some bad luck with the women. He has wives that give him endless trouble. Whereas I can appreciate that they have some very fine points." He dropped his hand and smiled warmly at me. "But come, you might find more about your blue tiles and gold domes in Damascus. Why don't you travel with us?"

I paused, still aware of the doubts that riddled my mind over whether the blue tiled dome was real and that it existed in Samarkand. I'd had no confirmation and had not the slightest inkling that Alessandra had come this way while heading to Samarkand.

Knowing I must decide quickly, I plunged in and thanked him heartily. He might be right. Though I had planned to head directly toward Palmyra, in Damascus I might at least get some more information. And it was a caravan of sorts and being part of it when reaching Damascus might assist me in securing a place in a caravan there heading east.

In some ways I was relieved it had been so easy to find a caravan, albeit a small one going only a small part of my journey. I was glad then, after confirming arrangements with the men, to return to my quarters with one of their slaves to collect my own goods to strap to two of the donkeys they were willing to loan me. At a price, of course. But I had expected nothing more.

～

The sun was strong, which helped to offset the wind that blew our robes about us and sent sand into my eyes. The road was dusty and the donkeys plodded through the swirling sand steadily, but with little speed. Laden down, but well trained, these donkeys moved at a pace slower than the horses that mounted the merchants and the soldiers. The terrain had been tough in places, especially when crossing Mt Hermon. It was behind us now and I was glad of it. We'd covered over half the distance to Damascus, but we'd been on the road for five days already.

I scratched the beginnings of the beard that had grown since my arrival at Tyre. I was tired and was ready to rest. It was nearing dusk and soon we would be setting up a camp as there was no caravanserai or village to house us. We waited a moment while one of the soldiers checked the terrain ahead, where in the distance a group approached from the east. Up to this point we'd met only a few herders and other inhabitants of the terrain we crossed and I realised that I'd begun to relax my guard.

But as this group approached, the tension that had gripped me on the first day or so of our travels rose again.

I strained my eyes to make them out. Some were armed, the glint of steel and a few bows strapped across backs evident at this distance. I touched the dagger at my side. Though it was of little use on a horse, at close quarters I was confident I could inflict some damage.

The soldier turned his mount and galloped back to us. He spoke quickly to ibn Allah, who I'd come to understand was the leader of this caravan. All the soldiers and the slaves answered to him. He provided the donkeys and made the arrangements at the caravanserai when we stopped. All for a price. That price, I'd learned, was an elusive sum that seemed to change as the days progressed and I was certain was the reason he'd encouraged me so warmly to travel with them.

Ibn Allah replied to the soldier and I tried to read the nuances in the tone. They spoke Sogdian, primarily because the soldiers originated from the east, but it was also the language of the caravans along these routes. Ibn Allah, once a soldier himself in his young years, had come from the region further east, near the Turkish lands, and though he'd lived in Tyre for many years, he was still comfortable with the language of his birth.

The tone, I decided, seemed neither fearful nor menacing. If anything, it was curious. Taking heart from that I urged my horse forward, nearer to ibn Allah.

"Do you recognise the group that approaches?" I asked him.

"I think not," said ibn Allah. "But perhaps one of our companions does. My man says only that he thinks it is a group of traders like ourselves, returning from the East."

By the time the group arrived it was clear the soldier had assessed the situation correctly. Ibn Allah made some polite exchanges with the leader of the other caravan and after a few minutes' conversation, ibn Allah's demeanour became friendlier and more open. Before long it was clear that we were to share a camp for the night. It made sense. It would provide us a chance to exchange news as well as share companionship and break up some of the tedium of the journey. But knowing this didn't help my uneasiness.

I'd watched ibn Allah throughout the journey, recognising the ruthless businessman in him, but always on the lookout for something more in him that would give me some indication of his designs regarding me. I was no fool to believe that he took me into his caravan for the small amount of money he would earn, or the goodness of his heart. With a keen eye to my goods that I had brought into my tent each night, I was careful never to give him an opportunity to assume I was a fool either. It might be that with this other caravan sharing our camp for the night he had been given an opportunity to profit in some way that didn't concern me, but I wasn't so certain.

Later, after the tents were erected, the meals prepared and presented to the group of merchants who gathered in ibn Allah's copious tent and I had finally retired to my tent, I thought I might have found the answer. A request arrived for me to return to ibn Allah's tent. There, engaged in a friendly conversation, were the three merchants from the other caravan, but there was no sign of Baati, or the other men from our group.

The reason became clear soon enough. They were seated on the piles of cushions as before, the thick brightly coloured carpet before them. Ibn Allah was intent on a serious game of cards involving stakes that were higher than any I'd played in Venice. Cards, I knew, were forbidden for the followers of Allah, and gambling was even more taboo. I eyed the merchants from the other caravan and realised they were more than likely of other faiths. Ibn Allah, a Mamluk convert of many years, had obviously decided that his faith took a lower priority to profit.

Ibn Allah was adept at cards. The three other merchants weren't. Two of them had the tilted eyes and flattened faces of the Far East. The taller one who had a long nose, possessed some skill, but it was nothing compared to ibn Allah's who had undoubtedly honed his abilities when he was a soldier. The third merchant, Petros Krestopolis, was an olive skinned grey haired Greek and he had only the rudiments of the game. I played my own game carefully, eyeing ibn Allah and his hands with a sharpness that he detected, but made no comment about.

"You have played this game more than once," said ibn Allah in Latin.

Latin was the language we agreed to speak, for the men from the east seemed to have some grasp of it, though sometimes the Greek man acted as interpreter.

I shrugged. "I have some acquaintance with it." I played a card, testing ibn Allah. He grinned. "You have your own particular skill," I added.

The card was picked up. Ibn All pretended to frown, glancing at his other opponents. They studied their cards carefully, considering my card and their own. Ibn Allah sighed and placed a card on the carpet. I blinked. Looked at my own hand and reviewed what had been played, even though I knew the answer. He was cheating. I regarded the other men, who seemed oblivious to what I had just discovered. I looked at him, careful to keep my expression bland. He grinned. He knew what I had done by placing down the particular card and why.

I considered my course of action. I had nothing to gain by exposing him as a cheat. These men would probably not thank me for revealing their ignorance of an obvious cheat, nor would the other merchants from my caravan appreciate that a complete stranger had exposed their trusted companion and fellow Muslim as a gambler.

One of the servants from the other caravan entered and bowed. Krestopolis looked up and beckoned the man forward. He whispered into his ear and Krestopolis nodded, then turned to ibn Allah.

"I must beg a favour. My sister travels with us and she has come to hear there is a Venetian travelling with you." He gave me a polite smile and nod. "We have some distant cousins in that city and she would like to speak with Domine Bonavillagio, if you would be so good as to excuse him from our company for a short while. And if Domine Bonavillagio is agreeable."

Ibn Allah gestured widely in my direction. "Though it might pain us to be deprived of your company and card playing, we must of course accommodate a beautiful woman, especially if she is your sister, Domine Krestopolis. Domine Bonavillagio, I'm sure you won't mind visiting the lady?"

I bowed my head in affirmation, and smiled wryly. "Of course. It would be my pleasure."

I scooped up my small winnings, rose and followed the servant out of the tent, thankful I at least had my decision deferred about any action I should take. Perhaps I would be allowed to seek my bed after exchanging a few pleasantries with what would assuredly be a grey haired old matriarch who would tire easily.

The tent, though smaller than ibn Allah's, was luxuriously appointed with expensive thick carpets and silk cushions. A scented brazier burned warmly, mixing with the heavy perfume that hung in the air to create a cloying atmosphere. Silver plates filled with figs and dates and cooked dishes were scattered in a corner. In the centre, reclining on brightly coloured silk and tasselled cushions was a woman dressed in a deep red silk gown and a matching veil that covered her head, shoulders and was draped across her face so that only her kohl rimmed eyes showed.

After I bowed, she beckoned me forward, the silver bangles on her arm jingling loudly. I approached her and at her indication took a seat on a cushion placed beside her. She snapped her fingers and waved at the attending female servant. The servant, a Greek by all appearances too, with her dark curly hair and simple dark gown, bobbed a curtsey and followed the male servant out of the tent, leaving the two of us alone. Curious, I looked over at the woman whose eyes were filled with laughter.

"I fear I have shocked my servants beyond recovery," she said, in Italian, her voice high and bright.

"I'm sorry madam, I fear you have the better of me," I replied in Italian, striving to keep my tone even and light. "Shall I address you simply as Signor Krestopolis's sister?"

She gave a trill of laughter. "Oh, please don't. For it isn't true. You may call me Pania."

"Signora Pania," I repeated dumbly. I studied the lively eyes, the slim figure, the young hands. "Did I misunderstand? You're his wife? Forgive my mistake."

The laugh came again. "Oh, no. Not his wife. Though he might wish it." She removed the veil, uncovering her face and long, luxurious black hair, the oiled ringlets shining in the light of the oil lamps. Her shoulders, no longer covered by the veil, were as smooth and flawless as the voluptuous breasts that the low cut of her gown revealed. Her mouth, pouting softly was full and red, and her cheeks glowed softly.

She stroked my cheek with her hand. "You are as handsome as they said."

I cocked my brow. "They?"

She smiled. "The servants."

"Should I be flattered?"

"Oh you should. You most definitely should. It's not often I take an interest like this."

"And why am I so honoured then?" I gestured to the luxury around us. "I am hardly a rich merchant, or a lord that would clearly have you bestir yourself in my direction."

She dismissed the room with a wave. "Oh be certain that Petros has my ultimate loyalty. For now." She ran her tongue along her lips. "But I sometimes crave a little taste of the exotic."

"I am exotic now, am I?"

She fingered one of my curls. "Oh, I believe so." She touched my beard. "Though this, I think, must go."

I gave a short laugh. "I think that might be a decision for me to make." I smiled politely. "While I am not unaware of your charms, I hardly think that Signor Krestopolis would appreciate it if I was to sample them."

She tossed her dark curls. "Oh let's not become fussy, now. Be patient, you'll see that it will be worth your while to do as I wish."

She leaned forward, her breasts in danger of tumbling out of her gown and her scent filling my head. "You are special, am I not right?"

A small wave of unease rose up in me. "Special?" I said cautiously. "I assure you, there is nothing about me that is particularly special."

Still leaning towards me, she took my hand and placed it on top of her breasts. "You can see into my heart," she said with a flirty laugh. She slipped her hand inside my robe and along my tunic. "I can see things too," she whispered.

I pulled back and her hands dropped away. I studied her face, trying to discover if there was more meaning behind her words. "I'm afraid you've lost me."

"Perhaps, but you do see things, do you not?"

I gave her a puzzled look, determined not to understand. "I see you before me, a beautiful woman with a generous patron who for some reason wanted to speak to me."

She grabbed my hand, this time an earnest expression on her face. "I had to be sure it was you. But I'm certain I'm right. I can tell. You are the one who has the sight."

I withdrew my hand and frowned. "No, you are mistaken."

She shook her head. "I know that I'm not." She bit her lip. "I have the sight as well. And I saw you. As soon as you entered the tent I was sure you were the one, but I had to be certain."

"The one?"

"You seek something, isn't that right?"

I shrugged. "Perhaps. Don't we all seek something? Right now I would seek a comfortable bed."

She gave me a brief provocative look, but abandoned it when I didn't respond. She sighed. "Well I thought I might have some fun as well." She fingered one of my curls. "Since you are undoubtedly a tempting dish. But I see you will not play."

"Signora," I began. "Pania, what is it you want with me?"

She crossed her arms and her face went into a sulk, revealing her extreme youth. Was she even sixteen? How had she come to this pass at such an early age? I supposed it could only be the ripe, beautiful body and desire for wealth.

She took my hand again and squeezed it. "You must believe me, Giacomo. I may call you Giacomo? But I too have the sight and these few weeks past I have continuously had a vision. A vision of you, in great danger."

"I am in danger?" I quipped lightly.

"Yes," she said solemnly. "I was scrying, you see. In my wide silver bowl that I use. It's something I do betimes when things are dull. And I saw you being attacked by several assailants." A tear formed and she blinked it away artfully. "It was awful. They had large daggers." She held out her fingers, demonstrating their length. "And they were plunging them into you repeatedly."

"What was I wearing?" I asked.

"What?"

"Can you describe my clothes?"

She paused and then gestured towards me. "I don't know. Something like you are wearing now. I was too caught up in the attack to pay much notice."

I smiled smoothly. "I only ask because it gives me some clue as to where the attack might take place, or if it has already happened."

She gave me a puzzled frown. "But surely you haven't been attacked in such a manner before?"

I considered a moment. "Not by several men armed with daggers, I suppose. But I have been attacked."

Her mouth formed a small "oh" and then she recovered herself. "But this danger is to come, that I know."

"I see. And do you know where this danger lurks?"

She nodded eagerly. "The road you follow now."

"The road to Damascus?"

"No, no. Further along."

"You know I'm going beyond Damascus?"

"Of course. I saw it in the vision. You head east, *si*?"

"*Si.*"

"You must turn back, Giacomo. It isn't safe. Those attackers will kill you." She rubbed her hand along my arm. "And I wouldn't want that to happen." She took my hand and licked one of my fingers. "Why don't you accompany us to Tyre? I can promise you it will be a highly pleasurable journey."

"As much as your offer tempts me, I'm afraid I must refuse. I have matters that compel me to journey on."

She pouted a moment. "Will you at least give me a kiss of thanks?" She leaned forward and placed her hand around my head and pressed a kiss on my lips. Caught off guard, I fell forward and she took advantage of the moment and pulled me on top of her.

"There," she said. "That isn't too awful is it?"

She started to slip her hand inside my robes again, but I caught her wrist and pulled it away. With as much delicacy as I could manage I extricated myself from her and rose.

"My apologies," I said. "I'm afraid I've eaten something that doesn't agree with me and I lost my balance. If you will excuse me I will go to my tent and retire for the night."

Even with her hair tousled and her gown askew there was no denying the voluptuous beauty I was refusing. She seemed to know that and arched her brow, smiling.

"Such a pity. But then some dishes can prove too rich for those used to only rough fare."

I bowed. "Exactly." I turned and made my way out of the tent, more puzzled than anything.

Back in my own small quarters, I lit the oil lamp and was gratified to see my bed roll was laid out and someone had loaned me cushions as usual. Taking up most the room were the three sacks of pepper I'd managed to obtain in Tyre. I'd traded them for Murano glass and velvet cloth that I'd brought from Venice. I still had some glass and velvet cloth left, as well as kersey in the chests beside the pepper sacks, but it was the pepper I thought would bring the money I needed.

I moved over to the pepper sacks and looked for the tell-tale blue marks that I'd hidden at the end of a top corner in each of them. They had vanished. Just to be certain I checked every corner but there was no blue mark on any of the three sacks. I drew out my knife and carefully, on the nearest sack, unpicked the heavy thread that sewed it shut. When the gap was wide enough I wet my finger, pushed it in the gap and then withdrew it. I examined the yellow grain that clustered on the tip of my finger. Gingerly I pressed it to my tongue. Sand.

Was that the point of my summons to Pania's tent? Keep me occupied long enough that sacks of sand could be substituted for sacks of pepper? It was clear to me that Pania had no more gift of the sight than the horse I rode. Was it ibn Allah who wanted rid of me quickly now that he had my sacks? I found it hard to believe he'd have that much cunning and foreknowledge to arrange for Pania's little show. He had summoned me to a card game. Pania's invitation and revelation must be something else. Could it be I finally had a sign that I was on Alessandra's trail?

CHAPTER EIGHT
DAMASCUS, LATE WINTER, 1448
BARNABAS

By the time I woke up the next morning, the other caravan was only a storm of dust in the distance, leaving me to speculate that something had been put in the small flagon of wine so thoughtfully placed by my bedroll. Whether Pania or ibn Allah, it mattered not, because I had no desire to chase after them to see if my pepper was hidden among their goods. I thought it more likely that ibn Allah had it among his own sacks. I would find my opportunity.

In the meantime, I concentrated on the rest of the journey, giving the impression that I had no suspicions of ibn Allah's duplicity. I studied all the donkeys, carefully marking out which merchants owned each of them and the type of goods they carried. In one sense I found it amusing that a donkey was carrying sacks of sand over terrain consisting of that very same sand, though I knew I was the one funding such a feat. But my state of seeming oblivion allowed me to pat each donkey and rub my hand along their backs while subtly checking how securely they were strapped. I determined that, unsurprisingly, some slaves were more diligent than others.

While a plan was forming in my mind, and in between exchanging pleasantries with ibn Allah and the others during meals, I pondered over my meeting with Pania. Clearly someone wanted to warn me away from Samarkand. And the only person who would wish to do such a thing would be Alessandra. Only she would arrange with a young woman who so obviously was a courtesan of a sort to create such a distraction to warn me off by one ruse or another, on the off chance she should meet me on the journey. But then Alessandra knew me. She knew what I'd read, what I had speculated about and half wished for when we'd shared a bed before the fire had injured her. She also must have realised I would follow her. Perhaps she wanted me to. Perhaps the whole reason for kidnapping Eleanor was to lead me on a chase of her own design.

Eventually, I decided against getting caught up in the double twists and turns of my thoughts. I recalled that decision as I sat in my tent, the oil lamp lit, on the night before we were due to arrive in Damascus. I must not get caught up in the whys, I reminded myself, but take comfort from the certainty that Alessandra was ahead of me and Eleanor too. She would keep Eleanor with her, I was certain.

I looked at the metal bowl beside the bed, holding figs that Baati had pressed upon me. On impulse I dumped the figs on the bedroll and poured water from the small ewer that was meant for the ablutions before prayer. Though they knew I wasn't of their faith, the servants assumed I would pray to my own god in the privacy of my tent and wash beforehand like they did.

The water swirled around the bowl and settled. I drew the oil lamp closer and peered in. I hadn't attempted to scry at all since I'd left Venice, unwilling to tempt fate and unable to bear the others' scrutiny. To fail in front of Alys after all I had insisted they do was more than I could stomach. Now, though I was certain of Alessandra's movements, suddenly I was less certain of Eleanor's. Would Alessandra have left Eleanor behind?

I stared at the water, opened my mind and shut out the sounds of music that echoed outside. The servants had a little talent, though their singing was not as accomplished as the singing I'd heard at the court of the Grand Vizier. I thrust the thought away, along with the images that surged up in front of me. I focused on the water instead, and the copper finish of the bowl's interior, glinting in the glow of the lamp.

It was only a fleeting glimpse. A carved wooden box with hasps and an intricate metal piecework covering it. Hands reached out and, with a few twists and turns of the metal fastenings, the box opened. The vision vanished before I could see the interior. I blinked my eyes, tried to re-focus, but it was no use. There was no more.

I lifted my head thoughtfully. Suddenly, I had no doubt what the vision meant. Though it wasn't the reassurance I was seeking about Eleanor, it gave me the means I needed to reach Samarkand and Alessandra. And once there, surely Eleanor would be with her.

I gave ibn Allah a deep bow. "I owe you much for your generous hospitality, my good friend. You have protected me and my goods well in this journey and provided me with pleasure in the process." I patted the small bag of gold coins that I'd won playing cards with him.

"I was glad to be of service. You have proved a worthy companion and a good traveller," said ibn Allah. "I would that all my paying travellers were so well behaved and such good company."

We were in Damascus outside a large building near the bazaar, waiting while the donkeys were unloaded and all the trade goods placed in the warehouse nearby. I had decided to take my leave of them here, before they had arranged for me to stay with them, declaring I had need of a few quiet days in which to gather myself.

"Ah you flatter me sir," I said. "But since you have been more than kind enough to arrange for my transport on another caravan heading to Palmyra, I must insist that you take my sacks of pepper in payment and I shall hold on to the meagre sum of coins I have, though it will bring me no further profit."

Ibn Allah flushed. "But that is too generous."

Baati clapped ibn Allah on the back. "Nonsense, take the man's offer for what it is. His repayment for all that you have done for him. You provide a good service but we all know you don't provide it cheaply."

The other merchants added their support to Baati's encouragement while ibn Allah shook his head.

"If you insist on turning down his generosity, ibn Allah," said Baati, "why not just give him a small chest of your finest spice to compensate? The frankincense. I'm certain you mentioned you had a chest of that."

Annoyance flashed across ibn Allah's face, to be quickly replaced by a smile. "Of course," he said hoarsely. "But it is the custom of my people to be generous and I wouldn't want to give you discomfort by pressing it on you. I'm sure you would rather not burden yourself with such a thing. It has value and some might find it too much to worry about. Thieves would be tempted."

"Though that's an important point to consider," I said. "I'm afraid that in due respect to the custom of people I must accept your offer and once again be reminded of your generosity of spirit."

Ibn Allah gave me a grudging smile and bowed his assent. He issued some orders and the small chest was removed from one of the donkeys and placed at my side. I now had two chests to take with me, the goods of greatly varying worth, but light enough not to be too burdensome on the journey east. I'd arranged for one of Baati's servants to carry the chests until I found appropriate quarters.

It didn't take as long as I thought. Though the bazaar was large, the stalls weren't as numerous as would be expected for its size. Baati had complained that the wealth of Damascus had declined after the sack of Timur's soldiers and it appeared he was right.

Now I had not only the gold, but the chest of frankincense as well, though the frankincense was acquired unwittingly after I'd taken the gold . Without even trying too hard, I had earned a profit beyond my imaginings on this journey. Would that it might stand me in good stead for what I was to face.

My newly acquired goods checked, I glanced at my surroundings and found the small cot and carved chest sufficient for the time I hoped to spend here and, with the bag of coins from the card playing, I made my way outside.

The streets were busy enough, especially as I closed in on the bazaar. Though I had pretended to accept ibn Allah's arrangements for me to join the caravan heading towards Palmyra, I'd decided I would be safer if I found my own group to travel with. And visiting the bazaar might just provide me with the opportunity to inquire about Samarkand.

I entered the bazaar and glanced around. Stalls of every assortment were arranged in several lines. On impulse I made my way down a line of stalls selling cloth and trimmings, some piled on rude carpets and others on tables, thinking I might find something unusual and interesting to add to my store. There was cloth of all kinds, including fine watered silks from Venice, I noted, and silks of unusual shades whose dyes may well have come from far Cathay.

I walked along, noting everything but captured by nothing in particular. The stalls became filled more with trimmings and then leather goods and eventually exchanged to scribes writing letters for illiterate people, and then manuscripts, codices, and other types of texts. Intrigued, I stopped at one stall and began examining the texts and scrolls piled on the table while an old, bearded man with spectacles talked quietly to another dark haired young man in Arabic.

"Isaak, you are most generous to let me borrow this for a few hours so that I might study it," said the young dark haired man. He drew his richly made robe closer to him against the small draught that caught it.

"Of course I would. I know you are trustworthy, my friend," said Isaak, his accent thick. "And I am most interested to hear your conclusions."

"You are too kind," said the young man. "I am grateful for the opportunity to read such important work on the heavens. His theory on the placements of stars and planets is fascinating."

"But is it plausible?" asked Isaak.

The man nodded slowly. "As much as my calculations can fathom, I believe so. But I am no expert."

I stood there listening with increasing interest until I could contain myself no longer. "I beg your pardon for my forwardness, but you have piqued my curiosity. May I ask what book it is you're discussing?"

The two men turned to me, their expressions warm and open. I bowed and introduced myself, adding. "I have a great interest in texts of this type."

"It is always a pleasure to meet a fellow scholar," said the young man, handing me the text. "My name is Abdul ibn Kasim.

"And I am Isaak Joseph, a humble bookseller."

I looked down at the work. "Not so humble, judging by the quality of some of these texts," I said.

"Are you based somewhere? Padua, perhaps?" asked Abdul. "It has the makings of a fine library there."

I smiled, appreciative of the subtle comment. While Padua might be growing in fame and renown, it couldn't match the libraries that had been once in Alexandria and other parts of the Arab world.

"I have been to Padua, and other libraries in the West. But they were no match for the library of the Grand Vizier's in Hüdavendigar."

"Then you have seen some impressive works," Isaak said. "I'm privileged here that I meet worthy scholars and my trade allows me to examine rare and wonderful tomes." His eyes twinkled. "And even keep one or two for myself. But Abdul is most blessed in that he is able to travel long distances with his father to visit the best libraries in the world in the pursuit of his studies."

Abdul gave Isaak a kindly smile. "I am indeed so blessed. Fortunate in my father and his vocation." He looked at me. "Is this your reason for travelling to Damascus? I would be glad to show you places of learning."

"Alas, though I wish it were true, it is not. But I would be interested to see these places. I have spent much time studying mathematics and sciences."

Abdul brightened. "Is that so? Then you would of course be interested in that volume. It concerns astronomy and there is much about mathematics in it."

I regarded the volume in my hands, nodding. "I could see that." I handed the book back reluctantly. "But though it tempts me greatly, I have little time or money to spend on such things at the moment. I must go east, to trade. And with God's blessing," I added with a smile, "I might then be able to afford such things."

"Ah, but we are headed east as well," said Abdul, his eyes aglint with possibility. "Travel with us. We would be able to enjoy discussions and I'm certain my father would share some of our texts."

"Where are you headed?" I asked. A small kernel of hope formed inside, but I shoved it down.

"Bokhara. It is known as a great place of learning. Scholars gather there from many regions and such is its fame that my father and I are determined to go and spend as much time as possible there."

"Bokhara?" I could hardly fathom my luck. "Isn't that near Samarkand?"

"I believe so. They're both part of the Royal Road, I'm told. But I'll check with Father. Why, is that where you are destined for?"

"Yes, I hope to reach Samarkand. Tell me, have you heard tales that there are domes of blue tiles to be seen there?"

Abdul shrugged. "I can't tell you, I'm sorry. But my father might, or one of his companions."

I felt more cheered than I had in a long while. I grinned. "I would be more than grateful to you, my good friend and I thank you for your invitation. I am happy to accept."

∽

If the son was anything to judge by, I felt the journey would provide some real enjoyment, beyond anything I could wish for. It was with some surprise then, when we met the next day, as arranged by the son, that I found the father disgruntled and embittered. Nothing like the gentle son.

He introduced himself as with a curt bow, as Kasim ibn Mansur, outside their quarters, just some few streets from the main bazaar. He was tall and wiry with a hooked nose and wore a dark voluminous turban like his son and a dark, wide-sleeved robe. His beard was grizzled and his eyes were heavily lined.

"My son has invited you to join us," he said in a resigned voice.

He glanced over at his son, who suddenly seemed tongue tied after his brief but hurried explanation of the invitation he'd extended to me.

"Your son was very generous," I said. "But possibly impulsive. Perhaps it would be an inconvenience. I am happy to seek a caravan elsewhere."

"No, no," he said and forced a smile, straightening. "You must forgive my manners. It has been a long and tiring journey and lately I have suffered with my back. We are happy to have your company."

The tone was still surprisingly grudging and I put it down to his ailment. Arab scholars prided themselves on their courtesy and cultured manners. "There is no need to apologise. Where have you travelled from?"

Kasim grimaced. "Just lately from Tunis. But we began our journey at our home in Morocco. At Tangier."

I bowed slightly. "I have heard that Tunis boasts some very fine madrasas renowned for their learning. Tangier, I'm sure has the same."

"Mister Bonavillagio has a great interest in mathematics and astronomy," said Abdul, his composure recovered. "He has studied at some very important places in the West. Padua."

Kasim raised his brow. "Indeed? Padua?"

I nodded. "Have you visited Padua?"

He raised his brows slightly. "It hardly seemed necessary since most of the texts of any worth that they possess would be copies of original texts that will be in the libraries we have already visited, or plan to visit. But we have little concern with mathematics and astronomy. Our interest is in theology and the law."

"Of course," I said.

I looked at Abdul a moment, but his eyes were downcast, though his face was flushed. I wondered if the son felt the same passion for theology and law as Kasim thought he did. If nothing else, our journey would certainly not lack interest. I had a feeling I would be questioned and tested in more areas than just trade and commerce.

CHAPTER NINE
THE ROAD EAST, EARLY SPRING 1448
BARNABAS

I wiped the sweat from my brow with the loose cloth that hung from my turban, feeling the sand that had stuck to it grate across my skin. Despite the covering I knew there was sand in my hair, beard and mouth. The sun was strong, and had grown increasingly hotter as we progressed into the desert landscape and the days passed towards spring. The caravan in which we travelled was small, but well-armed, carrying gifts from a wealthy merchant to a noble in Bokhara and for that I was glad, for it meant that we could set a fast enough pace on camels that could cover twice the distance, and more, than the pace the donkeys had set in the short journey to Damascus.

"You are tired, my friend?" asked Abdul.

"I am, but it is nothing." I smiled at him. There were probably only a few years between us, but he seemed much younger than me sometimes. His enthusiasm was boyish, his energy high and though he'd travelled widely enough, he still had an air of innocence about him. And now, there was no trace of fatigue or discomfort at all. This hardiness was in contrast to his father, who sat hunched over his camel, barely hanging on, clearly exhausted.

We were halfway to Bokhara. The Tigris River had been forded and Hamadan was also now behind as well. We'd used part of the trans-Persian Khurasan Road, stopping at caravanserai along the way.

To ford the Tigris River, the chests and other goods had been unloaded and floated across on a raft, while the camels were allowed to swim to the other side. I chose to cross on the raft for the sake of my chests as much as anything else. Eventually, we reached Hamadan, a city that had once been a marvel, as had so many others in the regions before they were overrun by Genghis Khan and then Timur. Though the Timurid rulers had restored some cities and regions, Hamadan hadn't quite recovered. Šāhrok, the Timurid prince who ruled the region had recently died, and an air of uncertainty hung about the city, compelling us to leave as quickly as we could.

Now we travelled in the open desert, no caravanserai station or town visible in the distance and it made me uneasy. Though the dusk approached and part of me would have liked to stop, the other part of me felt compelled to travel whatever distance might be needed to take us to a populated place. But it was a foolish thought, I knew, for dusk, when it came, lasted for only a brief time and then darkness fell like a black curtain draped across the landscape. Nightfall brought dangers that would only increase if we were still travelling, better to defend ourselves in a camp than strung out along the desert.

I glanced at the soldiers who guarded us. Clad as they were in belted short tunics over leggings and leather boots, bows slung across their backs and swords at their sides, they were prepared to defend. But not one of them appeared worried and that gave me some comfort. Kasim seemed more tired than troubled but the wealthy merchant, Usef ibn Battuta, with his precious chests of jewels and gold, squinted into the distance. I'd spent little time talking with Battuta since the journey had begun, primarily because Kasim, and by default his son, chose to keep a polite distance from him. Kasim had, however, decided my company was acceptable and many entertaining hours had passed in the evenings when we weren't too exhausted from the journey to seek our beds immediately upon stopping.

Tonight, I felt restless, my nervous energy due to my unease, and I was happy enough when Kasim suggested I join them in their tent for a meal. I was about to accept when Battuta came over to us and issued his own invitation. To my surprise Kasim only hesitated a moment before he accepted and then I did the same.

As I made my way to Battata's tent, I noticed none of the soldiers were at their ease. Though, a few squatted before fires eating, it was hastily done and they were still armed with swords or bows. Others milled about, checking the camels or scanning the horizon as the darkness fell. The soldiers who officially stood watch did so at a distance and there were more of them than usual. Was this change anything to do with Battata's invitation?

When I entered Battuta's tent some time later I was surprised at how well appointed it was. For some reason he'd struck me as an ascetic man with his simply wrapped turban and plain robes. By Kasim and Abdul's expression they were equally surprised and Kasim's face took on a more hospitable look.

Battuta bowed his welcome and gestured for us to be seated. I was happy enough to sit opposite, further away from the table filled with a variety of tempting fruit, grain, cheese and meat dishes, but in a position to observe Battuta himself. I was curious to know what had prompted such a sudden invitation. An invitation that had never been issued in the near month we'd been travelling together.

His expression at the moment was pleasant enough but I could see a trace of concern in his eyes. Battuta gestured to the dishes, offering them out to us. Kasim eyed them with pleasure and helped himself to generous portions. Abdul, followed his father, but his portion was more moderate. Though hungry, I was more sparing in my approach. I was more interested in my host.

"Your invitation was most thoughtful," I said carefully. "I welcome an opportunity to get to know you better. I have admired the capable manner in which you have handled our journey."

Battuta held up his hand in dismissal. "It is kind of you to say so, but it is no more than others would do who have travelled these roads."

"You have travelled these roads often?" I asked.

He nodded. "For many years."

"Ah, but you must find it difficult to bear," said Kasim, frowning. "Even in places such as Hamadan, the grammar is just appalling. Can no one speak properly any more in these parts?"

Battuta gave Kasim an amused smile. "They have had much to overcome. A good portion of their city was destroyed with Tamerlane's forces, so maintaining madrasas and other places of learning became secondary to finding enough food to eat."

Kasim shook his head. "But learning is the very foundation of a society. Surely that should be a priority too?"

Battuta shrugged. "It may be easy to feel so from this distance. But then perhaps I must warn you that you may feel even more aggrieved in Merv where hundreds upon hundreds of women and children were slaughtered and the men killed in the most appalling manner."

"How awful," said Abdul. He'd been quiet up until now, but the remark seemed to come unbidden from him. He cast his eyes down modestly when his father frowned at him.

"We are going to Merv?" I asked.

"Yes," said Battuta. "If all goes well we should reach there in a week's time."

"Do you expect any trouble that might slow us down?" I asked.

He looked over at me, considering his answer. "Expect? I wouldn't say that. I hope that there is no trouble, but it's best to be prepared."

I decided to rephrase my question. "Do you have any reason to think there might be trouble?"

"There is always reason to think there might be trouble on this road. There is much unrest, people find it difficult to support themselves in their former manner. All the farms and other types of livelihoods were destroyed some thirty years ago and now only a meagre living can be had in this region. It leads to desperate acts."

"Do you think there will be an attack tonight?" asked Kasim, a note of fear in his voice. "Is that why you have asked us here?"

"There is no cause for alarm. I am just taking extra care, as would any responsible person."

"If you should need my assistance, I would be happy to help," I said. "I have some skill with a sword and dagger. I can retrieve it from my belongings."

Battuta raised his brow. "Indeed? I thought you were a scholar, like your companions."

I gave an easy smile. "You are too generous. No, I am a merchant, like yourself, though I have spent time as a scholar."

"A merchant?" He looked at me keenly. "And your first time travelling east? You must excuse me for saying this, but your goods are few to journey so far. Do you hope to purchase a sizeable amount of goods in Bokhara that would make it worth your while, for I hate to disappoint you, that place is more a centre to study theology and other learned subjects, rather than trade."

"I travel beyond Bokhara, to Samarkand. At least that is my wish."

"Samarkand? Well that has more promise for trade. Their ceramics are judged to be very fine and many goods that come from Cathay can be found there as well."

I blinked, cursing myself for a moment that I hadn't sought him out sooner. "You have been to Samarkand?"

Battuta nodded. "Once. I go there now in the hopes that I might speak with Mīrzā Mohammad Tāraghay bin Shāhrukh, Ulugh Beg, the Timurid ruler."

"The Timurid ruler?" asked a surprised Kasim. "Why that is a very ambitious desire. Will it be easy?"

Battuta took a deep breath. "Well, I hope that my goods might tempt him."

"You hope to tempt him with the jewels and gold you carry?" asked Abdul. "That would place you in a good position I'm sure."

"Jewels and gold?" said Battuta. He looked at Abdul, for a moment puzzled and then gave a hearty laugh. "Is that what you thought my chests contained? No, my friend, nothing so grand as that. At least grand in the way most men would think, but precious nonetheless to some. No, my friend, I carry ancient texts on astronomy. I understand that Ulugh Beg has a great interest in astronomy. In return I hope that I might persuade him to give me some other ancient texts that I have on good authority he possesses."

"Ulugh Beg is a man of learning?" I asked curiously.

"He is reputed to be. He built an observatory some twenty-five years ago and has assembled astronomers and mathematicians to plot the night sky. He is a mathematician himself."

"He built an observatory? Is it in Bokhara?" asked Abdul eagerly.

"It is in Samarkand," said Battuta.

Abdul's face fell and I recalled the book he spoke so enthusiastically about to Isaak.

"He sounds like a real man of learning." I looked at Kasim. "Such a man of learning would surely have scholars of all kinds gathered around him. Even theology and law. Perhaps you might consider travelling onto Samarkand after you've spent time in Bokhara, Kasim."

Kasim frowned. "It wasn't part of the plan to go there."

Abdul, his eyes now alight, leaned forward. "But consider what may be learned there, Father."

Kasim gave him a speculative look. "I doubt that theology would hold much place there with Bokhara so close."

"It's something you can consider," I said. "There is no need to decide now. It might be once you reach Bokhara you will have a clearer understanding of the worth of travelling onto Samarkand."

Kasim nodded, but his eyes showed doubt. I thought best to shift the subject to one that had pressed in on me since Battuta had revealed he'd been to Samarkand.

"Would you recall in your previous visit to Samarkand if they have a building with a dome covered in blue tiles?"

Battuta smiled, curious. "Blue tiles?"

"Yes. I have heard there is one such building in Samarkand. But the person might have been mistaken."

"No. Your friend wasn't mistaken. There is indeed a blue tiled dome there. It's the Bib Khanum Mosque."

It took a few moments for the words to sink in. I'd been so prepared to hear a denial or at least a lack of certainty or doubt, but to have it finally confirmed so completely had left me breathless.

I blinked at him and forced a smile. "In truth? It sounded like too much of a fantastical tale to take as nothing more than a flight of fancy. Or an exaggeration. I look forward to this place."

"You are there to view the sights as well as trade?" Battuta asked in amusement. "Or did you say that you weren't trading?"

Battuta knew I had said nothing in either regard and I gave him a rueful look. "No, I didn't say. But I too am hopeful of gaining knowledge and have only a few things to tempt any purveyor of such knowledge."

"You have manuscripts to trade as well?" asked Kasim, bewildered.

"No, my friend. I have some small goods and some gold. But my hope is to purchase some precious knowledge with it. And perhaps some of the goods our friend here has spoken about."

"I see," said Battuta. "A scholar and a merchant. But I think a scholar first."

I inclined my head. "A scholar first."

∞

I'm not certain what woke me. A movement, a small sound, but my eyes flew open and I saw a shadow looming over me brandishing a dagger. Quickly, I reached for the dagger tucked under my pillow and blocked the thrust that was aiming for my heart. Surprised by the resistance, the man stumbled backward and I took advantage of his unbalance and kicked my leg into his. He fell over awkwardly, the dagger still in his hand.

I rose quickly and went over to him, restraining him with my knee pressed against his chest and my dagger at his throat. He stared up at me, his eyes slowly clouding. It took me a few moments to see that he was dead, his dagger protruding from his side, blood pouring from it.

Stunned, and still somewhat muddled from being wakened suddenly from sleep, I rose slowly and went over to light the oil lamp at my bedside. Once lit, I took it over to the body and kneeling, held it up to the face. It was a man of perhaps middle age, with threadbare clothes and a drawn face, half obscured by a beard. He was no one from our travelling group that I recognised, a fact confirmed by his manner of dress. Instead of robes, or wide legged pantaloons he wore trousers and a simple tunic.

The tent flap opened and Battuta came in, bareheaded and wearing a hastily donned robe. A soldier stepped in behind him.

"Omar said there was a commotion in your tent." He glanced over at the body at my side. "I see he wasn't mistaken."

"Do you know him?" I asked.

Battuta came over and studied the body carefully. "No," he said finally. "He is probably from the region."

"He was trying to kill me," I said. I rose and gave him a kick.

"Kill you? Why would anyone want to kill you?"

It had puzzled me since the man had stopped breathing. "I don't know."

"It seems unlikely that it was because of the gold coins you carry. He would have just taken them, rather than bothered to kill you."

"Exactly so. It wasn't theft. Clearly he was intent on murder. But he is no trained killer, that's certain."

"Fortunate for you, my friend, or more than likely you wouldn't be here now to puzzle over his motive. Who among your acquaintances know you were on this journey and why would they want your death?"

This man was no fool. He had honed in on the precise point that was forming in my mind. Though only three people knew about this journey, I would count none of them among the suspects. But what I could count on is that Alessandra knew enough about me, my scrying and that I would stop at nothing to find her. If there was any question in my mind that I was on the right path it had vanished now. Alessandra was in Samarkand and she was doing all she could in her power to prevent me from going there.

CHAPTER TEN
MEDITERRANEAN SEA, LATE WINTER, 1448
ALYS

Tomaso wound his fingers in Alys's hair from his perch on top of her shoulders, picking and plucking as though she were covered with fleas. It felt restful, and it seemed as though Tomaso knew that she needed comforting against the strain of her world falling apart.

In front of her, at a small table over by a porthole that looked out onto the sea were Hal and Joanie, attempting to play a hand of cards to distract themselves and her from the increasing pitching motion that had overtaken the ship since early that morning. In light of the rolling and rocking motion, the ship seemed to have shrunk and felt less secure in the tumultuous waters of the Mediterranean Sea in winter.

"I do believe you're cheating," said Hal.

Joanie snorted. "Says the expert. I'm only defending myself."

Hal gave her a look of mock hurt. "Are you saying I'm cheating?"

"I don't need to say it. It's plain as anything."

Hal looked at Alys. "Am I cheating?"

Alys laughed. "Let me just say I'm no longer sure of the rules of the game you're playing."

Hal placed a hand over his chest and looked crestfallen. "That hurt me, sister."

"Aw, go away with you," said Joanie. "If you don't want anyone to beat you at your game you may as well play with Tomaso here."

"Now that's an idea," said Hal. "We could teach Tomaso to play and charge people to watch."

Joanie laughed. "I would enjoy more watching you teach Tomaso to try to play cards. That would be worth charging for."

Alys gave them both a fond smile. They were trying so hard and she appreciated it. She felt fortunate that they were with her to support her in the past week since they'd left Tyre. The journey had been difficult with lack of wind at first and now it seems there was too much wind, rain blowing in with it a few hours earlier. All of these things hadn't stopped her from worrying about Barnabas, fearing for his safety and sanity and wondering what she could do even now to coax him back from the East. She had told him she was leaving and had boarded the ship only in the hope that it would force him to come with her. But once committed to that extent she felt compelled to see it through, and she only hoped it was the right decision.

Suddenly the ship swayed at an alarming angle and the banter between Hal and Joanie halted. They glanced at each other.

Hal rose. "I'll just go above and see what's what."

Joanie put a hand on his arm. "Is it safe?"

He glanced at Alys. "I'll soon see. If not, we should take precautions."

He disappeared through the door and up the small ladder to the deck above. Joanie came over and sat beside Alys, taking Tomaso from her shoulder.

"We should put Tomaso away," she said.

Alys nodded. She watched as Joanie opened the small wooden cage and tucked Tomaso inside. He gave a few screeches of protest, but then settled down. Even he sensed the prospect of danger, it seemed.

Hal returned a few moments later, drenched and with a disgruntled look on his face. "They sent me right back down. Said I was more 'indrance than 'elp. Felt I was best served looking after you two, even though I told them I used to be a seaman."

"And they were right, too," said Joanie firmly.

"Is it bad?" asked Alys. "Are we in danger?"

Hal turned to her, concern written on his face. "The storm has kicked up fierce. One of the masts 'as a split, but they've strapped it up good." He glanced around. "We should put everything away and tie the rest of the stuff down, as best we can."

The three of them set about packing away the cards and any other loose items they could find amid increasing pitching and roiling. It was difficult as they swayed and tried to keep their balance, but they managed it in the end. All clothes were stored in the chests and the chests secured and strapped to the table leg, which was nailed to the floor.

By the time they had finished, the three of them could hardly stand and Alys was getting worried. Tomaso screeched and whimpered in his cage, secured to the table leg. Outside, the storm roared and then a piercing crack split the air. She looked at Hal in alarm and could see the horror written on his face.

"It's the mast, isn't it?"

He opened his mouth and then shut it and just nodded. "It's not good. I'll go above and see what's going on."

Before she could protest, he was gone and she and Joanie sat, their hands clasped. The ship pitched violently again and the wind screamed above them. The small window blew in with a gust of rain, the shattered glass scattering across the room.

The door burst open and Hal entered. "Come. They are thinking to leave the ship."

"But our things?" asked Joanie.

Alys rose and went over to the cage, and bent to unfasten it. "Tomaso. We must take him."

Hal frowned, "Quickly then. There's not much time."

They grabbed their cloaks and followed Hal out of the cabin and up the stairs. Once above deck, the wind blew so strongly Alys found it difficult to keep herself upright. She was drenched almost instantly and her hair, braided and tucked carefully inside the hood of her cloak, was whipped out and blew across her face, obscuring her view. Hal turned and tried to speak to her but she couldn't hear him for the wind. He grabbed her arm and shoved her forward and she tried to help, but a gust blew her backwards and she lost her footing, skidding on the wet planks and falling hard. Her head banged against the rail and that was the last she recalled.

∽

It was dark when Alys woke. Her hair and clothes were drenched, but she felt no pitching or roiling beneath her. The wind was gone and the sound of lashing rain with it. Her mind was fogged with the dream she'd just had of

Eleanor. Sweet Eleanor now a small child, playing with a wooden doll, her golden curls catching the light. She'd looked up as hands reached down to pick her up. Hands that weren't Alys's. She'd choked in pain at the sight. The pan was still lingering in her when she opened her eyes carefully, conscious now of a great throbbing in her head as well. In the poor light, she managed to make out Joanie's face hovering over her.

"You're awake," she said softly. "How do you feel?"

"Wretched," said Alys. "But alive."

She lifted her head carefully, wincing at the pain that shot through her skull.

"Careful, now," said Joanie.

"Where are we? What's happened?" she asked.

"Shhh. Just rest now. All is well," said Joanie. "Or as well as it can be. We lost a mast, but there's still one good one. The captain says we aren't far from Cyprus by 'is reckoning, so we can limp there and get repairs."

"And Hal and Tomaso?"

"They're both fine, though Tomaso looks none too pretty. A little bruised maybe, from tumbling everywhere and a little seasick with it. We'll see more when the daylight comes." She smoothed the hair back from Alys's face. "Now lay quiet and get some rest. There'll be enough to do when the time comes."

It was three days before one of the seamen sighted land. In that time both Joanie and Alys had been put to work repairing sails, while Hal had joined the men dealing with the heavier repairs that could be managed on board. The ship had inched slowly towards its destination, the split mast looking wounded and forlorn in the presence of the other mast whose sails were furled wide and full.

When Alys stepped on to the dock at Famagusta, the large port city of Cyprus, Tomaso's cage in her hand, it was with great relief. In some ways she was glad they would have to spend some time ashore while the ship was repaired. She would need that long to gather her courage to undertake the remaining part of the sea voyage back to Venice. She knew winter was not the time for such journeys and Barnabas had warned her too, but it couldn't be helped. One part of her was impatient with any delay, and the anxiety it brought only added to the restless spirit that had become a familiar part of her since first learning of Eleanor's disappearance.

The city was walled, with a high fortified castle and a large imposing cathedral at its centre. Perhaps she might steal a bit of time and venture into the cathedral to see their paintings, she mused. It would provide some distraction, if nothing else.

Hal came up beside her. "Let me take you and Joanie somewhere safe first before I search for a place for us to stay. Then I'll return for our baggage."

Alys nodded and let him lead her and Joanie away towards the street. It was crowded with seamen, carters and other people bound to serve the needs of a port. The stink of rotting fish and waste assaulted her nose. She was about to suggest they go to the cathedral first and beg help of someone in authority there when the sound of rapid footfall close behind caused her to turn. The ship's captain, red faced and out of breath, stood behind her.

"Signora," he said, in Italian. "I beg your pardon. I meant to speak with you earlier, but I was detained by a port official."

"Yes?" Alys regarded him coolly. She'd exchanged barely a few words with him the whole voyage. It was Hal who had acted on her behalf whenever the need arose to convey some small request, or seek information.

"I-I. That is the ship's owner, Signor Ravello, I'm certain would wish that you are accommodated here as befitting your situation. He has…a particular lady friend who lives here under his care. She is of noble birth, you understand, otherwise I wouldn't dare to suggest that I arrange this. I mean, I'm certain you would feel no unease." The captain reddened again.

"That is most generous of you," said Alys. She glanced at Joanie who gave a barely perceptible shrug. "I'd be happy to accept."

The captain looked relieved and gestured ahead of him. "Please, I will show you the way. I took the liberty of sending one of my men ahead to alert her to your arrival."

Alys nodded and allowed him to escort her through the streets. Her leg was a little stiff and precarious, but the captain seemed to accept it as a natural occurrence after the sea journey. The streets were crowded and narrow at first, but gradually the thoroughfares widened slightly, and the houses became a little more spacious, with some breathing space between them. But as the size increased, so did the number of churches she counted.

"These people must be either very sinful or very holy to need so many churches," she murmured to Joanie.

The captain gave a small smile. "It is the merchants. They build the churches to demonstrate the wealth of the city. It has prospered over the years from the trade in silk and other fine items."

Alys sighed. Trade. Was its importance always to be thrown in her face?

They halted before a large carved door and the captain pulled the bell cord beside it. A round faced serving woman opened it and gave a deep curtsey when she set eyes on the group.

"I am here on your master's business," said the captain in Italian. "I sent word earlier to your mistress."

"*Si, Capitano,*" she said. She opened the door wide and indicated they enter.

The hall was tiled, as were the walls. They left the hall, Alys struggling to disguise her limp after their journey through the streets. They entered a sizeable room with doors that faced onto a small courtyard with a fountain at its centre. Though the doors were closed, Alys could hear the faint trickle of its spray. Except for the brightly coloured swirled decorations painted on the wall tiles that exuded a more exotic flair, there was a distinct flavour of Venice about the house.

Sunlight poured through the doors into the room. Plush carpets in rich designs covered the tiled floor and the walls were hung with paintings and tapestries worth a small fortune. In a corner, reclining in a heavily cushioned long bench, was a beautiful golden-haired young woman, delicate as the porcelain china ornament on the table beside her. She rose to greet Alys, huge grey eyes fixing on her with simple joy.

"How marvellous to have you stay," she said with a smile that displayed an enchanting set of dimples.

Alys put down Tomaso's cage, moved forward and gave a small curtsey. The young woman, who really was no more than a girl, barely came up to Alys's shoulder.

"You are most kind to offer your hospitality," said Alys.

"Oh, no, no. Cesare would have it no other way, were he here." She took Alys's hand kissed it. "It's as though I was granted a sister. I've always wanted a sister. Say you will stay a good while, so that I might call you thus."

Alys regarded her carefully. Was she truly that simple and good hearted? In her experience she had learned to trust little of courtier's words.

"I would of course be flattered you would consider me a sister," said Alys, with a little laugh. "Especially if you could tell me your name."

"Oh, how silly of me. You must think me very rude. Cesare is always calling me his feather brained little goose," she said, her eyes twinkling. "I am called Floramundi. A silly name for a silly girl." She giggled. "But call me Flora. That's what everyone calls me."

"Flora," said Alys. "I am most pleased to meet you. I am Alys." She turned to Joanie and Hal. "And these two are my travelling companions, Joanie and Hal. We are all under the protection of Signor Giacomo Bonavillagio."

Flora nodded and giggled again. "Oh. That's wonderful. Three guests in my house. I will do my best to keep you all amused." She clapped her hands and looked down at the cage. "And what is this delightful animal?"

"It's a monkey," said Alys. "His name is Tomaso."

"Tomaso!" she gave a little squeal. She knelt down and regarded Tomaso in wonder. "And he is yours?" She began to reach her fingers through the cage and Tomaso screeched at her.

"Have a care, Flora. He's generally friendly, but suspicious of strangers. He might bite your finger."

Flora withdrew her finger immediately and stood up, directing a wary glance at the cage. She turned to Alys, her expression cleared. "You must introduce me to him formally then, after you and your companions have refreshed themselves. And you also shall tell me all about your own travels and how you came to be shipwrecked."

Alys caught Joanie's glance that hinted at raised brow. Her own amusement, she suppressed. Flora might be a flighty, empty headed person, but she could see no ill intent in her. And for that she felt some relief.

ᴗᴥᴗ

Alys stared at the paintings above the cushioned bench that held Flora, now changed from the simple flowing silk gown of deep blue into an ornately embroidered velvet sarsanet with seed pearls sewn around the low neckline and cuffs. Her hair was elaborately dressed with curls and braids, seed pearls woven into them.

Alys smoothed her own gown which had been hastily donned after she'd had a brief wash and food on a tray brought to her room. Joanie had done her best to brush out the gown, but it still bore some of the effects of its confinement in the depths of the chest. It was a dull brown, a colour that suited her mood and had seemed practical at the time. After the informal greeting she'd had from Flora, it seemed entirely appropriate for a comfortable afternoon of storytelling. But now, faced with Flora's sumptuous attire she wondered if Flora was dressed in that manner on a whim, or if there was something else afoot.

Alys studied the paintings while Flora chattered on to offer more effusive greetings and recounted some mishap by the servants in the kitchen that caused Alys's fare to be so simple. The paintings were surprising in one sense. The colours were fascinating and artfully blended, the proportions accurate and the scale impressive. It was the subject matter that held Alys's gaze and provided distraction from her growing unease. They all depicted mythic battles, a strange subject matter for one of Flora's temperament and function. For a house that was supposed to seduce, or at least provide comfort, the paintings fell well short of the mark.

Tomaso stirred in her lap and she gave him a soothing rub. He'd been a bit skittish since the storm, careful of his surroundings and alert to any loud noises or people approaching. Flora had tentatively stroked his head when Alys had first appeared with him, but she seemed content, now, to admire him from afar.

"You are perhaps wondering why I haven't insisted you begin your tale yet," said Flora, changing the subject abruptly. "But I have a glorious surprise for you."

She giggled again and Alys wondered if she thought and felt everything in hyperbole to make it so wonderful, marvellous, glorious, but suppressed the notion quickly as unkind.

"What surprise is that?" asked Alys. "I'm certain I will enjoy anything you arrange." Was it some sweetmeat, or confection and its creation had caused chaos in the kitchen?

Flora clapped her hands together. "Oh, but you will surely enjoy this surprise. I have invited my dear friend, Valentina, to come here this afternoon. Imagine, she knows King John! Though he is old and hardly wields power since his dreadful wife Queen Helen became regent. Do you know the Queen bit off the nose of the king's mistress? Well that caused a stir, but that was before I came here. It was Valentina who told me that story. So you see, she would be thrilled to hear your tales, since she has so many wonderful tales herself."

Alys listened to Flora's outpouring of words with a mixture of amusement and frustration she might feel with a child. There was no doubting Flora meant well, but Alys would much prefer to spend her time here as quietly as possible and with only the barest company deemed necessary.

"Is Valentina a member of the court here?" asked Alys when she could get her breath.

"Well, not exactly. But she knows many members of the court. Queen Helen, you see, takes a dim view of her since she is a great beauty and might attract the attention of the king, though Valentina herself says she would no sooner bed him than she would bed a bear." Flora giggled again. "Valentina now is under the protection of a very rich and powerful patron. Though he isn't as nice as my Cesare. But she is still in demand, for her taste and charms are very great. She can play the lute like an angel and her voice is as sweet as a songbird's. She is perfection itself."

The door opened and a servant entered and bobbed a curtsey, trailing a statuesque, dark-haired woman with a full mouth and dark, kohl rimmed eyes. Her gown outmatched Flora's with its array of semi-precious stones that edged the neckline and high waist of the ruby and gold thread brocade garment. The pattern was full of bold swirls and curls, expensively made and flamboyant. This woman was one of the few who could carry it off. Even the hair piled high on top of her head and adorned with feathers of peacock and ostrich seemed a perfect complement to the confection, rather than a garish addition to an already overblown dress.

Flora jumped to her feet and rushed to the woman. "Valentina. You are here at last. Come meet my guest, Alys. And look – she has a delightful companion. It's called a monkey. Is it not divine? Though you mustn't get too close, because it doesn't like strangers. But you won't be a stranger long, will you, since Alys will be staying with us for some time. Her ship has lost one of its masts in a storm and is in Famagusta for repairs."

Valentina laid a hand on Flora's arm. "My dear it's too much. You must let me catch my breath."

Flora put her hand to her mouth. "Oh, I'm sorry Valentina. You tell me often enough not to speak so much, but I do forget. Please forgive me."

Valentina patted her hand and released her, and took a seat in a large carved chair that was clearly her usual place to sit. She turned to Alys. "What a delight to meet you. Flora was so kind to invite me here and allow me too to hear your tale." She eyed Tomaso. "And seeing your little friend, already I am intrigued."

"It's a pleasure to meet you. From what Flora has mentioned of your own experiences, I'm certain mine would only pale in comparison."

"No, no, don't say that," said Flora. She lifted a flagon on the table before her and poured wine into three glasses. She handed one to Alys and another to Valentina. "You must have a drink first. It is my Cesare's favourite from his own vineyard. It's very fine, I assure you."

Alys took a sip and found that Flora spoke the truth. Valentina's sip was careless and uninterested. She looked at Alys.

"Tell me, how is it you came by this monkey."

"Tomaso was a gift," said Alys.

Valentina arched a brow. "A gift? That person must have very strong feelings to give such a gift." Her smile was warm, but there was an underlying edge to it.

Alys forced a calm smile, her sense alert. "He does."

"Would that be Signor Bonavillagio?" asked Flora. She flushed. "You said you were under his protection."

Alys nodded, stroking Tomaso, who was starting to fidget, sensing her unease. "Signor Bonavillagio and I have a long-standing, strong bond."

"Signor Bonavillagio," said Valentina, her tone musing. "I'm certain I've heard that name before. Is he a merchant? Is that why you were on board a ship?"

"Yes. I was travelling with him as far as Tyre. Once there, it was deemed unsafe for me to travel onwards with him, I turned back with my companions."

"Onwards? Was he heading further eastward?" asked Valentina. She took another sip of her wine, her eyes watching Alys carefully.

"Yes." She was determined to keep her answers brief.

As if sensing her reluctance, Valentina switched tack. "Bonavillagio. Yes, I know now. He trades in Venice, does he not?"

Alys's fingers stilled in Tomaso's fur. She nodded.

"Yes, he was associated with Alessandra Cardina, the famous, or should I say, notorious courtesan."

"Valentina, you know everyone," said Flora, her tone excited. "Oh Alys, is it not a wonder that she knows your Signor Bonavillagio?"

"It is a wonder," said Alys blandly, her eyes fixed on Valentina.

"Ah, but you don't know the tragedy, *cara*," said Valentina. "For Alessandra was burned in a terrible fire and the scars were so bad that she was compelled to wear a veil to cover her once beautiful face."

"How awful," said Flora, raising a hand to her own cheek.

"One would lament the loss of such beauty, and more important, such income from the beauty. But Alessandra was too cunning for that. She took on a young girl, some say a girl more beautiful than Alessandra herself, and fashioned her into the most perfect courtesan Venice has ever seen, thereby earning a handsome income for

Alessandra. She was fair-haired, like you…Alys. Her name, I recall, was Maria."

"How fascinating," Alys said. "You seem well informed. How did you come by such details?"

"Oh, I have many friends," said Valentina. She gave Alys a long look. "This particular friend visited me recently. Tomaso Cortini. Do you know him?"

Alys schooled her features to betray nothing. "His name is familiar. It might be that I've heard him mentioned."

"Do you play cards? Tomaso is a skilled card player. You may have met him that way."

"I do play cards. Perhaps it is as you say."

Valentina nodded. She leaned over to Flora and patted her knee. "You must allow me to invite Alys over to my home tomorrow for a game of cards. I won't trouble you to come because I know you find card games tedious. But you will allow me this small bit of entertainment?"

"Of course, Valentina," said Flora. "You are so kind to invite Alys and allow me to stay at home. I do find cards boring, but only because I'm so very bad at them. I know you would get cross with me if I played, and I don't want that." She beamed at Alys. "You will go, won't you?"

"Of course. I am delighted to accept Valentina's gracious invitation," said Alys. Her hands were clammy, but she forced a smile. She had no idea what was behind the invitation, but she couldn't pass up an opportunity to discover exactly why Tomaso had been in Cyprus recently and what he might have said to Valentina.

CHAPTER ELEVEN
CYPRUS, EARLY SPRING, 1448
ALYS

This time Alys dressed with care. Her gown was made of dark silk and finely made, but not overly elaborate. Though she hadn't anything that matched the sumptuous quality of Valentina's the day before, she hardly wanted to call attention to herself and would have declined to wear such a gown if she had owned one. This dress and the braided hair woven with a matching silk ribbon showed she was refined enough, but not the matchless courtesan Valentina had spoken of.

She appeared at Valentina's home, at the appointed time, led there by the escort Valentina had provided. The nerves that had risen up in her from the moment she'd awakened that morning suddenly disappeared, to be replaced by a deadly calm. What, after all, could this woman do to her?

Alys was ushered through a rabbit warren of rooms, all abundantly decorated with expensive paintings, silk hangings, intricately carved chests, and tables adorned with glass, porcelain and carved jade. It was a haven of the exotic from all corners of the world.

She ended her journey at a large room that, like Flora's, looked out on a courtyard. The wooden doors of the room were beautifully glazed with coloured glass rims leaded in leafy shapes. Silk drapes hung around the room, drawn back in places with a silk cord, as if to provide little private sitting areas. Long benches filled with silk cushions were placed in small groupings. At the far end, near a brazier, sat Valentina in a cloud of heavy musk scent.

Her gown surprisingly was more modest than the one she'd worn the day before, but only just so. Instead of the brocade, she'd settled for gold silk, with a length of matching fabric woven in her hair, so that it tumbled down from her head, like some sort of ancient Grecian goddess Alys had seen depicted in one of the texts in Alessandra's library. Some part of Alys itched to paint the woman. She was spectacular and possessed her own unique beauty. She could see why Tomaso might have taken the opportunity to come to Cyprus to visit her. But was that the only reason? And where was Alessandra?

"You are so good to come," said Valentina. She gestured to a bench beside her. "Please, be seated and make yourself comfortable."

Alys forced a smile and did as she was bid, walking carefully. She had deliberately rested and massaged her leg rather than have any hint of a limp for Valentina or her staff to detect. She wanted no assumptions made or questions asked on any account.

She selected a cushion to place behind her back so that she was looking directly at Valentina. "You were kind to invite me. Will others be joining us for the card game?"

Alys surveyed the empty table in the middle of the grouping of benches.

Valentina waved a hand in dismissal. "Ah, that was merely a ruse to allow me to have your company all to myself." She cocked her head. "I would like to know you better. As I said, you intrigue me."

"I'm not so intriguing as I may appear. I fear you can lay claim to that sort of description, more than I."

Valentina gave a throaty laugh. "I? I am exactly what you see. A courtesan who enjoys what she does and is privileged to be patronised by the company of some very wealthy men."

"I have no doubt they are privileged by your company," said Alys carefully.

"But I think perhaps others have been privileged by your company in the past, possibly under the name of Maria?" Valentina smiled faintly. "I don't mean your Signor Bonavillagio."

Alys made an effort to keep her voice calm. "I'm flattered you should think so."

"I might not know for certain, but my suspicions are strong. Though you are a trifle windblown, shall we say, your beauty is evident. Your colouring matches the reports I've heard. And you were recently in the company of Signor Bonavillagio."

Alys gave her a cool look. "Is it important who I am?"

"Perhaps not, but I am still intrigued. You see I like puzzles, especially ones whose solutions might benefit me."

"What puzzle do I pose that its solution might benefit you? That in itself is a puzzle, I think."

Valentina gave an amused noise. "You aren't without humour. I like that. No, I might have some pieces for your puzzle."

Alys gave her a direct look. "You know Tomaso well?"

"Yes. I know him particularly well, as I mentioned."

"You have seen him recently?"

Valentina's eyes sparkled. "You are catching on, *cara*."

The last words had an edge to them. Alys's senses were alerted to every nuance. She was certain that Valentina was not a friend, despite the endearment. She was someone who was deriving great pleasure from drawing out the pain of this conversation.

"He has told you some things you think I might be interested in," Alys said patiently, her voice and expression giving away nothing.

"I have some understanding of your situation and I want to be as helpful as possible," said Valentina slowly. "I can't imagine what it would be like to lose a child, and though I would never trouble myself to have one, I'm certain that it must be very difficult for you."

Alys gave a small smile, giving away nothing. "I appreciate your sympathies. You can imagine, then, how much I would value any information you can give."

"Of course. But first, perhaps you would be so kind as to satisfy my curiosity. Where does Signor Bonavillagio fit in all this? Why has he taken it upon himself to assist you to reclaim a child someone else has fathered? A Venetian patrician who refuses to acknowledge his own brat."

She studied Alys, her eyes curious and penetrating. Alys adopted her old Venetian manner and gave a noncommittal shrug.

"He is a good man. We share a past and, well, he cares for the child as if it were his own," said Alys. She knew this woman would give away nothing.

Valentina raised her brow. "Perhaps the people of Venice have the information wrong?"

"What did Tomaso tell you?"

Valentina gave a dismissive snort. "He has no liking for Signor Bonavillagio, and said much about him, but very little about you, *cara*."

"What did he say about Signor Bonavillagio?"

Valentina waved a finger at Alys. "Ah, ah ah. We have the puzzle to solve first." She cocked her head. "But perhaps you have given me the piece. Signor Bonavillagio is the father." She nodded slowly, studying Alys carefully, her eyes narrowed. "Yes, I believe that I have it, though without the cooperation I requested. And it is such a shame you wouldn't share that information with me, especially after I asked so nicely. It seems then, that I won't be able to share with you the information you seek. It's only fair."

Alys made a calculation and rose. "Well, since I no longer amuse, I must go."

Valentina smiled at her silently, her finger to her chin, pretending to consider. "Well...I could make you guess."

"I'm afraid I left my guessing game with my childhood. Just tell me. Did Tomaso say where my child is?"

Valentina shook her head slowly. "No."

Alys frowned, trying her best to retain some control of the conversation.

Valentina tsked. "Oh, dear. Let me just give you a little tease. Our dear little courtier, Tomaso was on his own. Yes, I think I can tell you that much."

"Then Alessandra had left him, or he had left her. Did he say anything about Alessandra?"

"As a matter of fact he did. He spoke quite venomously about her." She put a hand to her mouth. "Oh dear, I might have given away too much."

Alys paused, mulling over the bits she'd been given. He'd be ready to betray Alessandra, perhaps even to Alys, if she caught up with him. She stared at Valentina. "You know where he is?"

Valentina smiled widely. "Oh, even better than that."

"You know where she is, what her plans are."

Valentina clapped her hands. "Very good, you have it, though it took you longer than I expected. Such a shame."

"What did he say?"

"I'm afraid I can only tell you for a price."

"What's your price?"

"Two hundred ducats."

"Two hundred ducats! I don't have two hundred ducats," Alys said, striving to keep her voice calm while a knot formed in her stomach.

"A pity. I'm afraid I can't tell you then."

Alys clasped her hands tightly searching her mind for a way." Would you not consider something else instead?" She glanced at the art work on the walls. "I have some paintings I can send to you from Venice. Good ones that you can sell."

Valentina shook her head. "I have enough paintings. No, I think I must insist on the ducats."

Alys looked down at her hands. Her rings were worth only a little. She had sold all she could before they went on the journey. Now, she had only the money that would see her back to Venice and it was little enough.

"You do have something I might find worth the information, now that I think of it."

"What?" asked Alys warily.

"Your little friend, the monkey. What is his name? Oh, yes, Tomaso. How amusing he has the same name as the man whose information you seek. And I can provide. I think that's rather fitting, don't you?"

"Tomaso?" Alys forced a little laugh. "But what would you want with him?"

"Amusement, of course. Surely you can see that. What other use could he be? Is there something more to him that makes him more valuable?"

"No, of course not."

"Then shall we agree?"

Alys stared at her. "I have to consider this. He isn't entirely mine, you see."

"But you told me he was."

Alys shook her head. "He is also Signor Bonavillagio's. And he would be most distressed to hear that I parted with him."

"But surely not as distressed as he would be if he knew you would pass up an opportunity to learn how to get his child back."

Alys took a deep breath. "As I said, I need time to consider. I might be able to gather two hundred ducats instead."

Valentina shrugged. "I can be generous. Let me know by tomorrow evening. You can bring either the two hundred ducats or the monkey."

Alys nodded and rose. "Until tomorrow."

CHAPTER TWELVE
CYPRUS, EARLY SPRING 1448
ALYS

"Two hundred ducats!" said Joanie. "Is that woman mad?"

"Just greedy," said Alys.

She straightened the coverlet on the bed for the tenth time, her hands casting shadows in the candlelight. Joanie stood above her, fists on hips, full of indignation. Hal leaned against the wall of the bed chamber. His face was grim and worried.

"I knew that woman was trouble from the first," said Joanie. "When you told me about 'er I thought to myself, this woman is sly and cunning. Didn't I say to stay well away from 'er?"

"It's no use lamenting it now, Joanie. It's done. The choices are clear."

"Can you ask Flora for the money?" asked Hal.

Alys looked at him, considering. "I don't know."

"Tell 'er you can send a painting, like you did the other one," said Joanie. "She may go for that. She likes paintings, too."

"Or she may just lend you the money outright," said Hal. "She's soft touch that one." He knelt down by Tomaso's cage. He was curled up, asleep, so innocent looking. "Though why I'm so concerned about keeping this one, is more than I can see. 'E's more trouble than 'e's worth."

Alys gave him a fond smile. She knew Hal was just as fond of Tomaso as she was, but she appreciated his joking manner. Some of the tension eased inside of her.

"I'll try. Though I wouldn't put my hopes on Flora. She's not the most reliable sort of person, though she is kind."

Alys found Flora lounging against her cushions as always in her reception room just off of the garden, nibbling on some grapes. She looked up when Alys entered the room.

"Oh good," she said. "I am glad for some company. I was becoming thoroughly bored and was wondering if I should call one of the servants to paint my toes. Do you know it's become the fashion in some circles?" She gave a little giggle. "Can you imagine? Do you think Cesare would like it, though? I don't know. He can be a bit old fashioned sometimes. It could be very enticing. But would it be so on me, do you think? Or perhaps I might even go so far as to paint some henna designs on my skin, like those Moghul women I hear do in the East. It was Cesare who told me that."

Alys took a seat next to Flora and murmured some response or other while she waited for Flora's prattle to halt. Finally, when her monologue seemed finished, Alys spoke.

"Your beauty will shine through with or without any of those things, and continue to charm Cesare. But I've come to ask you something, if you'll hear me."

Flora eyes widened and looked at her inquisitively. "Of course. You can ask anything of me. You are a dear friend. What is it? Do you require more clothes? I have plenty and am happy to loan you several, if your own are too travel stained to be of use. Or perhaps you need a change of room? There is one overlooking the courtyard that gets the sun, though it isn't as large as the one you have now. Or do you need a particular kind of food? I am happy to try and provide it, if I can."

"No, no. My clothes are sufficient to my needs, I assure you. And the room is perfect, as is the food you have provided for us. No it is something much different. A favour."

"Of course. What favour?"

"I need the loan of two hundred ducats," Alys said carefully. "I can repay you with some paintings I have back in Venice. I promise I will send them to you as soon as I return there and they will be equal to the value or more."

Flora blinked at her, for once speechless. "For what purpose would you need two hundred ducats here in Famagusta?"

Alys spread her hands out, feigning helpless dismay. "The captain. He is pressed for money and so presses me. I owe him for some goods that were lost on the voyage, things I spoiled through my own carelessness. He demands I pay him now."

"But can't you promise him the paintings instead?"

Alys shook her head. "No, he needs it immediately. And besides, he isn't someone who would have interest in paintings, valuable or not. He is no merchant or person of culture. He is only a sea captain."

"Oh, I see. Of course." Flora knitted her brow and pouted. "That is too bad. And so worrisome for you. I only wish I could help you, but I can't. I don't have two hundred ducats."

Alys glanced around her. "But…"

Flora followed her glances. "You mean all this? The household, my clothes? My jewels? Yes of course I live in luxury, but I don't pay for it. You must realise that. It's all Cesare." She waved her hand. "He takes care of everything. I have no head for such things. If I want something in particular, then I have only to say to him on his next visit. He arranges for all of the rest to be paid by his man."

Alys forced herself to speak. "I know it is an imposition. But perhaps one of your jewels? I could find some buyer and—"

"Oh, no. I am *desolato*, but I cannot. Cesare would find out and then where would I be? No, it is impossible." Flora reached for Alys's hand and gave her a pleading look, tears in her eyes. "You do understand don't you? Say you do, so that we can continue to be dearest friends."

Alys swallowed her disappointment and anger. "Of course. We are still the dearest of friends."

❧

Back in her chamber, Alys knelt beside Tomaso. He chittered happily to her while she opened the cage and took him up in her arms. She stroked his head, noting the feel of the soft fur. A tear welled and slipped down her face and onto his back.

"The answer was no, then," said Joanie, her tone matter-of-fact.

"The answer was no," said Alys. She turned and bowed her head out of Joanie's view.

"So you'll do it then? You'll give 'er Tomaso?" asked Hal.

"She has no choice," said Joanie firmly. "It has to be done. For Eleanor."

Hal started to say something but changed his mind. He shrugged his shoulders. "The sooner the better. Let's hope her information is worth it."

"If it isn't, I'll kill 'er myself," said Joanie.

"If it isn't, she won't get Tomaso," said Alys.

"Either way Tomaso still comes back to us, though I like Joanie's idea better."

Alys laughed weakly and nodded. "I do as well, but we must be practical. It would cause a mess." She stroked Tomaso one last time, speaking small endearments and with a sigh returned him to his cage. "As you say Hal, we'll do it now, before I change my mind."

The servant ushered Alys into the same chamber as she had visited some hours before. Tomaso had shifted restlessly in his wooden cage as they entered the house, as if he sensed what was about to happen. Alys stood just outside the small cluster of cushioned benches, set Tomaso down on the floor and nodded to Valentina. Hal stood behind her, a support and comfort, but also a message, Alys hoped.

Valentina, reclining in a different gown to the one she'd had on earlier, which revealed even more cleavage if that was possible, looked at her in surprise.

"You are here so soon. You surprise me. From your reluctance, I would have thought you would spend as much time as you could before you brought me your little monkey."

"I might have been bringing you the money." said Alys with studied calm.

Valentina laughed. "You would have agreed immediately, if you had it with you. And where else would you obtain two hundred ducats in such a short time?"

Alys remained silent and Valentina studied her. "Oh my, you didn't ask Floramundi, did you? But you did! I can see it in your face. You must have been so disappointed. Poor Flora, she has no sense, except when it comes to self-protection. She would never do anything to jeopardise her comfortable situation. But I suppose you understand that now."

Valentina glanced behind Alys. "I see you brought some company. And such handsome company. So well built. But I think he does not rival Signor Bonavillagio quite so much. There is perhaps a touch of the coarseness about him, no?" She looked at Alys. "Is he your protection? Surely you don't fear me in that way. But that is too much." She gave another throaty laugh and patted the seat beside her. "Come, sit here beside me and your companion can sit across from us. That way I can whisper the secrets you so desire and admire him from afar."

Alys and Hal took the seats indicated, Hal's expression grim. Alys schooled her own face to a more pleasant look and steeled herself for what was to come. Valentina leaned forward to Hal, her breasts threatening to spill out at any moment. She gave him a sultry smile.

"She neglected to introduce us, I'm afraid. I am Valentina, in case you haven't been told."

"I have been told," said Hal in his rough Italian. "'Al."

"Al? How charming. Is that short for Alberto?" asked Valentina.

Hal gave her a dark look. "No."

Valentina took a deep breath and sighed. Alys swore a nipple peeked out at that moment. "Oh, dear, have I angered him? I am sorry. You perhaps have an aversion to that name?"

"Perhaps he would rather that we turn our attention to the purpose of this visit. We're not here to exchange pleasantries."

Valentina pouted. "But we are mannered people. And there are courtesies." She gave an elaborate sigh."Very well though, if you insist."

"You have what you wanted. What is it you can tell me about Tomaso Cortini and Alessandra?" said Alys.

"You don't want refreshments first? A glass of wine? A little food?"

"Thank you, but no," said Alys.

Valentina, leaned over again, this time taking the glass of wine from the table. She sipped it. "You know Tomaso and Alessandra were travelling together after they left Venice."

Alys nodded. "Yes, we'd established that."

"Can you imagine those two together? Why, it makes me laugh just thinking about it."

"I'm glad you derive amusement from it."

"And with a child in tow, too. Tomaso can't abide little children."

Alys tensed. "He talked about Eleanor?"

"Eleanor? Was that her name? I forgot. Yes, he did mention her. He said she was constantly fussing and demanding attention. He found it most irritating because Alessandra and he, well, the child, let's say took some of the pleasure from any intimate encounters they had."

Alys restrained herself with great difficulty when all she wanted to do was lunge at this hideous woman and rip out her throat. She forced herself to put these comments aside and think about them later. Tomaso gripped the wooden slats and started to screech.

"My, my, he does have a loud voice when he wants to. Can you give me any guidance about that? Does he like particular titbits?"

Hal rose and went over to Tomaso and calmed him, stroking him and making soft noises.

"Oh that is touching," said Valentina. "Perhaps I will keep you as well."

Hal gave her a dark look and resumed his seat.

"What else did Tomaso say? Did he mention where Alessandra went after they parted?"

"You see, I think that's what finally finished them," said Valentina. "She was just spending too much time with the child. That, and the fact that he felt used, unappreciated. He was to be a full business partner and she refused in the end. After she'd had what she wanted from him."

"A full business partner?" Alys said, her tone expressing only mild interest.

"Did I not say? The two of them, together. She offered Tomaso a partnership in her trade, in return for his…countenance."

"Countenance?"

"Well, you know how these men can be, especially in the East. They will hardly trade with a woman, will they?"

"East, where?" asked Alys, her breath gone for a moment.

"Oh, I don't know. Some very foreign sounding name. But the point is they have valuable goods that she wanted to bring back and trade."

"So she's coming back?"

"I assume so."

"But you don't know where she is now."

"For all I know she might be somewhere in Venice now. Though Tomaso did say she was planning to go north to trade these goods."

"North where?"

Valentina shrugged. "Again, a place whose name I now forget, if he said it. But I don't think so."

"And where is Tomaso now?"

Valentina paused and considered. "He said he was going home."

"To Venice?"

"No, the place of his birth. His family are still there, I believe."

"Where is that?" Alys's patience was growing thin and she fought the urge to slap Valentina. "West of Venice, I think. Let me see…"

"Spit it out," said Hal. "You've had your fee, now stop toying with us and get on with it."

"He speaks again," said Valentina blithely. "And with such ferocity. Now, where was I? Yes, Tomaso's birthplace. Mantua, I think."

"Mantua," said Alys. She'd heard of Mantua. The Gonzaga family and its head, the Lord of Mantua, lived there and so did many of their retainers. "He isn't related to the Gonzaga family is he?"

"Well yes, I believe he is, but don't let that worry you, it's only a distant relationship. It's what gave him access to the best circles, you understand, but he still hadn't any money to speak of, so he lives by his wits. And apparently his wits deserted him when he decided to ally himself with Alessandra. But then he was always blind when it came to her." She gave Alys a sweet smile. "And all the more so when his appetite for her was increased after your Signor Bonavillagio appeared on the scene and stole her away. And if that wasn't enough humiliation, he beat him badly at cards and took all his money. Tsk, tsk, your Giacomo made a bad enemy there."

Alys ignored Valentina's barbs. "So you think Tomaso is in Mantua?"

"Well, I cannot say, *cara*. I can only tell you what he said his plans were."

"And Alessandra is heading north to trade?"

Valentina nodded. "Perhaps Tomaso can tell you exactly where. I, alas, cannot. But I think I have given you a fair bargain, have I not?" She looked over at Tomaso and smiled. "Can you bring him here? I would like to have him in my lap so we can become properly acquainted."

"Get him yourself," said Hal. "We've filled our part, and you've had your say. There's nothing more to be done here so we'll be on our way."

He moved over to Alys and held out a hand to her.

Alys took it and stood, turning to Valentina. "I'm afraid I can't say it was a pleasure to meet you, or that I wish we will see each other again. I can only hope that you will treat Tomaso with the kindness and attention that he is worth."

"Oh, you can be sure I treat all things of value with extreme care," said Valentina. "I look forward to hearing how you fare. You are an interesting and determined woman. I have to say, though, I'm not certain how this will play out with Alessandra as your adversary."

Alys turned away and walked out of the room, her hand on Hal's arm and only a brief glance at Tomaso. He began to screech, and the screeching followed her down the hallway and to the door outside while she fought back the tears.

CHAPTER THIRTEEN
SAMARKAND, SPRING 1448
BARNABAS

Samarkand was everything and nothing I'd expected. Though Genghis Khan's destruction of the city during his invasion centuries before was still in evidence, it was a magnificent city. Under Timur, the city's location had slipped south when he'd decided Samarkand should be his capital and his additions had contributed to its grandeur. Mosques and minarets dotted the landscape, along with richly decorated palaces and noble homes. And clearly visible was the blue tiled dome that had haunted me and given me hope since I'd left Venice.

We approached the city from the northern outskirts, proceeding along roads lined with trees of seemingly mountainous proportions, and gardens that obscured the houses and palaces behind them. We entered through the Bokhara gate, coming as we did from that city. There were four gates in all guarding each direction, all passing over a moat. From those gates, six main stone-paved streets proceeded through squares containing fire brick constructed fountains, mosques, minarets, madrasa, mausoleums, caravanserai and bathhouses. The six streets ended at the domed trade gallery at Samarkand's centre, the Registan. And there, within the citadel, bordering the western wall, stood the four-storey Kok Serai, the Blue Palace. In the shadow of the Registan was the main bazaar, a vaulted street running across the length of the city, built by Timur himself. It was his grandson, Ulugh Beg, who ruled now.

People bustled around dressed in all manner of unfamiliar fashions, marking their origins in lands I probably wouldn't know. Battuta pointed out the Chinese from Cathay who were, by his account, the best craftsmen and traders in the most precious items like stained glass, rubies, musk, diamonds and pearls. He pointed out the traders from India who brought nutmeg, cloves, mace, cinnamon, ginger and many other spices.

He'd arranged for us to stay in a fairly comfortable caravanserai, each of us with our own room at a cost less than I had imagined, given the luxury and prosperity the city seemed to imply. But as I looked closer at the buildings, and then the stalls, and every other aspect of the city I could see the cracks. Faded and worn tapestries and silk hangings covered the cracks on the walls of my rooms, and cracks were also evident in other parts of the building. Cracks in a more abstract sense were also evident when I noticed that some of the caravanserai appeared to be housing few travellers, with little comings and goings, some with vacant or boarded windows and some looking closed permanently.

All this I noticed from my window, after settling in and contemplating the character and size of the city and its truly exotic quality. Though I'd seen some very surprising buildings and places in my travels, this was far and above anything I'd imagined or seen previously. Bokhara, where we'd only stopped briefly, held marvels of architecture, but nothing of the flamboyance and size that I'd viewed in Samarkand.

A tap came at the door. I shook myself from my musings and went to open it. Abdul stood there, his face alight with eagerness. In the two days that Battuta had allowed us to remain in Bokhara, Abdul had diligently followed his father to the mosques and madrasas that gave the place its fame as a theological centre. His father had made use of the time and did his best to convince his son that this direction of study was best, what Allah would approve of. But as the days unfolded and we'd moved ever closer to Samarkand, it was clear Abdul still held his passion for topics of a more scientific nature. When his father was out of earshot he'd pressed me for more information on my own studies and what I'd concluded.

"Father is resting," Abdul said. "But I am too upset to find that appealing."

"Upset? Why?"

"Didn't Battuta say? He can't gain us entry into the observatory, or the madrasa. The person he hoped would oblige has died."

I shook my head. "Battuta didn't mention it." I gave him a reassuring smile and gestured for him to enter my room, though my plan had been to go out and begin my inquiries. There was nothing to be gained by showing impatience. It would have to wait a little longer.

Abdul took a seat in an elaborately carved lattice work cushioned bench that was at the far end of the room and matched an equally impressive carved bed. I sat beside him and poured some wine from the flagon provided, which sat on the table beside a plate of grapes and figs. I offered him a glass. He hesitated and then relented, sipping his drink carefully. I wasn't certain how abstemious he was at heart and this was a gesture of hospitality and curiosity at a youth testing his own resolves.

"I'm sorry he has disappointed you," I said finally. "But perhaps he didn't mention it to me yet because he hoped that he could gain us entry through another method."

"Do you think so? It would be awful if we came all this way and weren't able to see anything." he asked. He glanced out of the window. "Though even what I've seen so far is magnificent. Don't you think?"

I nodded slowly. "It is impressive. But you have travelled yourself, you must know how it compares."

"I haven't travelled as you have to such varied places. My travels have always been with a particular religious view which doesn't always mean an impressive city. Just impressive texts."

"But haven't you been to Mecca, made your pilgrimage to the Haj?"

Abdul shook his head. "No, we are to do that on the return journey. Our travels thus far are to prepare our minds and bodies through study before we reach Mecca." He sighed, not entirely convinced, I could see.

"I have no doubt you will find Mecca equally impressive, though perhaps not in the same way," I said neutrally. I didn't want to alienate his father completely. I was already receiving dark looks that I knew he wouldn't dare direct at Battuta.

"Perhaps. But I can't help but think that I will find everything dull after this." He bit his lip. "Do you think I could persuade Father to allow me to stay behind?" He looked at my sceptical face and rushed on speak further.

"To study for a time. I would certainly return and perhaps we could go to Mecca then. I would be able to find a path that serves both Allah and my own interests. Surely Allah would want us to make sense of the stars? And is not Ulugh Beg a believer too?" His words tailed off.

I patted his arm. "Perhaps you may persuade your father. You are his son and I'm certain your happiness is important to him. A few days in the city and all that it has to offer may be all you need to support your wish." I had no belief in my words, but I wanted to give him some comfort.

Abdul nodded, forced a smile and made an effort to change the subject. "Do you know any ways that Battuta or yourself might gain permission to visit the observatory?"

"Let's see what Battuta says in the morning. There is probably a protocol on gaining entrance. I have given him some names of people I've studied with and the texts, in the hopes that the scholars will see we desire to pursue our knowledge and aren't frivolous visitors. Maybe someone can direct him to an appropriate person."

"Will that take long?"

I shrugged. For me, a few days would be welcome, so that I might make my own inquiries and inspect the city for more than just cracks in the walls. If it didn't happen, well, then it would be a pity, but not something that would distress me. Alessandra was my main concern.

"I'm certain it won't be too long," I said. "But in the meantime it wouldn't hurt to rest ourselves, so that we have plenty of energy for what's ahead."

I rose and gave a small yawn. Abdul took the hint and shot up from the bench. "Forgive me, I have kept you. I will leave you in peace. Perhaps now I might be able to find my own repose in my room. Thank you for listening to the ramblings of a foolish young man."

I shook my head. "It was no trouble at all, my friend. You're not foolish at all. Just enthusiastic. And that in itself gives welcome energy to others."

He smiled and left, hopefully more at ease than he'd been before. I sighed as the door shut behind him. My own task lay ahead, its own proportions almost unimaginable. But it must begin somewhere.

It would be difficult to enquire after Alessandra. The language would undoubtedly be an issue. I'd managed to acquire some words of Sogdian that was the primary language, especially among those who worked and traded regularly along the Royal Road and some areas of Transoxiana but I had no idea what manner of language was spoken in the bazaars and everywhere else. The people of Timur were Turkic from what I could gather, layered on top of myriad other peoples settled here over the centuries. I needed to discover what I was up against.

❧

Hearing shouts I turned, thinking it was me they called, the Arabic language a familiar sound to my ears, but when I looked I saw it was someone behind me. The man halted and smiled, his fingers moving the string of beads in his hand as if they worked independently.

On the other side of the street two Chinese men walked in the opposite direction, their long silk robes flapping against their legs. The face of one was weathered as if he'd spent long hours in the wind and sun, but his companion was youthful and his features were less distinctively Chinese, his nose more pronounced and his eyes rounded. Other men, of Turkic background, milled around looking at the various stalls. Only a few women, obviously servants or members of the poorer groups, were in evidence.

Would Alessandra have dared to venture out on the streets of the bazaar in the face of this preponderance of men? Perhaps, heavily veiled. Or would she have used Tomaso instead? I found it difficult to believe she would have relied on Tomaso to do her trading. I could only hope that she would have met with the merchants herself, in a back room with Tomaso to act as her mouthpiece at the very most.

A man exited from a building which had an elaborately carved doorway. His robes were long and rich, his appearance marking him as most probably from the Levant, his black hair curling. I smiled and greeted him and he gave me a cursory nod, but answered me nonetheless in the Arabic I'd spoken.

The aromas wafting from the door told me what trade they dealt in and I took a chance. "My friend, I am newly arrived. I am a scholar foremost, but a trader second, and though while I am here to study at the observatory, I wish to trade for a small amount of goods. As much as my humble sum allows. May I take it from your happy countenance that you would mark this as a good establishment for such trade?"

The man blinked, his eyes quickly assessing me, and made a decision.

"You may take it so," he said. "But he may not trade with you. Would you have anything that vouches for your sincerity?"

I gave him a winning smile. "My wit? And of course my gold. Would that suffice?"

The man paused a moment and then laughed. "I would say that will take you far. Especially with Xuan

Zang." He bowed a moment. "I beg your pardon. I am Hosan Nador."

I returned the bow and introduced myself. He clapped me on the back lightly and urged me into the building, following behind me.

"I will take you directly to Xuan Zang, past his servants and clerks. They will only keep you dawdling just for show. No need to waste time with them."

"I'm deeply indebted," I said.

He led me through a labyrinth of corridors filled with clerks and servants who each bowed in turn to us. Hosan barely gave them a nod. I caught glimpses of spacious rooms lined with large chests and sacks, all, I suspected, filled with various spices and other items I had yet to discover.

We climbed stairs and travelled along another corridor that led to carved double doors. Hosan tapped on them. A moment later a Chinese man, clad in rich crimson silk robes opened the doors. He gave a short bow and, recognising Hosan with a smile and lift of his brow, ushered us in. At first I thought he was Xuan Zang, until we entered and I saw a man sitting at a large carved table filled with documents and rolled parchments. His hair was dark, but the light caught a scattering of silver strands. He wore a thin moustache and a wispy beard that trailed down below his chin.

He rose when we entered and greeted Hosan, his Arabic heavily accented, clearly surprised to see him so soon after his departure moments earlier. They exchanged bows.

"You wish something more?" he said after his greeting.

"Only to introduce my friend. A scholar, like yourself. When he mentioned he was here to study at the observatory but also wished to purchase some goods, I thought to myself there is only one person he should meet."

Hosan bowed again and introduced me.

Zang bowed, his eyes alight. "Master Bonavillagio, you are a scholar?"

"I aspire to it."

"I am certain you are being too modest," said Zang politely. "You are interested in the stars?"

"I am fascinated many things," I said. "But yes, the stars and the planets interest me very much. I have studied mathematics with some very fine scholars, both in Padua and at the Grand Vizier's library at Hüdavendigar."

Zang raised his brows at the mention of the latter, clearly impressed. He posed a few mathematical questions relating to calculations for stars and planets. I did my best to answer, though some were beyond my understanding. Eventually he nodded, satisfied.

"You have studied widely yourself?" I asked. "You're obviously a scholar of some depth."

Zang gave a small self-deprecating smile. "You are kind. I have been privileged through my life to have been able to consult many texts and have conversations with many learned men."

"And yet you have found time to be a prosperous merchant? You are indeed a marvel."

Zang laughed briefly. "No marvel at all. It's the trade that has enabled me to travel and support my studies. I suspect it might be true for you too?"

"To a degree. It has certainly served me here. You are familiar with the observatory?"

"As my friend Hosan here can tell you, I have been fortunate to visit there on occasion."

Hosan moved forward, smiling. "He is too modest. He's a frequent visitor. There is a community of scholars who attend there regularly, along with the ruler Ulugh Beg."

"Ulugh Beg attends there regularly?" I asked, surprised.

"He does of course. It was under his direction that this observatory was built and he still takes a keen interest," said Zang, his tone polite. "He is a man of learning, himself, and an enthusiast for astronomy and mathematics."

"A man of ideas," said Hosan. "And the power to carry them out, though as I understand it his abilities in astronomy may not match his enthusiasm." His tone held some condemnation, and something else that took me a moment to name. Bitterness.

Zang made no comment, his expression neutral. There was an undercurrent of sorts that I wasn't able to decipher. "Would I be able to gain entry to the observatory?"

Zang bowed. "I would be happy to take you with me and introduce you."

I gave my own bow in thanks. "I know an enthusiast who would be more than appreciative if he were able to accompany me. He is young and a budding scholar who is particularly taken with this area of study. May I bring him?"

"I'm certain that won't be a problem," said Zang. There was a light in his eyes, barely perceptible. "I know what it is to be young and enthusiastic, thirsting after knowledge."

"Well it's an indulgence that not everyone can afford." Hosan gave a small sigh. "But who's to say we haven't all benefitted from those who can afford it?"

"Exactly," I said, in an effort to help reclaim a more positive atmosphere. "And trade is certainly a benefit to many, my friend," I said to Hosan. "I am indebted to you for your help in both my endeavours."

Hosan nodded and smiled, his expression softening. "It is my pleasure. I'm glad that I was able to introduce two like-minded people."

"I am privileged to be able to discuss matters of the mind as well as those of trade with you," I said to Zang, hoping to get back onto trade.

"Are you interested in anything in particular that I deal with?" asked Zang.

"Spices. Most specifically cinnamon, nutmeg. Things of that nature. Easy enough to carry."

"Of course. I also have some particularly good satin silk that I've recently acquired. Others have asked for it, but I wanted to save it for someone who might appreciate its true worth."

I nodded and gave a faint smile. I had no doubt that the quality was good, but wondered at his flattery. "I would appreciate its worth, I can assure you. I have dealt in cloth frequently." I paused as if a thought had just occurred to me. "Would you perhaps have had dealings with a certain woman from Venice? I haven't encountered her in some time, but she had mentioned that she was travelling here with her trade partner. She would be distinctive."

"A woman?" Zang shook his head and frowned, puzzled. "I've had no dealings with women, Venetian or otherwise."

"Perhaps her trading partner, then. A Venetian, with a love for gaming."

Zang studied me and then shook his head slowly. "I don't believe so. At least not directly. I could inquire of my staff, if it's of importance to you."

I waved my hand in dismissal. "No, it is of no matter. I was only curious because they are both particularly interested in fine cloth."

Zang nodded. "Of course." He gestured to the door. "Would you like to try a sample of the spices and make your decision? And then if you would like to consider the cloth, I can show you that as well."

I bowed again. "I would be honoured if you would do that. And I would like to view the cloth. It sounds unique and special enough that I am certain I will want to purchase it. I have some items I brought with me that you might be interested in."

Zang gave a slight smile. "Of course. You have intrigued me now."

I followed him out of the room, Hosan trailing behind us. He took his leave once we were in the corridor and Zang led me in a different direction, down a back stairs to some remote rooms. The man was a puzzle. His response about Alessandra was puzzling in itself. I was certain there was more going on in his thoughts than his words suggested.

CHAPTER FOURTEEN
SAMARKAND, SPRING, 1448
BARNABAS

The grandeur and size of the buildings of the Registan, the public square, was overwhelming. Though its meaning denoted "sandy place" it was at the heart of Samarkand. Opposite the square was a lofty-domed *khanaga*, a hostel for Dervishes. At the edge of the square rose three monuments, haughty and proud, each a complex of towers, domes, gateways and high walls covered with detailed mosaics, arabesques studded with gold, amethysts and turquoises and intricate calligraphy. Among them was a blue domed building.

On the west side of the square was a beautiful madrasa, a school of great learning, built some years before by Ulugh Beg himself. I was told it housed at least 100 students under the tutelage of the finest scholars to be found, teaching the subjects of both Islamic and secular sciences, including astronomy. Azure stars decorated the school's huge portal, indicating the importance placed on astronomy among the subjects studied. A Kufic inscription read "this magnificent facade is of such a height it is twice the heavens, and of such weight that the spine of the earth is about to crumble." Tiles of earth tones with glazed green, turquoise, yellow highlights amid shades of light and dark blue covered it. Mosaic and majolica panels shone with floral motifs, and the Kufic calligraphy, as well as geometric patterns, stretched across the walls and up the minarets flanking the building.

Through the portal entrance was a square courtyard from which four vaulted arches opened onto fifty student cells over two storeys. Under the corner domes were spacious lecture halls, while the western axis concealed a five bayed mosque.

It was into this massive complex that Zang ushered our little group a few days after my initial encounter with him. We were greeted by one of the madrasa servants. Abdul could hardly contain his excitement, while his father looked pensive and perhaps a little wary. As we made our way along the halls I was distracted, as well as wary of Zang and frustrated by my lack of progress in finding Alessandra. Battuta had seemed relieved when I'd told him about meeting Zang and obtaining an introduction to the madrasa and the observatory. He'd said that Zang was well known and very reputable as both a scholar and a merchant, though Battuta had no personal knowledge of him.

Now I glanced at Zang and could see no reason to distrust him or the scholar he was about to introduce us to, but some instinct told me that things may not be as they appeared.

The servant halted in front of a door and gave a soft knock. A moment later it was opened by a man wearing a large turban and long dark robes. His beard was grey and myriad wrinkles covered his face, but his dark brown eyes were lively. He smiled at us and greeted Zang warmly, then beckoned us all into the room.

It was no student cell, though its size perhaps was only slightly larger, or it may have seemed small since every possible space was piled with codices, scrolls and pieces of parchment fragments, except for a narrow path that led to a dark wooden table where a huge piece of parchment, a small astrolabe and some other tools lay spread.

He introduced himself as Razim Neẓām-al-Molk, an astronomy teacher and Zang introduced us in turn. After the bows and greetings were complete, Razim cleared a small bench and bid us sit.

"I would not trouble you ordinarily, Razim," said Zang. "But I know you are eager to meet and discuss other institutions and their progress, so I felt compelled to bring my friend to meet you." He glanced beyond me at Abdul. "And his eager young companion and the father, who I believe are both seekers of knowledge."

"I am a student and compiler of Hadith," said Kasim, drawing himself up. "I put the interpretations and understanding of the Koran above all."

"A worthy vocation, and one from which we all benefit," said Razim, his tone neutral. He looked at me. "You have studied elsewhere?"

I bowed slightly. "I have been fortunate."

"May I ask what manner of studies?" His eyes were alight, eager again.

"Mathematics and many of the sciences."

Razim nodded. "Under whose tutelage?"

I gave an apologetic look. I rattled off a few names from the men who'd taught me in Paris and Padua. "I'm not certain you would have heard of them."

"But you also mentioned you were at the library of the Turkic sultan's Grand Vizier," said Zang.

"I was. There I studied for a short time with a man called Habib. Most of my studies were with someone else, though." I forced out the name of the man I'd sworn to kill and finally had. "He called himself Master al Qali, though he went by other names. He was African, and I believe he studied at the libraries in Timbuktu."

Razim's expression was keen, his eyes fixed on me. "How interesting. Interesting indeed. I haven't met anyone who has studied there. Did your mathematics lead you to astronomy?"

"The stars and their arrangement in the skies, yes, but not the study of the heavenly bodies to predict the future in relationship to particular people, though some might call both astrology." I'd made a point of stating the clarification just to be certain he wouldn't expect any kind of prediction from me. I had no desire for anyone to even suspect I might possess any precognitive abilities, whether they had faded or not.

"Oh, I mean the arrangement of the stars and the heavenly bodies, of course," he said. "I have no interest in the other."

I smiled and nodded. "Yes, I had some interest, so my tutors, including Master al Qali, indulged me." I gestured to Abdul. "And I believe my friend Abdul has perused some texts he's encountered."

Razim returned my smile. "You are very welcome, my friend. I look forward to many discussions with you."

The door burst open and two soldiers entered, announcing something in a language I didn't know. A moment later an older man of no particularly height, but richly dressed, with a jewelled turban and an embroidered coat entered. Immediately Razim and Zang prostrated themselves on the floor and the rest of us, slightly bewildered, followed suit.

"Ulugh Beg," said Razim.

I kept my head down, momentarily full of wonder. It was Mīrzā Muhammad Tāraghay bin Shāhrukh, known as Ulugh Beg, or "Great Ruler". Such a ruler, so renowned, yet here he was, striding into the rooms of a madrasa teacher.

Ulugh Beg waved his hand and bade us rise. "No need to stand on ceremony here. We are all scholars seeking learning," he said, his accent thick. "I heard you were to explain some new theories today so I thought I might come and ask you about them."

I glanced at the two soldiers who stood silently at attention by the door. I guess by Ulugh Beg's standards this was a meeting without ceremony. We all rose and Zang, Kasim, Abdul and I remained by our bench while Razim stood uneasily before Ulugh Beg.

"Nevertheless, we are honoured by your visit here at the madrasa," said Razim. "You will forgive me, but I was just greeting some guests who are also interested in astronomy." He nodded in our direction.

Ulugh Beg turned to study us. I lowered my eyes, experience cautioning me that it was best not to look directly at anyone of such noble birth.

"This particular guest," Razim said, pointing towards me, "Master Giacomo Bonavillagio, has a background you might appreciate as well." He described my academic pedigree and I flushed, not knowing whether to be flattered or worried.

Ulugh Beg smiled at me and I dared to raise my eyes to his face. It seemed friendly and open enough, but I knew better than to use that as a guide.

"Master Bonavillagio, you have come to Samarkand to study? With such a background we are pleased to welcome you."

"Yes, I'm here to study," I said. "But also to trade." I gave him a remorseful look. "To support such a pastime I require some income."

"Of course," Ulugh Beg said. "And what are your theories on the planets and their orbits? Have you seen some of the calculations and conjectures of our fellow scholars?"

"I have read Archimedes' report on Aristarchus's heliocentric theories," I said. "And adding that to the writings of Martianus Capella, a convincing argument forms."

"So you refute Ptolemy's assumptions," said Ulugh Beg.

"I find it interesting to read a variety of opinions."

"Opinion?" said Ulugh Beg, amused. "Have you read anything of the Maragha School of Astronomy?"

"I am aware of it, as I am aware of the problems of Ptolemy's theories. I believe an Arab scholar wrote a critique of it, outlining some of the issues."

"So you think the planets revolve around the sun and not the earth?" asked Ulugh Beg. There was a challenge in his voice.

"I think that the earth revolves. And rotates," I said carefully. "Based on the mathematical models I've seen."

Ulugh Beg nodded. "Good. Then you must see our own records at the observatory. Come tomorrow. We'll expect you there in the morning." He turned to Razim. "You as well, Razim, and tell us both your latest theories. I wager our friend might have some interesting comments about them."

"May I bring my friends here?" I said, venturing this request. "They are most desirous to see the observatory as well."

Ulugh Beg glanced over at them. "Perhaps another day." He looked at Razim. "You can take them in a few days' time. I want to have you and Master Bonavillagio completely at my disposal tomorrow."

He gave a nod and turned to his soldiers, still standing at attention by the door. Without a moment's hesitation they opened the door and he strode out, before any of us could prostrate ourselves.

"A man of action," I said softly.

"Indeed," said Razim. "And most supportive of our work. He compiled a very fine star table some years ago. I'm certain he'll show it to you. He's very proud of it and the work that is done."

"How admirable. You are fortunate to have such support for your work," I said.

I glanced at Abdul and Kasim. I could see the happiness shining in Abdul's eyes and a glimmer of hope. I knew in what direction that hope was cast. Kasim on the other hand looked troubled and wary. I could imagine the discussion on the placement of the heavenly bodies might have indicated something less than holy to him, and perhaps leaning towards blasphemous. Would it contradict the Koran to state that the earth wasn't the centre of the heavenly bodies? The main issue, I told myself, wasn't what the Koran said, but what *hadith* Kasim had learned and taken as truth about it.

In the meantime I was drawn into the sultan's sphere whether I liked it or not. It could be the most fortunate encounter of my entire journey, or the most unfortunate, leaving me exposed to conspiracy and danger. My past time spent with noble company had never led to anything good, and more often than not it had put my life in danger.

✦

My mind was afire with the possibilities and the wonder of it. At least that's what I thought upon my arrival when I first saw the observatory, rising northeast of the city against the foothills in all its majesty. The thoughts and worries about my child, about Alessandra, that had been a running narrative in my mind, had gone for the moment.

It was difficult not to be impressed, to feel awe at the mere presence of the power of its conception. It was a cylindrical building, three storeys in height, the walls ornately tiled similar to the other buildings. Rising from inside, through its uncovered walls, was the largest sextant I'd ever seen, its sides fashioned from marble and oriented north-south by my calculations.

I stopped my escort and pointed, my mind racing with questions. "What radius? What diameter?"

I got a shrug for my answer. It might have been the language. I had no grasp of any of the Transoxiania languages to make headway with him, and could only hope those inside might be able to help. I wasn't certain if Ulugh Beg's invitation meant he would actually be present, or if he merely was extending me the opportunity to admire his work.

I sighed and followed my escort inside. The weather was warm, a Samarkand spring having taken a firm hold here. Open to the sky, the interior was bright and welcoming. A few servants milled about, assisting the three men who stood silently over a couple of tables to the side, parchment, reed pens and ink at their elbows. One looked up when I entered and made his way over to me hastily.

He bowed low when he reached my side and dismissed the escort with a nod. He was younger than I had imagined, his dark eyes alert under his simple turban and his beard barely showing any hint of grey.

"Forgive me," he said in careful Arabic. "I was caught up in my work. I am Ali Qushji, astronomer here at the observatory, by the grace of Allah and Ulugh Beg. You are come at Ulugh Beg's request, I believe?"

I bowed my reply. "Yes, a request that I was happy to comply with. I am Giacomo Bonavillagio. "

"Yes, he mentioned that. I understand you have an impressive scholarly background?"

"Ulugh Beg was being generous," I said. My initial impressions convinced me that I would find it difficult to match my knowledge with any of the scholars here. Still, my curiosity was great. "Is it possible for you to show me the sextant?"

Qushji smiled faintly. "I'm afraid we must wait until the sultan arrives."

I nodded. So he was to come here. "Has he been detained?"

"Possibly. Though he is a man who has great energy and will brook no distractions if he has his mind set on something."

As if on cue, the door opened and the sultan entered, flanked by his customary soldiers with a few more added for extra measure this time. They remained at the door while Ulugh Beg strode over toward us and we prostrated ourselves on the marble floor. With a wave of his hand he bid us rise immediately, while a servant brought forth a chair and cushions so that he might sit down next to one of the tables. He took the seat with a weary sigh, worry and fatigue carving great grooves on his face and made more prominent in the raking light. The rich brocade long coat he wore hung from his frame loosely.

"Good," he said, looking at me. "You are come."

"I am honoured you have seen fit to invite me." I gestured around. "It's truly magnificent. A marvel."

Ulugh Beg brightened. "It is, is it not? I am most proud of it. It is a great centre of scientific learning. No one can dispute that."

"Not at all. I assure you I have seen nothing like it."

"That is because it is the best in the world. You will see nothing like it ever again."

"Without a doubt," I said, hiding a wry smile. I was certain he was right, but I found it interesting that he seemed insistent I should know.

"But we must demonstrate how magnificent it is."

He nodded to Qushji who stepped towards me and guided me towards the sextant. The next hour flew by as Qushji demonstrated the sextant that was really a quadrant, though all 90 degrees couldn't be used, and showed the calculations that could be derived from its size. He also showed me the star tables, Zīj-i Sultānī is a Zij, the astronomical table and star catalogue which described 1018 stars, the constellations' locations with coordinates and a defined length of the star year. Ulugh Beg himself had worked on this and I gave him all credit for it.

Ulugh Beg had monitored the demonstrations and explanations, interrupting to add his own comments on occasion like an excited puppy. There was no denying his enthusiasm, his interest or, surprisingly, his knowledge. I warmed to him, appreciative that such a man might take it upon himself to choose this area to make his influence felt.

"You must come at night," he'd said at one point, interrupting Qushjiin the middle of our discussions on the star chart and I vowed that I would.

When the explanations were finished Qushji excused himself, but not before thanking me for the interest and keen eye I had displayed. "I have enjoyed this very much," he said, his eyes twinkling.

"Certainly not more than I have. You were very kind to spend the time with me."

"But your knowledge is wide and worthy of such time. Your questions so full of insight and consideration."

I felt myself blush at such praise. It had been a long time since I had the opportunity to really push my mind and exchange views and question someone in such a manner. I'd been eager to please, to show off, almost, a feeling that gave rise to complicated emotions. The last time I'd done that it had been for al Qali, a man whose memory I now despised, a man who had coloured with caution or derision my view on pursuing any kind of knowledge. But this man, Ali Qushji, seemed cut from an entirely different cloth than al Qali. His comments seemed genuine, not born of any ulterior motive. I forced myself to accept the praise in good spirit and gave him a smile, bowing low and murmuring my thanks for his words.

Qushji bowed again and then, turning to the sultan, took formal leave of him. With a wave he gathered the other scholars, who scooped up rolls of parchment and their writing and calculation tools and followed him out of the observatory. Two of the servants remained behind, but they kept a discreet distance.

Ulugh Beg indicated the carpet at his feet. "Sit," he said.

Puzzled, I did as I was told. Was this to be an extension of the discussion about astronomy? Or was there something else on his mind? My mind flashed to Alessandra and Eleanor.

"It isn't often that Ali Qushji offers such praise. He thinks highly of you and your ability."

"I am indeed flattered by his praise. He's a man of great learning and it's been a privilege to meet him. Though not compared to your own abilities," I added tactfully. "You are without peer, both as a scholar and as a truly enlightened leader."

Ulugh Beg smiled faintly. "There are many who have no appreciation for what I do. Even among my family." His eyes darkened, his expression drawn. He sat for a moment, his mind somewhere else. Finally, he looked down at me. "You are married, Master Bonavillagio? Do you have children?"

"I have a child and a wife." In my mind as well as in my heart, Alys was my wife. I thought of our bitter parting and the pain that had been a dull ache since she'd left sharpened.

"I hope you are fortunate in your child and your wife. Families can be a burden just as much as a blessing."

"My daughter is very much a blessing, as I'm sure your own are," I said carefully. I studied the sultan, uncertain about his questioning.

"Daughters can be good. I am fortunate in a few, though I see them little now. Beautiful, charming and difficult."

I nodded and murmured some agreement. "Do any of your sons take the same interest in astronomy as you?" It seemed a safe, neutral answer so I was surprised by the bitterness and sadness that crossed his face.

"They do not." He looked in the distance for a moment, then, collecting himself again, forced a smile. "To have a son as you, so obviously possessing a thirst for knowledge is a rare blessing. Your father is fortunate."

I started to open my mouth to say I knew neither of my parents, that I was an orphan, but recalled myself in time. While my own past was that of an orphan, Giacomo, my invented self, had a family, of course. "My family are merchants. That's what takes their energy and effort. They have little appreciation for my interests and studies."

"A pity, for them and for you." He reached over and patted my head. "We share that feeling then." He gave me a soft look that I found at once disarming and alarming. "You will be like a son to me, for as long as you stay. Just as Ali Qushji is a younger brother."

I flushed and lowered my eyes so that he couldn't see the surprise and confusion on my face. Was this man so impulsive he would pronounce such words on someone he hardly knew? Before I could reply, he reached inside his coat and withdrew a chain with a small gold handled mirror dangling from it. Carefully he put it around my neck and I looked up at him in astonishment.

"A token to show my appreciation of you and mark our relationship," he said.

"My humble thanks are not good enough for such notice," I said. "I am a stranger and hardly worthy of such a gift, Ulugh Beg." I reached up to remove it. "Please, it's too good. I cannot accept."

Ulugh Beg's eyes clouded. "You will accept. You're not a stranger, for our minds have met and they are alike."

I relented and nodded. It had been foolish to protest a gift from Ulugh Beg and only an unguarded reaction had prompted my initial refusal. Getting hold of myself, I suppressed the urge to continue.

I fingered the small mirror that now hung around my neck. "I thank you most sincerely and will treasure it always."

Ulugh Beg nodded. He rose. "You will remain in Samarkand and we will assuredly no longer be the strangers you seem to think we are. You will come here again tomorrow at the same time."

I quickly prostrated myself as he strode from the building, the soldiers taking up their places beside him. The door shut behind them, leaving the observatory in a deafening silence. I rose to my feet slowly, staring at the door and absentmindedly fingering the gift now hanging around my neck. What had happened? Was this sultan so deprived of friends and people who shared his interests that he would take up a complete stranger on a whim? Or was there something darker at work here?

CHAPTER FIFTEEN
SAMARKAND, SPRING 1448
BARNABAS

"I think my father might allow me to remain," said Abdul. "Especially if you are here with me."

I gave Abdul a vague smile. We were in my rooms, which were now in a more spacious and richly appointed accommodation nearer to the madrasa and the company of Razim. Abdul and Kasim had rooms there as well, all three of us the guests of Ulugh Beg. The days passed and I became a frequent visitor of the observatory, most of the times in the company of Abdul and Kasim, after the initial permission had been obtained from Ulugh Beg. Ulugh Beg wasn't always there at the observatory or the madrasa but he attended often enough to make his partiality towards my company clear.

My elevated status and undisputed learning had gained Kasim's grudging admiration. Any remaining complaints and objections had been silenced when he was allowed access to the *hadith* and the theological teachers at the madrasa. But I was still sceptical he would allow Abdul to remain behind for any amount of time.

"Perhaps if he found additional reason to linger here, you might gain more time," I said. "But I doubt that my presence would count towards convincing him. Besides, I don't plan to be here that long."

"But surely you are here at the sultan's pleasure? It is up to him to give you permission to leave and he is clearly much too fond of you to allow you to go yet."

I frowned, knowing his statement to be true but still frustrated by it. I leaned over to pick at the dish of dates on the small table before me, avoiding the charts, diagrams and calculations that had taken up so much of my time.

"I am here to trade," I said. "I must take some time and see Zang to complete my order."

I also wanted time to myself to question other traders, stall keepers and anyone else I could think of who might have seen Alessandra. My days spent at the observatory and madrasa had begun to leave me feeling anxious, constrained and frustrated. I felt I was losing valuable time and with each hour, each day, I was further away from getting Eleanor back.

"You might send Zang a message. Have him meet you at the madrasa."

"Perhaps," I said. I patted Abdul's shoulder. "But it's not for you to worry. I'm certain I will be able to make my arrangements and leave in good time. I just wanted you to realise that you can't count on my presence when you make your case to your father. Perhaps you could ask Qushji to speak with him."

"No, no, I couldn't do that," said Abdul, flushing.

"But you have spoken to him about remaining behind?"

"Well, no. I-I thought I would obtain my father's permission first."

I repressed a sigh. "It might be best to check that it is permitted. Approach Razim then. Or even Zang. Either one of them will know the best course to take."

He gave me a bright look. "Yes. Yes, you're right. I'll do that."

I gave him a benign smile and watched as he rose eagerly, already keen to take the next step to achieve his great wish. I hoped that it might come to pass. He was a good person, who deserved a chance to develop his talents. Perhaps Ulugh Beg would take an interest in him. I decided I would explore the possibility.

I pulled the chain over my head and the small gold handled mirror fell against my chest. I straightened it and began to turn it over so that the mirrored side was facing my chest and the ornate embossing was outwards. It caught the light, flashing in my face and I halted, pulling it away from the beam. I glimpsed an image and stopped, transfixed. I had avoided looking at the mirror, somehow knowing that it held a message for me. A message I wouldn't like. Now, compelled, I studied it carefully. A small unicorn sat surrounded by a wall of flames, its head bent, its eyes round and filled with pain. My breath stopped. I angled the mirror carefully peering closer. There, at its right haunch, was a small wound seeping blood. Anger seized me. I would kill her. Kill Alessandra if she'd hurt Eleanor in any way. For that's what I knew, what I had been dreading to see. There was no doubt in my mind that the unicorn was Eleanor and somehow she wasn't just captive, she was hurt. I had to find her soon.

The dust irritated my eyes and I wiped them carefully, looking once again for some vendor or stall keeper I hadn't yet asked. I tried to repress the desperation growing inside so that it wouldn't affect my manner or my words. I knew I was taking risks on so many counts. I had told the escort who came to take me to the observatory that I had some stomach ailment and needed to rest, before going out to comb the bazaar and anywhere else I could think of that might offer up some clue to Alessandra's whereabouts. But I had tried to steer clear of any person connected to the sultan, knowing that any hint of my ruse would undoubtedly enrage him.

I also had no wish to alarm anyone I questioned, in case they reported me to the authorities. At worst that might alert Alessandra to my presence, at best I might be hauled away and asked uncomfortable questions, which could also result in alerting Alessandra.

I was still certain she was here, or at least something of her lingered for some reason. Why, I didn't know, except that I felt there was some important clue, some reason why I needed to remain in Samarkand until I discovered what it was.

I wandered a little further until I heard someone hail me. I turned and saw Battuta coming up behind me.

"My friend," he said. "You are well? I have seen nothing of you since you were taken under the wing of the sultan."

I gave him an apologetic smile. "Yes, I'm sorry for that. I have been remiss. You are making prosperous trades I hope? Your manuscripts, were you able to exchange them as you hoped?"

"I was. I think perhaps some of your fortune is rubbing off on me. But you were hoping to trade too, I recall." He gave me a searching look. "Did you find suitable wares at Zang's warehouse?"

"I did but I haven't finished my selection and trade yet. It was fortunate meeting Hosan outside the warehouse. His kindness in introducing me to such an illustrious merchant as Xuan Zang I shan't forget."

Battuta put a hand on my arm and looked at me directly. "Prosperous, yes. And also renowned for knowing how to make favourable trades. But for a reason. This is what I've heard. Be careful, my friend. He has contacts in high places who allow him this success, but it has its price and he is willing to pay it."

I stared at him, trying to make sense of his words. "I thank you for this warning, Battuta. I am always watchful, always careful, though."

Battuta shrugged. "I think you're a good man, though troubled. In this case, I think you must be more than watchful and careful. I wish you well, in any case."

I forced an amused expression on my face. "But I have the sultan's ear. Surely that counts for some protection?"

Battuta shook his head. "No, I think it brings you greater danger. There are many who plot in his court, among his harem, even among his own sons."

"I understand. Your words are wise and be sure they'll be heeded."

"For your sake, I hope my fears are unfounded. Alas I can discover no more than that. Go with God, my friend."

I thanked him and bid him the same, watching him retreat down the street, until he disappeared into the crowd.

I sat in my chair with a sigh. It had been a particularly gruelling day, fraught with efforts to conceal my growing anxiety over Eleanor, to perform calculations for Qushji to support his theories on the Earth's rotation. It was important work and at any other time I would have revelled in it, but I knew I wasn't doing it justice because of my distraction.

My desperation to find information had even extended to quizzing Qushji and his colleagues, as well as Razim, at the madrasa. All had led to nothing. It had been foolish to expect men whose main concern and focus was intellectual pursuit, an area where no woman could tread in the company of men, would have heard of a foreign woman in search of a good trade.

Now, it seemed I had reached my end here. What more could I do? I hadn't dared to ask the help of Ulugh Beg, in part because I feared what such an obligation might lead to, but also because I had little reason to believe he would know anything.

There was a knock at the door. I opened it to find Abdul on my doorstep, his face creased with anxiety.

"Abdul, what is it?" I asked. "Your father, he is well?"

"My father is well, thank you. No it is something else. May I speak with you?"

"Of course."

I gestured for him to enter and he went directly to the window and peered at the street below. I glanced out of the window beside him, but I could see nothing that would cause him alarm.

"Has something happened in the street?"

"No – I just wanted to be certain no one saw me enter this building."

I gave him a puzzled look. "But you live here. Why wouldn't you enter it?"

"Yes, I mean I wanted to be certain that no one followed me here."

I glanced in the street again but could see no one lurking. "I think you're fine." I turned to him. "Now, tell me, what's this about?"

He left the window and sat on the nearest bench, putting his head in his hands. "I am a wretched person, Master Bonavillagio."

"That's nonsense. You're a fine young man and no one can doubt it."

"You don't understand. You don't know the temptation that is before me now." He raised his head, his eyes baleful. "Temptation to which I am very nearly succumbing."

"Come now, it cannot be so very awful. You're here, obviously wanting to resist it. Tell me, what is tempting you?"

He reached his hand slowly inside his thick sash and withdrew a small folded parchment, sealed with wax. He held it out to me. "This."

I took the packet and turned it over in my hand. There was nothing that marked it as particularly tempting, but without knowing its contents I could hardly judge. I looked at Abdul and raised my brows.

He looked away. "They want me to give it to one of Ulugh Beg's servants at the observatory next time I'm there."

I refrained from an impatient retort and strived for calm. "Who is pressing you to do this and why?"

Abdul looked down at his hands, twisting the ring on his little finger. "Zang," he said softly. "I went to him as you suggested and asked if he could arrange for me to remain to study at the madrasa and the observatory. This was his price."

"To hand a small packet of unknown contents to a servant of Ulugh Beg?"

Abdul nodded. "I'm certain it can mean nothing but ill."

"I'm sure you're right." I started to break the seal.

"You can't do that!" said Abdul. "He will know that I've tampered with it. Who knows what he'll do to me then?"

I frowned at him, my patience gone. "Unless you actually plan to go through with it, there is no reason to count what Zang may or may not do. I will not be a party to it, nor will I allow you to be."

Before he could protest further I opened the packet and laid it out on the table so that I might examine its contents clearly. A small heap of powder, grey in colour, sat in its middle.

"Poison," I said.

Abdul paled. "How do you know?"

"I know."

Months in the company of the Grand Vizier and all his plots had taught me much. I didn't have to test the contents of the packet to confirm that the intention was to poison the sultan. I could imagine there was some reason that Zang would find profit in the sultan's death, but something this risky had to be part of a bigger plan.

I folded the piece of parchment and tucked it in my waistband. "Leave this with me. I'll take care of it."

"What are you going to do?"

I put my hand on Abdul's shoulder. "Don't worry. I've handled men like this before."

There was no Hosan conveniently emerging from Zang's building to usher me straight to Zang. Nevertheless a servant spotted me as soon as I entered the building, and

I was assured I would be seen promptly and led up the stairs. It was as though I was expected and all the things I had guessed at or suspected in my journey here were being confirmed, the pieces starting to fall into place.

Zang bowed and gave me a pleasant greeting when I entered his room. He dismissed the servant who had escorted me and the scribe who'd been scribbling away at Zang's dictation. I noticed the scribbles were nothing like I'd seen, neither Arabic script nor those of Christendom, or of the ancient Greeks. The assistant possessed the same type of eyes and facial structure as Zang and I could only conclude it was the language of his birth.

I sat at Zang's indication and decided I would dispense with the preliminaries and go on the offensive. I withdrew the packet from my sash and placed it on the table before him.

"You've been expecting me."

He raised his brow briefly. "Very good, Master Bonavillagio."

"You knew Abdul would come to me, that he wouldn't be able to go through with your plan and I in turn would be forced to come to you."

Zang opened his hands wide. "I am a student of human nature."

"You want the sultan dead and you want me to assist. Why do you need me?"

Zang shrugged. "It has become necessary to use you. The sultan has lost interest in my views. He finds yours more enlightening. Alas, I cannot pretend to know what I do not."

"Why would I help you?"

"You mean you cannot guess?"

I shook my head slowly. I had my suspicions, but I waited for him to say it, to dare to tempt me with the only possibility that would have me consider taking part in his plan.

"I have information you desire."

"Information?"

"Come now, you surely cannot play the innocent with me. It is no secret. You've spent weeks questioning everyone, including me, about a certain woman – covered with severe burns, I think you describe her."

"You know something of her? But you protested you knew nothing when I first asked. Why should I believe you now?"

"Because, my dear friend, you are desperate. Anyone can see that. And I have taken it upon myself to make enquiries, to confirm suspicions and to assemble it into a very clear picture."

"She has been here then. Is she still here? Does she have a child with her?"

"Ah, and there we come to the nub of your desperation, I think."

"What do you know of the child?" I fought to keep the edge from my voice. It was important that I keep control, to avoid giving him any advantage.

"Eleanor, I think the child is called."

I blanched, tightening my hands into fists.

"Yes, you see, I have your attention now. All you have to do is comply with my wishes and you will have all the information at my disposal. An amount well worth the price I ask."

He pushed the packet back across the table towards me. "A small packet, passed on to a servant."

"A servant who will then empty its contents in the sultan's next drink."

"Perhaps, perhaps not. I don't ask you to speculate. I only ask you to convey the packet."

"And you don't think they will suspect me once the contents are drunk?"

"A small risk, but then there will be so much chaos…so much opportunity. Opportunity that could include you, should you wish it."

"I can imagine the various opportunities." I reached forward and took the packet, tucking it back into my sash. "I have your word that you'll tell me all you know about the woman in question after I've given the packet to the servant?"

"You have my word."

I rose, forgoing any formalities. "I'll take my leave then. I don't think there's anything to discuss."

"We have a bargain then."

"We have a bargain," I said and strode from the room.

I found my way back down to the street, my mind reeling. I was certain that death was at the top of the list of opportunities offered by poisoning the sultan, whether it came from the sultan's soldiers, or if I was lucky enough to escape, from Zang and his cohorts who would rather not leave me alive with the knowledge I had, regardless of the part I'd played. I had to figure out how to get the information in Zang's possession so I didn't have to give the packet to the servant – because somehow, I knew Zang would never tell me. I'd never live that long..

CHAPTER SIXTEEN
MANTUA, EARLY SUMMER, 1448
ALYS

"A masquerade?" said Alys in disbelief. She wiped her paint brush and put it down on the table beside the nearly completed painting. Though the brush was scarcely bigger than her hand, it still required painstaking precision to use.

"That's what Tomaso Cortini told me," said Joanie, her tone dubious. "'e said you're to meet him at the Gonzago's palazzo at the masquerade."

"And this masquerade is tomorrow."

"It is. At least that's what 'e says. I did check with one of the servants as well, just to be sure and they said it was true. Lord Gonzaga is 'olding a masquerade tomorrow and you're to meet him there, telling them that you're there at 'is invitation if you're questioned."

Alys frowned. Somehow this wasn't what she'd envisioned when she'd made the journey to Mantua to obtain more information about Alessandra's location. It had been easy to find Tomaso. Hal had sniffed him out in one day's outing into the market. The Cortinis were well known and Tomaso's flamboyant nature and notorious reputation were difficult to hide.

She had planned carefully. A discreet meeting with Tomaso, seemingly a chance encounter in the Piazza Sordello, where there was certain to be numbers, but no one to recognise her with her veil and sedate clothing. Information for a small wrapped painting, carefully exchanged in the view of all, but the knowledge of none. A painting that he could easily sell and secure himself enough money to return to Venice, instead of kicking his heels tethered to the home of his disapproving father.

She'd composed her note carefully, reminding him of her connections to Crivelli, the access she'd had to his works and suggesting she might have one particular small piece that would be his if he could part with something that would cause him no trouble to share. After all, she understood he no longer owed any loyalty to Alessandra.

Instead, when Joanie had delivered the note directly into Tomaso's hands she'd received this cryptic verbal message back.

"How did he look? Did he look pleased? Does he mean to tell me what I need to know?" asked Alys.

Joanie looked thoughtful. "I wouldn't say he looked pleased. More surprised. At least at first. Then his eyes darkened and he came over all sly. You know what 'e's like. 'e used to get that way when 'e came to her parties. With you all in your fancy clothes, 'alf undressed."

"So you think he still desires me? Is that what's behind this? He wants me to come to this masquerade so he can seduce me?"

"I don't know. I only know what I said. But I'd be surprised if 'e didn't want something. Don't forget the man's a gambler. 'e loves any kind of game of chance."

Alys sighed. "I wouldn't forget that. But I might be able to turn that to my advantage. In any case, it appears I shall have to attend this masquerade if I'm to have any hope of getting this information from him."

"What will you wear?"

Alys gave a bitter laugh. "There's little to choose from. I've only the one gown that is anywhere near suitable. It will have to do, I suppose."

Joanie patted her hand. "Leave it with me. I shall contrive something. A few pieces 'ere and there and let me see if I can find anything in the market that might 'elp."

"Thank you Joanie. You are so good. If anyone can make something of that old gown, you can. But don't worry too much. I have no intention of causing a stir. If anything, I want to be as inconspicuous as possible. Get the information and give him the painting."

"Well you best get on with the painting then, 'hadn't you?" said Joanie with a wicked laugh.

Alys smiled at her quip, glancing at the painting in front of her. She was pleased, overall. It had been months since she'd picked up a brush and when the idea had first come to her she wasn't certain she could carry it off, but Hal's confidence and Joanie's persuasion had convinced her it was worth a try. Hal had obtained the necessary supplies and she'd spent the past few days working on it. It was drying quickly enough, the summer weather and the tempera medium allowing her to create the illusion that it had been painted a few years earlier, not a few days ago. But the only person she had to convince was Tomaso, and he was no expert.

～

Alys was grateful it was only a short walk to the palazzo, through the archway and along the cobbled piazza. The summer evening was still bright enough that she had no need of a lighter boy carrying his lantern to ensure she didn't break her ankle in her effort to keep her skirts and good slippers clear of the dirt. She fought to keep her gait even, though she could feel the tension in her leg, causing it to ache a little.

She tugged her neckline up, feeling the light breeze on her breasts. Even with a veil, she felt bared to the world. After months of covering up and concealing anything that revealed her womanhood, it was strange to be accentuating it. Joanie had worked a few miracles with skilful needlework and trimmings, borrowing seed pearls from her other gowns and hair ornaments and contriving something that approached the fashionable trends she'd remembered in Venice.

She was under no illusions about the masquerade and the type of women who would be attending. The masquerade pageant was for one of the cousins of the Gonzaga family on attaining his majority, she'd discovered. That told her more than anything what to expect. Especially given that she was asked to arrive after the official family feast and celebration. No, though there would be elaborate costumes on display to tell some fable or other, she had no doubt, the festivities would take on a different turn once the darkness fell and the hidden corners of the pleasure gardens could provide convenient places for seductive trysts. She planned to be long gone before that.

She lifted her gown against a questionable stain that clung to the ground and joined the small group of richly clad men and women who were heading towards the palazzo. The women wore decorated cloth masks across the upper half of their face, but she suspected it was more in the way of being mysterious than to conceal any particular identity. Their role inside was clear enough from the cut and vibrant colour of their gowns. Laughter and bawdy comments drifted to her ears.

She touched the small painting, now dry, which was stowed in a bag that hung from her waist, tucked below the velvet overdress she wore. It would be awkward, but she could see no other way to manage.

They entered the arched portico and the main door of the Magna Domus opened. The group entered and she slipped in with them, happy not to have announced her connection to Tomaso. She preferred to make this as quiet and unobtrusive as possible.

Carefully, she scanned the small groups that clustered inside and then followed her own group as they climbed the steps slowly to the floors above. For a moment she thought her leg might give out, her muscles were so taut, but she allowed herself a pause and climbed onward with no mishap. They emerged into a large, crowded hall that appeared to run the length of the building. Perfume hung heavy in the room, doing little to disguise the odour of too many bodies confined in a closed space. Conversation drowned out the music that wafted from a distant corner.

Alys searched the room, but the crowds pressed in on her and made it difficult to manoeuvre easily. Her body heated up quickly in the warmth of the room, though she couldn't envy those women in filmy gowns of sheer silk who might have been cast as nymphs in the pageant.

She felt a hand on her shoulder and turned to see Tomaso giving her a sly grin.

"Madonna, you have come," he said with a slight bow of his head. "You look enchanting as always." He laid a finger on her cheek and she refrained from flinching. "Though perhaps your adventures have left their mark a little. Are those freckles on your face? Tsk tsk, what would Alessandra think?"

"I can ask her, if you can tell me where she is."

Tomaso laughed and ran his hand along Alys's chin and down across her collar bone. This time she couldn't help the slight flinch. He was wearing a dark burgundy velvet doublet, and hose of a light colour that showed legs of passable quality, thought Alys, but perhaps a little on the spindly side. She thought of Tomaso, the monkey whose namesake stood before her and a bitter rage that he was now lost to her took her for a moment.

"There is time enough for that information. First, I think, we must enjoy ourselves a bit. Get reacquainted. It's been some time since I had your undivided attention."

He took her hand and pulled her towards the dancing at the far end of the room, near to the musicians. They were playing a pavane, its stately moves so at odds with her fast beating heart. She allowed him to draw her into the processing dancers and went through the motions, curtseying at the appointed time, bending and walking. Her leg managed well enough and it seemed to ease some of the ache.

She was glad, though, when the dance concluded and she began to walk away, but he clutched her hand and smiled the same sly smile he'd initially greeted her with. The music struck up again and this time it was a livelier galliard. The galliard had only recently come into fashion and she'd barely danced it before, especially with her injured leg, but Tomaso drew her in, made the advances in this courting dance so suggestive, so full of innuendo that she was tempted to walk away and leave the palazzo. Around her she could see the other couples dancing just as suggestively, the young Gonzaga, the main celebrant, being the most outrageous.

It was the world Alessandra had groomed her for, one she'd reluctantly inhabited, and as she went through the dance motions half-heartedly, she knew nothing had changed in that regard. She would much rather retreat to her modest dress, her modest food and be surrounded by people she loved. She thought of Barnabas and anger and longing gripped her hard. And then she thought of Eleanor and she nearly came apart. But there wasn't time for those thoughts. They would be for later.

She went through the steps awkwardly, conscious of the bag that hung from her waist and with growing concern over the leg that it occasionally bounced against. The bag hung only a short way down from her waist, so the danger of it swinging wide was minimised. Still, she would rather it not be in any danger of revealing itself to Tomaso before she was ready.

The music came to an end and she steeled herself. She would do what she needed to do. Avoiding his hand, she walked to the edge of the room, away from the dancers, away from those who feasted on the selection of dishes arrayed on the table along with the flagons of wine servants poured into any empty cup available.

Tomaso came up behind her and gripped her arm. "To the garden then? But that's a wonderful idea."

He steered her towards the stairs, his hand a vice around her, his pinching grip a message that left no room for doubt. His support helped her to negotiate the stairs but she knew it was not meant to help.

Torches were lit at the garden entrance, but as they emerged she could see the shrubs, trees and other plantings, so carefully placed for shade and pleasure in the day, now provided such extreme dark and shadow. They made her hesitate. Other couples strolled leisurely, their laughter and murmuring voices drifting towards her. She could see the outline of shapes in the more remote reaches, while some embraced or caressed each other openly on benches.

Firmly Tomaso moved her forward and she slowly walked further along, until he took her hand and led her towards a darkened area. He put his arm around her now, a clear statement of possession. He stopped by a small lemon tree, its fruit already showing signs of ripening. Only faint light from the nearest torch illuminated them both.

Tomaso turned her to face him. His hand moved to her face and clutched her chin. He leaned down and kissed her. She bit his lip. He pulled back, anger flashing across his face. A moment later he attempted a smile. "Now, madonna, that's no way to behave. Especially if you intend to ask favours."

"I'm not asking for favours. I said I intend to pay you for your information."

He gave her a speculative look. "Yes, a painting you said. One of Crivelli's."

"That's right. But only if you can tell me where Alessandra is. And I must be convinced you're telling the truth."

"Where's the painting?"

Alys shook her head. "Tell me where she is first."

"What makes you think I know where that daughter of a she dog is?"

"I know what happened. I know you were with her, that you parted on bad terms."

He gave a shrug. "So? Many people know that."

"I spoke with your friend." She put a special emphasis on the word "friend". "Valentina."

"You were in Cyprus?"

It was her turn to shrug. "It wasn't planned."

"You have wandered far," he said, a speculative look spreading across his face. "Perhaps I underestimated you."

She stared at him, refusing to be drawn in any manner by his words. "What do you know, Tomaso?"

"The painting first, *cara*."

She slowly reached for the bag and withdrew it carefully and held it up. "The painting."

He made to take it but she pulled it away. "Where's Alessandra?"

"How do I know it's really a painting? Or one of Crivelli's?"

Alys turned away and pulled the drawstring, shielding her actions with her body, ready to run should he decide to snatch the painting or try anything else. She stepped away and held up the painting, making sure she kept a firm grip on it. In this light it would be difficult to make it out with any great detail, but that served her well. It was a scene of the Annunciation, one she'd painted with Crivelli enough that she felt she could carry out his style with confidence. After all, his style to a certain degree had become her style, the two working together, furthering and inspiring each other's creative approaches. In the good times. That all seemed a lifetime ago now.

Tomaso closed the distance between them but he was leaning down, his eyes narrowed, studying the painting. She allowed him a short while only and then she whisked the painting back into its protective bag and clutched it to her.

"Satisfied?"

"It's small."

She sniffed impatiently. "But still would fetch a tidy sum that would more than offset your gambling debts, and perhaps even secure you back in your father's good graces. Or return to Venice, whichever you choose."

He grunted. "It looks like one of his. How is it you have it?"

She gave him a direct look. "I was his muse, his model for many of the paintings. It was a way he could show his appreciation."

He gave a snort. "I'd say you were more than his muse, though I wonder if Alessandra knew." He laughed sourly. "That has a certain appeal. That she didn't know." He gave another laugh, a pleased laugh. "I'm finding that I like this bargain, madonna."

"A bargain that is only yours if you tell me where Alessandra is."

He studied her carefully. "If you intend to find her, you should be careful. That woman has talons. Sharp ones. And that child – well Alessandra has some unfathomable liking for the brat. She won't give her up easily."

Alys suddenly felt angry and frustrated. How dare he say this to her? "Just tell me where she is and I'll worry about what she is or isn't likely to do."

"Yes, you should worry. She is a woman who seeks revenge. She may not harm that brat, but she'll stop at nothing to prevent you from recovering her. Or Giacomo. She has a real hatred for Giacomo, if only he knew." He laughed mirthlessly. "I thought I had reason to hate Giacomo and would find pleasure in getting back at him, but my own desire is nothing compared to Alessandra's. He thought she'd forgiven him, but he was easily duped. Using you was only the beginning."

Alys stared at him, the meaning of his words slowly sinking in. "Do you mean this was all her design from the first? Me, Giacomo, the child? All for revenge?"

Tomaso shrugged. "She is a woman who plans. But she also sees opportunities. I do think she has plans for the child, though. Perhaps if it had been a boy she might have let you keep it, but as it was, fortune smiled on her and she got the girl she wanted. A girl to fashion, to mould in the kind of perfect woman to tempt men, to extract money from them and more."

"But I thought she wanted to be a merchant, to expand and build a trading concern up north?"

"Oh, that too, so that she may fund her little schemes. Perhaps she means to send your daughter into the court of the Duke of Burgundy, and find a rich nobleman with a title to keep her in high style."

"So she has gone north. Where?"

Tomaso held out his hand. She placed the sack on his palm, but kept her own grip on it.

"Where has she gone?"

Tomaso sighed. "Well if you won't heed my warnings, it's nothing to do with me. She's gone to her sister. In Paris. At least that's what her intentions were."

"Her sister is in Paris?" Alys was surprised and a little doubtful.

"Her sister, as you may know, was the older daughter. There was only money enough for a dowry for her. And the lucky man was a merchant who later moved to Paris, to supply the royal family there."

She nodded. It seemed plausible, though she would confirm it if she could. "And the name?"

"Julia. She married Antonio Bargerigo."

She released her grip on the painting. "Thank you."

She turned to go, but Tomas put a hand on her arm. "Remember. Don't underestimate her."

She nodded and made her way back through the garden and through the passageway to the outside door. Once in the piazza she stopped and leaned against the wall of the palazzo, needing to rest her leg and take in all that Tomaso had revealed. Alessandra was even more dangerous and devious than she had thought, that much was clear. And in some ways she was glad Barnabas wasn't here to find out about her treachery, for he would surely seek her out blindly, without a care to himself and try to kill her. But Alys would do that herself, with as much cunning as she could manage..

CHAPTER SEVENTEEN
SAMARKAND, SUMMER 1448
BARNABAS

I prostrated myself for a few moments longer than usual, so that Ulugh Beg might understand that I had something out of the ordinary to discuss with him. I rose slowly, catching his puzzled look, and I forced a smile.

"I beg your pardon for my unannounced arrival. May I show you some of the calculations I made for your charts?" I said. "There is something I knew you would want to see right away."

"Of course."

He resumed a neutral expression and followed me to the table at the side. I eyed the one servant for a moment when he came to offer refreshment, but Ulugh Beg waved him away impatiently. The other servant was busy at the far end of the room tidying some of the scrolls, paper and parchments at my request. The astronomers were at the madrasa, I was relieved to see, so I was more or less alone with the sultan, apart from the two servants and the guards who were standing at the entrance. I had hoped his desire to finish a particular star chart himself would draw him to the observatory today.

I spread open a large piece of paper, filled with calculations and drawings I had made over the past few nights using the quadrant. Working here during the night, with the stars overhead to capture my thoughts had been the perfect way to escape my troubles for just a small amount of time, but in the end it had also given me the space to decide what I must do.

I pointed to a few of the calculations, murmuring my explanations, keeping my voice low, so that I might keep the exchange as private as possible. Ulugh Beg nodded, interested in what I had to say, but I could sense a tense awareness. He knew there was something else I wanted to convey to him.

He stroked his grey beard, his eyes keen and interested, despite the undercurrent. "That means the distance for this planet has been corrected?"

I nodded, pointing to a calculation for what we both knew to be a star. "It seems this planet has gone astray," I said with a laugh. "Following the previously calculated trajectory, it would have only headed to its death, knocked down by this other planet. Smaller, yes, but still deadly in the face of a direct hit."

"I see," said Ulugh Beg. "But you have corrected the calculations?"

"I haven't yet completed the corrections, but I will. I just need to substitute a few numbers."

Ulugh Beg gave an amused smile. "That is good. But, tell me, just out of curiosity, if this was the true trajectory of this planet, to when the death would have taken place? Do you know?"

"I have no exact knowledge. Only an approximate. It would depend on the small heavenly bodies attached to it. You see, they affect the planet's orbit, its speed."

He studied me carefully, his eyes assessing. I leaned over the chart, my body blocking its view from anyone else in the room and placed my hand on the paper, uncovering the small packet that I'd been holding in my left hand. Ulugh Beg came beside me, murmuring more about planet trajectories while he briefly examined the packet.

"You've changed the trajectory, but I'm not certain how you did that. Can you explain?"

"Well, as I say I haven't completed it yet. But if you substitute this calculation for the original one, you can see how the planet's situation changes completely."

I slipped another identical packet from my sash and placed it on the table.

Ulugh Beg fingered the packet, nodding slowly. "Yes, I see that now."

Quickly, I slipped the original packet back into my sash.

Ulugh Beg touched my shoulder, a high honour. "I am indebted to you for your assistance. I won't forget."

I bowed low. "It was an honour to be allowed to serve."

Ulugh Beg smiled at me, but it didn't reach his eyes. "Time to celebrate I think. A small victory, but worth marking, I think. Some refreshments?"

Ulugh Beg turned to study the chart once again and I nodded to the servants. One of them came scuttling over before I could even gesture. He bowed when he reached our side.

"Ulugh Beg asks for some refreshments," I said.

His back was to the guards, blocking their view of me. I lifted my brow and he gave me a barely perceptible nod. I quickly slipped the packet into his hand and he bowed again and made his way to the table where the small bowls and flagons of juices and wine were kept.

I watched him from my viewpoint, but there was little to see. A harmless filling of a glass, one with juice, the other with wine. The other servant came over to assist, filling small dishes with savouries to tempt the sultan.

The two made their way to us and Ulugh Beg turned when they arrived, indicating only with a flick of his head to put the refreshments on the table. When they had done he waved them away and lifted the glass of juice. He smiled and gestured a toast. I took my glass of wine and raised it to him, meeting his gaze.

"To a star-filled future," said Ulugh Beg.

"And to a most generous ruler," I said. "Who made it possible to map these stars." I took a sip and nodded to the chart. "And I give you my deepest gratitude for being a part of this. But I fear once these calculations are complete, I must leave, if you permit. I have pressing matters to attend to that I have put off long enough."

"Of course. And you have my gratitude. I shall ensure that you have a swift passage to wherever you need to go." He drank the rest of the juice and smiled again. This time it reached his eyes. "You may rely on the fact that you'll have everything you need for your journey."

I finished the rest of my wine, knowing that I'd been dismissed. I made my prostrations, rose and walked out of the observatory, uncertain of the future. Ulugh Beg had clearly understood my meaning. The packet I'd given the servant was harmless. But was telling him of the plan enough? Was he warning me that I was a dead man nonetheless? Or was I to be rewarded? Either way, I would leave the next day, keeping careful watch until then. I was all but ready. I would secure a camel and a guide. My goods were purchased and packed – a sack of cinnamon, no more, and a bolt of the finest silk. But the real task I had come here for hadn't been completed. I had no idea if Alessandra and my daughter were in Samarkand, or had ever been here.

Outside the observatory, I slipped into the shadows and hastily removed my long robe, turning it inside out, so that the rich red brocade silk was exchanged for the sand colour interior. My matching red turban was unwound and was exchanged with the white sash that had been around my waist. The end I wrapped around my face, seemingly against the dust that blew along the road.

I'd opted to walk to the observatory this morning, adopting sturdy sandals, instead of my customary leather boots to ride the horse that was usually provided for me. A surprise visit of sort, so no escort to see me to the observatory and none to accompany me back.

I moved through the shadows, adjusting my clothes and removing the dagger that had been strapped to the inside of my leg so that I now had it in my hand, blade hidden in the copious sleeve of my robe. I stepped out into the light, adopting a slight stoop and ambled my way down the dusty path, an aging man, returning to Samarkand.

Eventually, someone passed me on a donkey, but they took no notice of me, intent on their own destination. A group of boys went by the other way a few moments later. The noise of their carousing reassured me and I was tempted to smile.

A small group of horsemen approached, but I didn't look up. It was only as they passed that I dared to glance at them. Two of the astronomers, with an escort on their way from the madrasa to the observatory. They hadn't noticed me, I was glad, though hardly reassured, because they had no expectation or need to notice anyone on this road.

I picked up my pace slightly and as I neared the outskirts of Samarkand a group of men emerged from a large house, deep in discussion. They made their way in front of me, but with a few quick paces I was at their edge.

I greeted them politely, and bowed, excusing my boldness. The men returned the greeting, everyone bowing in return.

"Would you please direct me to the bazaar?" I asked. I had thrown out the most obvious destination. "I am new to Samarkand and came in this direction to look at the observatory, but now have found myself at a loss to know exactly how to get there."

The men laughed. "It is easy enough, friend," said the large one. "But come, join us. We are heading to the bazaar ourselves."

"I thank you."

The men absorbed me into their group and we exchanged pleasantries. My stoop remained, my steps deliberate. I invented a tale of a man travelling with his merchant son who hoped to see the famed sights of Samarkand.

When we arrived at the bazaar I parted from them and headed in the opposite direction. I weaved through the crowds slowly, discreetly scanning the people around for any signs of someone following or noting me. Eventually, in a very circuitous manner I ended up back at my quarters, camel arranged and waiting at a caravanserai. I would have to do without a guide for now.

I slipped inside quietly, careful to avoid any noise and crept up to my door. Pausing outside it, I put my ear to it and listened. Nothing. I clutched the dagger and pulled out the key, turning it quickly then flinging open the door. A man threw himself at me, brandishing a sword. Ready, I blocked his blade, twisted the dagger in the manner I'd been taught and the man, caught by surprise, dropped the sword. Immediately I had him in my grip, the dagger at his throat.

"Who are you?" I demanded. "Who sent you?"

The man struggled under my grip, and I held the blade closer. He was dressed in a tunic, turban and britches of an unremarkable brown and a short dirty white cloak belted at the waist with a dark sash. At such close quarters I could smell his rank breath and feel the scraggly beard against my hand. A hireling. One of Zang's or the sultan's? Or someone else?

I turned him around, gripped his tunic and held the blade point at his throat. I watched his eyes carefully. Fear? Cunning?

"I asked you, who it was that sent you. Was it Zang?"

His eyes revealed nothing. I pricked his throat with the dagger and a small bead of blood appeared. He blinked. I felt his weight shift, but before I could react his knee came up hard between my legs, I released the dagger with an outcry of pain. He reached for his sword. Still reeling with pain, I withdrew my dagger and moved quickly away from him until I could get my breath. He closed the distance and we were dancing around each other, while I tried to duck his attempts to swing his sword. He was clumsy, inexperienced and I took heart from that, risking a feint, and then attacking. His blade slipped along mine and I thrust it forward but it slid off his wrist, his grip loosened and my dagger plunged into his chest, my whole weight behind the thrust. He gasped and fell to the floor, his sword clattering beside him.

Stunned, I looked at him. His eyes fluttered a moment, then closed. A trickle of blood seeped from the wound. I knelt down beside him. His chest was still and I could hear no breath at his mouth. He was dead. There was no knowing who hired him now, though I had my guesses.

Quickly, I removed the dagger and bound his wound. No sense in him bleeding everywhere and perhaps alerting someone. I lifted him on the bed and pulled the coverlet over him. Let whoever decides to check in the morning think I was asleep. That might delay matters for a little while.

I packed my few things and lifted the sack of pepper and my sack of belongings on my back. The chest I would have to leave behind, but its contents were safely stowed with my belongings. With one last glance behind I made my way to the street. I regretted not being able to bid Abdul and Kasim farewell, but in view of the circumstances it was unavoidable and probably for the best. Abdul would have to dream of a different future.

Once in the street, I headed toward the caravanserai that held the camel I'd hired, making my way through the crowds, conscious of the sacks. A hand gripped my arm.

"My friend, wait a moment."

I stopped and turned slowly towards Battuta. He gave me a warm smile and pulled me to the side to a shaded archway.

"You need some help," he said.

"You are kind to offer, but there's no need."

"It is not my kindness, but that of a great friend you have. Such exalted company."

I studied him carefully. I detected only gentleness and a little concern. "What help are you offering?"I asked.

"You must trust me. I was told to help you. A task that I took on gladly. Come."

He spoke in a murmur, his words barely discernible in the noise of the streets. He led me away, his hand gripping my arm. Suddenly I felt too tired to argue. Perhaps it was time to surrender to the fates, to acknowledge that I had failed miserably and to use my last breath to pray that Alys would find Eleanor.

He led me down a side street and then another. My back felt the weight of the sacks and I sweated profusely in the late afternoon heat. He arrived at a large building that had seen better days and made his way to its rear. There, two camels were tied up, saddled and ready to ride, a large bundle tied to the end of the bigger one. I gave Battuta a puzzled look.

"I said I am here to help." He gestured to the camels. "Come, we will tie up your sacks and be on our way. We'll head to Bokhara and change camels there. We will travel quickly."

"But how? Why?"

"As I said, you have very exalted friends, though it doesn't always pay to have friends in such high places. But perhaps you have learned that now."

"I've learned that it is best to trust no one," I said evenly.

Battuta laughed. "A wise teaching. But in this case I think you can be reassured." He withdrew a folded and sealed parchment packet from his waist and handed it to me. "This may help."

I took the bulky packet from him, broke the seal and unfolded it. Inside were a note and a large ruby. I closed my hand around the ruby and slipped it quickly into my sash before Battuta could see it. I studied the note. It was written in Italian, the script careful.

I send this man to you in gratitude of your friendship and loyalty. You are like a son should be. And for that I send too a little memento of our time together. Not quite a planet or a star, but something I hope will be of use when you continue your search. That which you sought here has now gone back to its origins. The only trace of its existence is a record of a disguise taken and used to conduct a transaction of some wealth by a man only few knew in its true form. And the wealth was spent in some degree, planning and exacting revenge.

There was no signature, but I had no need of one. It was the sultan. I looked up at Battuta and smiled. Perhaps I was to have a reprieve. If only for a while.

I went over to my camel, got it to kneel and secured the sacks across his back with Battuta's help. Once both camels were ready, we mounted and made to leave.

"Where are you heading? To Tyre?"

"Whatever the fastest route is," I said. "I mean to go to Venice. Back to my starting point." That's where the sultan had pointed me and I had to trust that. Alessandra had been here, I was right about that. She'd just disguised herself as a man, made her trade, but not without a few making a note that she was a woman in disguise. Something the sultan would have made it his business to know. I hadn't asked him, for the exact reason that Battuta had said. It wasn't a good practice to be indebted to exalted people in that manner. To question them, to make bargains with them. That the sultan knew of Alessandra's visit to Samarkand and my quest for information about her told me I'd made the right decision. Ulugh Beg had decided to give me the information because he could bestow it upon me. A generous gesture from an exalted ruler.

"Did you get all that you needed here in Samarkand? It's a long way to travel for a small sack of trade goods."

I nodded. "I gained much here. It's a place of marvels."

"Marvels that nearly cost you dear," said Battuta softly.

I glanced at him and grinned. "Only nearly. And nearly is not enough."

CHAPTER EIGHTEEN
PARIS, LATE SUMMER, 1448
ALYS

To Alys, it seemed a lifetime ago since she'd been in Paris. So much had happened. Then, she'd been an innocent, posing as a widow and following her beloved Barnabas to the French capital in the hopes he would be glad to see her and wish to make her his wife. Now, as she looked out from the small window of the room she'd taken for herself and Joanie, she acknowledged that Paris had changed little since she'd been here last. It was she who'd experienced the change.

Hal had gawked like a young boy when they'd arrived yesterday, bone weary on the scrawny horses she'd managed to buy with some of their remaining funds. It was his first time in this large city, and though his home place of London was probably just as busy, he hadn't been there in a long time. In fact he hadn't been this far north in many, many years. His animated face and excited questions had even prompted a nudge in the ribs from Joanie.

Alys smoothed her gown and rose, giving Joanie a reassuring smile. "Would you go tell Hal that I'm ready to leave?"

"You're certain you're ready?" Joanie brushed an imaginary bit of dust from Alys's shoulders. "I wouldn't expect too much. It's possible that Alessandra never came here to stay with her sister."

Alys forced a smile. "Well, we have to try."

Joanie sighed and went to the door, pausing to turn. "I don't want you to get your hopes up, that's all. It's been some time now. And much could have happened."

"I understand, Joanie. But somehow I feel I would know if something terrible had happened to Eleanor. But I don't. And neither did Barnabas." Joanie nodded and left, obviously unconvinced.

Alys felt a pain in her heart at the thought of Barnabas. Where was he now? Was he safe? Would she know if something had happened to him? She tested the notion in her mind, but all she could conjure up were images of him being attacked and murdered on that trade route, or in some town or city, and she would never know. Her conviction about Eleanor suddenly seemed foolish. How could it be any different for her daughter? She was at the mercy of Alessandra as well as thieves and marauders.

She gathered up her cloak and draped it around her shoulders. The weather was warm, but somehow she felt the need of this protection against the dirt and odours of Paris. She closed the door behind her and joined Hal and Joanie.

～～

"It is such a delight to meet one of Alessandra's friends," said Julia in Italian.

She twitched at her skirts, straightening and smoothing them. Her hair was elaborately dressed in curls and small braids with a lace cap on top that did nothing to disguise the hint of grey that was threaded through it. Her gown was richly made of a deep blue that set off her olive complexion well. Her lips were full and her eyes were deeply set but it was the overall composite that revealed the resemblance to her sister.

The room was filled with small luxuries, a clear indication of Julia's status, even without taking into account her clothes. The room was panelled, the windows artfully glazed and the tapestries and paintings that hung on the walls were costly. The rich silk embroidered cushions at Alys's back were worth a tidy sum as well.

But it was the paintings that caught Alys's eye. One in particular. It was a scene of the Madonna and child. The rich blue robes, the shape of the child's face, everything was so familiar.

"It's so kind of you to welcome me into your home," Alys said, drawing her eyes away from the painting.

Julia smiled nervously. "I am happy to. It's not often I get an opportunity to speak my native tongue. And meet a friend of Alessandra's." Her eyes darted to mine. "I-I don't believe Alessandra mentioned you Signora, but then my sister is not one to confide much."

Alys gave her a reassuring look. "I do understand. Alessandra can be a bit difficult for anyone to know. I cannot say myself that we were close, but she did mention you to me."

"Did she?" Julia's eyes lit up. She leaned forward. "I thought perhaps she'd softened. I hadn't heard from her for some time. Years. We hadn't parted well. And then suddenly, a letter."

Alys tried to repress the tension that suddenly arose inside her and spoke calmly. "Oh, I am sorry. Family can be that way sometimes, I know. Why, my own brother was the same. He left when I was but a young girl and not a word from him for years. And then suddenly he writes. It seems he had apprenticed himself to a painter in Venice."

"You are not Venetian by birth. I thought the accent was a little different."

"You have a keen ear, Signora," said Alys. "No I am from further north. A small town outside of Genoa." She waved her hand in dismissal.

"But you went to Venice?"

"Yes, it was fortunate that my brother wrote to me at that time because my parents had just died. So I went to live with him and run his household." Alys nodded her head towards the painting that had caught her eye. "In fact, I believe you have a painting by the man to whom he was apprenticed. Signor Crivelli."

Julia looked behind her, her face really coming alive. "Oh, but I adore that painting. It's from Alessandra. That I am certain is no coincidence." She turned to face Alys again. "You know Signor Crivelli?"

"We are well acquainted. My brother is still his good friend and they have sometimes collaborated together." Alys leaned forward and pretended to study the painting, she knew very well it was mostly her own work. "In fact that is probably one such painting. Made just after my brother finished his apprenticeship."

"Oh, how wonderful. To have met the sister of one of the artists," said Julia. "Is your brother here, now? I only ask because you mentioned in your note that you were here for an extended stay possibly."

"He is with me, but of course how long we stay depends on the number and types of commissions he receives. And he is very shy. A stutter, you see. He hates to speak to anyone outside the family. Perhaps Alessandra might advise us of potential commissions, if you could give me her direction."

Julia's face looked puzzled for a moment. "Oh, but didn't you know? Alessandra did write to me to say that she was coming. But she hasn't arrived yet."

Alys put her hand to her mouth. "Oh, my mistake. Perhaps I misunderstood. You see she hasn't been in Venice in some time. She went on a lengthy journey, but I understood that she was here in Paris now."

Julia shook her head. "She isn't here. I'm not certain when she'll come, she didn't say. The letter took a while to reach me."

"Where was it sent from?" Alys tried to appear casual.

Julia gave a shrug. "She didn't state. I only know that it took some time to arrive. A man coming from Marseille brought it. He'd disembarked from a ship that originated in Alexandria."

Alys studied Julia, considering her words. She fought off the sigh of disappointment that threatened to escape. But something wasn't right.

"But I shall let you know when she does arrive," said Julia brightly. "In the meantime, I would be happy to do my best to assist you and your brother. I'll speak to Antonio. I know I can persuade him to commission a painting. Especially if it is of the quality of the one Alessandra sent."

"Was the painting sent with the letter?" Alys asked.

Julia shook her head. "No that was later. It arrived less than a month ago. Whereas the letter was two months ago."

"And she said nothing more when she sent the painting?"

Julia shook her head. "No. Does it matter? There was only a note saying that it was an apology for her silence for all these years."

"Oh, how lovely. Such a wonderful painting, too. One of their finest works, I believe."

Julia flushed with pleasure. "I am glad you agree. But then you know your brother's talents. And Signor Crivelli's. What did you say your brother's name was?"

Alys blinked a moment, scrambling for a credible first name instead of 'Regina' with which she signed the other paintings. "Reginaldo Gregis." It was awful but it was the best she could do.

"I will be certain to arrange it soon."

"I'm very grateful. You are too kind."

"Oh, it's my pleasure. I look forward to making your acquaintance further."

Alys forced all the pleasure she could into the smile. "I do as well. I shall await your word in the meantime."

"Oh, but you must come again soon," Julia said with a sudden twinkle in her eye and Alys could see then what had captured the rich man's attention all those years before. "We can discuss what painting would suit. Then perhaps your brother can consult with my husband once we've decided."

~

She wiped a finger on the rag that lay on the table, removing the dab of paint on its tip. The odour of linseed and turpentine hung in the air, filling her nose and probably embedding itself in her hair. Alys didn't mind, in fact it made her smile. To be painting once again was more than enough to make up for odours or any other discomforts that came with it.

"I think that's your best painting yet," said Joanie, coming over beside her.

Alys turned and smiled at her. "Do you think so?"

"Well yes, especially considering the subject."

She looked over at Hal, who stood posing with a wooden slab with a handle attached, his head bent over it as though it were a lute. She'd arranged him like that, his lovely hair glowing brightly in the sun that streamed through the window.

She was excited about this work. It was a secular piece. A musician with his lute, strumming the music of the heavens. She'd chosen board, since it would require less preparation than the canvas and it wasn't very large. She didn't want to test her skill too much, especially given the kind of subject matter.

The choice of the type of painting had arisen more out of a general discussion with Julia than a planned design for a work. A note had been delivered only a few days after their initial meeting and when Alys arrived Julia had just dismissed a servant carrying a lute. Alys had remarked on it, lamenting that she'd had to leave her own lute behind in Venice and it emerged both Julia and her husband played. Music was a pleasure they shared and they often hosted entertainments that featured musicians. Alys marvelled at their mutual interest, feeling some seed of friendship and connection with Julia.

It was Julia who suggested a lute player be the subject of the painting after Alys had mentioned that a musical topic might suit. She'd been thinking of one of the muses, but the moment Julia mentioned a lute player she knew instantly what she would paint. It excited and scared her. But Julia was adamant and didn't even want to confirm the subject matter with her husband, so certain was she he would be agreeable.

If only her worries and anxieties about Eleanor and Alessandra's location didn't cast such a large shadow over her pleasure at painting. There was still no sign of Alessandra and she was becoming concerned that something had gone wrong.

"Aw, Alys, can't I stop now? I've been in this position for an age," said Hal. "My fingers are getting numb and my back 'as gone stiff."

"Ach, you big oaf," said Joanie affectionately. "It's not been that long."

"It's all right Hal, you can rest for a little while. I have the main colours and shape for your pose. I'll fill in some of the background for a moment."

Hal stretched his arms and eased his back before walking around the room and shaking his legs.

"Is that a new dance?" asked Joanie.

He gave her a wry smile and continued his progress around the room, until suddenly he scooped her up and started whirling her around, Joanie laughing with her head thrown back. Alys looked on at their antics fondly, glad her companions could find some relief in the long, arduous path they'd travelled for these many, many months.

The couple whirled a few more times and then Hal placed Joanie down, smoothing her hair affectionately.

"I'll have Alys to ask you to pose all the time, if this is the result when you finish," said Joanie, winking.

Hal kissed Joanie on the head and Alys raised a brow. She'd noticed the increased public affection they'd shown each other lately, and though it reminded her of missing Barnabas, she was still glad the two of them could find such affection in one another.

Joanie caught Alys's look and raised brow and her face softened. She came over and put an arm around Alys.

"Ah, my sweet, I'm sure it won't be long before your daughter and Barnabas are reunited with you."

Alys nodded, surprised by the sudden tears that came to her eyes. "I hope you're right, Joanie. But I can't help but wonder if we should go to Marseille and perhaps Alexandria. It might be that Alessandra has decided to remain there."

Hal came over and squeezed Alys's arm. "Nay, I think we can't be certain that she was even in Alexandria. Just because the ship came from there, doesn't mean that she was there too. It could 'ave been given to the captain by someone Alessandra paid to take it there, with another sum to see it safely to here. We don't know where she was, when she sent it. And don't forget the painting."

Alys nodded. "I haven't. We don't know that she didn't arrange to have the painting sent from wherever she is now. Alexandria, Venice, Lisbon. Who knows?"

"The best thing to do is to stay 'ere, near the sister," said Joanie. "You have the commission to find out if the sister has any news of Alessandra and also to give us enough money to continue the search. It makes the most sense."

Alys tried to extract reassurance from Joanie and Hal's words. They were right, but she did find it frustrating. She turned back to the painting, hoping that she might get lost once more in the technical skill and concentration required for her work. The colours she'd chosen were rich, with hues of ochre and burnt sienna for the lute, the highlights in white, the shadows of ultramarine and a hint of umber. She had the shape of the lute and shadows created from Hal's initial sitting when Julia had allowed her to borrow the instrument. But that had been returned and now the board played substitute.

His costume was also borrowed from Julia, but not required to be returned. Alys had been surprised when Julia had offered to provide the clothing. Though it was not an unusual gesture by a patron to supply a necklace, or some jewel to show off a particular bit of wealth, clothing was something she hadn't known was used. But she was happy enough, and glad in a way that she wouldn't have to scrounge in some second hand stall for suitable hose and doublet to hire for this commission.

Her pleasure at the painting was marred by another underlying unease that she hadn't mentioned to Hal and Joanie. Though Hal hadn't questioned her decision to use him to pose as the actual painter of the work, and even that she'd given him a false name on top of the deception, she hadn't explained that the few paintings she'd signed had been under that name. A name that would become more suspect if Alessandra ever did show up and see the painting hanging in her sister's house. Alys had no doubt that Alessandra would recognise the style. Wonder that it wasn't a Crivelli. And when questioned, it would become known that Crivelli's apprentice had painted it. The brother of an acquaintance of hers. And on discovering that, despite the name Alys had given, Alessandra would probably guess, upon extracting a description of Alys, who exactly it was that painted the new work. And that Alys was here, looking for Eleanor.

When she'd said her brother was a painter it had seemed like an ideal solution to pass the time here while they waited for Alessandra. And perhaps it still was. But she was mindful of Tomaso's warning and her own instinct. She would rather give as little foreknowledge of her plans to Alessandra as possible.

But still, it was entirely possible that Alessandra could arrive before the painting was completed and hanging in Julia's home. It was the best hope, but Alys's instincts told her that hope wouldn't come to pass. She would make enquiries. Find out more about how Alessandra had sent the painting to her sister.

CHAPTER NINETEEN
PARIS, SUMMER 1448
ALYS

Hal bowed low, sweeping off his cap, his blond hair swinging forward in a becoming manner. She was glad she'd insisted he keep the length that had grown on his hair since their journey to Tyre and back and to take on more of a gentleman's appearance than the scraggly sailor's attire that had been his usual dress. It enabled him to be more at home in the garments he had on at the moment and his air and manner seemed to follow suit. Maybe the long months spent in Barnabas's company had rubbed off.

Julia moved forward, extending her hand. Hal took it and kissed it with passable grace and Alys smiled, offering her own brief curtsey. Behind her, Joanie held fast to the now completed painting, wrapped securely in an oiled cloth.

"I am honoured to meet such a talented painter," Julia said to Hal. "I hope your sister told me how much I admire your work."

Hal glanced at his sister, a sly look in his eye. He nodded and smiled politely. "*Grazi*," he said simply.

Alys had instructed him to say as little as possible and if he could manage it, to stutter the words. She'd originally mentioned the stutter to Julia for just such an occasion, so that Hal's poor pronunciation and grammar would be less noticeable. His grasp of the language served him well enough in the gutters and alleyways of Venice and aboard ship, but it wouldn't suffice for refined Venetian company.

"He is honoured to meet such a fine patron," said Alys.

"I-I h-h-hope you l-like it," said Hal.

He flushed red and looked down, studying his hands. Alys marvelled at his acting.

"We are anxious to see your reaction," said Alys, smiling.

A flutter of nerves seized her for a moment. Her words were no lie. She was anxious to see Julia's reaction and to hear what she thought.

"Come, I am just as eager to view the painting." Julia gestured to the table by the window. "See, I have arranged for the painting to be viewed in the best light possible. If you could have your servant place it over there and undo it, we can view it in all its glory."

At Alys's nod Joanie placed the painting on the table, unwrapping it carefully. She stepped back to allow the other three to gather round it.

Julia turned to Joanie. "We'll be a while here. Why don't you take yourself off to the kitchens for some refreshments in the meantime? Let them know they can serve us in a quarter of an hour."

Joanie bobbed a curtsey and gave her thanks and left, giving Alys a glance and a faint smile.

Alys turned back to the painting and studied it in the light. Looking at it now, she couldn't help but feel a sense of pride. The folds of the cloak draped across the doublet looked well, as did the colour of the hair, under the plumed hat, and the way it caught the light

"But it's marvellous," said Julia. She clasped her hands together. "Truly, signor, you are a genius."

Hal blushed and bowed. "*G-grazi, signora.*"

"The lute, the clothes, they are all so real. My husband will be so pleased. You have captured the essence of a musician who loves to play. It is obvious you play the lute yourself. Am I correct?"

Hal looked at Alys. "M-m-m-"

"I do," said Alys, smiling. "He sees the passion with which I play."

"Of course," said Julia. "Still, the artistry of the hands, it's as if I can almost hear the music being played."

"He has watched me play often enough," said Alys.

Julia looked at him and paused. "But it is you! The painting is of you. How did you manage that?"

Alys laughed. "As you say, my brother is a genius. No, we were fortunate enough to acquire a mirror for the time. My brother could then have a model without any fuss. He used me to sketch in the basic placement, but the rest was from his own reflection."

Julia studied the painting again and then Hal, who reddened under her scrutiny.

"Yes, and so clever. You know your own features well," she said.

Hal bowed and Alys tried to repress a smile. "It is a good likeness, isn't it?"

Hal glanced at Alys and raised his brow slightly. "Don't try to be modest, you know you're talented," said Alys.

"I know my husband will agree. He'll be very pleased with this. I will have him send you the balance of what is owed, soon. You can be certain of that."

The door opened and a servant entered, carrying a tray of cups and a flagon of wine. He set the tray on a small table near the cushioned chairs and bench. Julia thanked him briefly and he left.

"Please, have some refreshments. We must celebrate."

The three took seats and Julia poured out the wine, handing a cup to Hal and then Alys.

"I only wish my husband could be here to see the painting, but he is busy at his warehouses."

"Of course," said Alys. "Perhaps another time."

"I hope so." She turned to Hal. "Have you managed to find any other patrons? I've asked my husband to make enquiries, but he has been busy."

"We have had a few possibilities, but nothing definite as yet," said Julia.

"Oh, such a pity," said Julia. "But I'm certain after my husband sees this painting he will be determined to find others who would be willing to commission you." She paused and then brightened. "We should have a little gathering. I'll ask my husband. Something to celebrate this lovely painting."

Alys looked at Hal and saw the slight shake of his head. "My brother doesn't feel comfortable going out into large groups, I'm afraid. But perhaps his company wouldn't be necessary."

"I understand," said Julia. She leaned over and patted Hal's arm. "It's a shame, but understandable. But, do not despair – we will have a gathering anyway. Perhaps your sister will come?"

Alys smiled. "I would be honoured."

Alys sipped her wine while Julia chattered on about the painting and the gathering, wondering if Alessandra would appear soon. She felt frustrated by her lack of progress, and despite the pleasure of resuming painting, she was beginning to think she should devote more of her efforts to something that would lead her closer to Eleanor than just waiting for Alessandra to appear and probing Julia for any clue that might reveal Alessandra's location.

She looked at her old painting. "Do you have a place in mind to hang the painting? Will you put it beside the other? The styles are similar, though the subject matter is completely different."

Julia studied the painting of the Madonna. "I do love that one, but perhaps it's best to put that in my bed chamber. I'll see what my husband thinks."

"If we are fortunate, your sister may be here soon and be able to attend your gathering," said Alys.

Julia frowned. "I fear that it might not come to pass. I've still heard nothing. And after all this time. It's been nearly three months now."

"I'm certain there is a simple explanation and she will come."

Julia gave a tight smile. "I hope you're right."

"Did your husband speak with the man who delivered the painting? Perhaps he knew where your sister is."

"He did for a few moments, though I don't know if he asked about Alessandra," she said, thoughtful. "He didn't mention anything. But I'll ask him."

Alys nodded. "It could do no harm."

She glanced over at Hal, who was attempting to look interested, but she could see his attention was elsewhere. He kept glancing at the door and it took Alys a moment to realise that he was thinking about Joanie. Judging by the intense expression, he was struggling with a mixture of emotions, one of which, she noticed with amusement seemed to be jealous anxiety. Did he think Joanie was at risk of being swept off her feet by some French servant? She nearly laughed at the thought.

"Your face is red. You can't deny it," said Hal.

"My face is red because I'm getting angry, you great oaf," said Joanie, her hands on her hips.

Alys stifled an amused laugh.

"You're telling me that fella who followed you out to the door didn't try a come 'ere m'lady with you?" said Hal.

Joanie frowned, anger clear on her face. "What he might 'ave done is beside the point. I did nothing but try and get information."

Alys's amusement vanished. "Information? What information?"

Joanie's expression turned smug. "Information about that painting. The one Alessandra sent."

"You got information about Alessandra? Oh Joanie, I could hug you!"

"Don't get too excited," said Joanie. She looked over at Hal and narrowed her eyes, before turning back to Alys. "I did the best I could, but someone saw fit to send for me before I could get the full story."

Hal gave her a dark expression. "Was he expecting favours from you?"

Joanie sighed. "No. I was well able to get 'im to talk with only a few admiring glances and a bit of praise, is all."

"Never mind that," said Alys. "What did he say?"

"Just that the man who delivered the painting wasn't the sort the master would 'ave in 'is best chamber so 'e sent 'im to the kitchens. There,'e complained about the woman who paid 'im to deliver the painting. Said 'is journey ended up twice as long because 'e 'adn't enough money for a decent 'orse."

Alys allowed herself a laugh. "That seems right. Did he say anything else?"

"Well, when I asked where the man came from the servant shrugged and said 'somewhere north'. I thought, 'ere now, that's different to what we know. But the servant was sure it was somewhere north of 'ere."

Alys's face brightened. "That's wonderful Joanie. That's the best progress we've made since we arrived."

"Yeah, but where north?" said Hal. He was still frowning. "It's information, sure enough. But does it get us anywhere?"

"Oh, don't be a grump," said Joanie. "You're just annoyed that while you were playacting I actually was doing something useful."

Hal sniffed but added nothing more.

"He is right, to a degree," said Alys. "We need to know where. He came by horse and it was some distance for him to complain about it. Where would he have come from that Alessandra would be? It would have to be a place big enough for commercial trading. Somewhere significant if she wants to build up her trade. A place where important merchants lived."

"Didn't Barnabas live in a place where he met Venetian and Genoan merchants?" said Joanie. "What was the name of those families?"

"He spent time in Bruges," said Hal. "He told me so."

"Bruges," said Alys. She considered it a moment and then turned to Joanie. "Do you think if you saw your Frenchman again he would remember if it was Bruges the man came from?"

Joanie nodded. "Yes, possibly."

"'e isn't 'er Frenchman, if you don't mind," said Hal, frowning again.

Alys smiled. "No, you're right, Hal. He is *our* dear, dear Frenchman. To whom I will be forever indebted if he remembers the city where the man who delivered the painting came from."

~

She should be enjoying herself. The small gathering Julia promised was a success, at least as far as the painting was concerned. They admired it even now, little clusters going past where it hung in the pride of place, instead of the other painting of the Madonna. That had been consigned to Julia's bedchamber, as if to remind Julia of the motherhood role she hadn't fulfilled. That was Alys's impression, at least. As she murmured her thanks to the various people who came up to congratulate her brother on his painting, she realised that she'd made the correct choice in making Hal her surrogate in this transaction.

"So unfortunate that your brother couldn't attend," said Antonio Barberigo. He pulled at the sumptuous burgundy cloak that did nothing to hide his girth, or the spindly legs that were beneath it. His neatly trimmed beard was, she suspected, dyed.

Alys gave Julia's husband a forced smile and ignored the censorious tone. "My brother is a man of many talents, but I'm afraid conversation with strangers isn't one of them."

He nodded politely. "We are of course happy that you are able to decorate our little group so beautifully. Has your brother ever painted you?"

Alys narrowed her eyes and looked at him. "He has, on occasion."

Barberigo studied her, examining every inch of her modestly cut gown, lingering on the neckline that revealed only a hint of her breasts. She endured this with all the patience she could muster and tried not to blush.

"Yes, yes, I see that he has used you for the subject of the painting in my wife's bedchamber, has he not?" His eyes darkened and his lips parted slightly. "A most stunning painting. And a most beautiful subject."

"Thank you," she said, her tone bland.

"I must have him paint more. Perhaps a companion to the Madonna. The Annunciation? Or maybe something entirely different. A classical theme. Venus? Or Diana the huntress? I understand classical themes are becoming a popular subject matter."

"Or maybe Judith and the death of Holiphernes," said Alys, conjuring an image of her holding Barberigo's head, after wielding a large blade to cut it off.

"Oh, that is amusing," said Barberigo. "But tell your brother I would have him wait on me in five days' time and we can discuss it."

"I know my brother will be gratified, though I'm not certain what his plans are. He did mention to me about a possible commission in Bruges."

"Bruges?"

Alys nodded. "A patron. They saw one of his paintings while travelling and inquired about it. A mural for their chapel."

Barberigo's face clouded. "A man of means."

"Yes, it would appear so."

"But it's yet to be confirmed. It is only tentative."

Alys shrugged. "I don't know."

But she did know. It would be confirmed. She wouldn't paint for this man. And now, in the face of these people who fawned over what they thought to be her brother's work, she realised it was a masquerade that could only lead to problems.

✦

Joanie slipped out of the door and joined her. The torch boy walked ahead and they followed him in silence in the direction of their rooms. Her leg was aching from all the standing earlier and her limp became more pronounced. Distant shouts and other noises of revelry greeted them in the warmth of the summer night. The odour of the nearby River Seine drifted to them.

Alys looked over at Joanie. Her face told the whole story.

"He didn't know?" she murmured.

Joanie shook his head. "It made no difference. He said it wasn't a question of remembering, he just didn't know."

Alys patted her hand. "Never mind. You did well. We know more than we did before."

Joanie bit her lip. "I tried to find out if he knew where he was staying, but he didn't have any information on that either." She looked over at Alys. "Perhaps Hal could inquire at some more of the inns, see if they know anything."

Alys shook her head. "No, we've tried that. There are too many places to keep trying that approach. No, we must act on what we have. We'll go to Bruges."

Joanie stopped dead. "Without knowing for certain?"

"Yes," said Alys firmly. "There isn't any other place she could be, based on what we know. It's our only chance and so we must go."

Joanie pursed her mouth and studied her. Alys took her arm, moved her forward and with only a moment's reluctance, Joanie allowed it.

"I pray that you're right," she muttered.

"It's our best hope," said Alys softly.

It *was* their best hope. Her best hope. She couldn't afford to be anything other than right. She'd come this far, it had to be the right course. She'd lost so much. Her daughter, her little monkey. Alys thought of Barnabas and his conviction in his own choice to go east, based on what she'd felt was flimsy and false belief, and suddenly she wanted to cry. How long before he found he was wrong? Had he discovered it yet? Or was he still ploughing onwards, putting himself in constant danger to chase a ghost? Or was he dead?.

CHAPTER TWENTY
VENICE, LATE SUMMER, 1448
BARNABAS

I rubbed the stubble on my face and gazed down into the canal. A distorted version of me shimmered, a true reflection, I thought. Distorted. I looked drawn, my eyes wide and glittering. I touched my side gingerly and felt the blazing heat coming from the bandaged wound there. I knew I must get someone to look at it again, but that was for later. Now, I had more important things to do.

I drew out a small flask and took a sip. The strong alcohol slipped down my throat and went someway to numbing the pain. As much as the grappa helped in that manner, it might have been better if I'd poured it on my wound instead.

Behind me, voices came closer, their joking tones loud enough to carry across the canal. I turned and plastered a smile on my face. Vito and Polo strode ahead, Pietro and Niccolo behind, the jokes now turned to a friendly argument.

"Hey, Giacomo," said Pietro. "We're sorry to be so late, but this one decided at the last moment he had to compose a poem for the fair Angelica." He looked pointedly at Niccolo.

"Angelica?" I said. "I thought her name was Frederica."

Polo and Vito laughed. "That was a few days ago," said Vito. "Tonight it is Angelica."

"And will this Angelica be there at this entertainment?"

Niccolo grinned. "If she knows I will be there, of course she'll come."

I clapped him on the back. "She will no doubt have heard of your wit and charm."

Pietro gave me a shove and I forced myself not to wince at the pain it caused. Though I'd taken the sword cut nearly a fortnight before, at Tyre, it was as though it was fresh. Or worse. I shoved the thought of infection from my mind and tried to concentrate.

"You look as though you've been to an entertainment already," said Polo. "Where was it? Shall we go there instead?"

"No," I said. "It was very dull. That's why I drank so much. Come, let's away now."

We arrived at the house where Niccolo's uncle lived, near the Grand Canal, alighting from the small gondola in fits of laughter. Behind us, shouts and laughter echoed eerily from the gondolas and barchettas while their lanterns bobbed, all of which added to the festive atmosphere, despite the foul odours of a Venetian summer that rose from the water.

The building before us was reflective of Venice's prosperity, defying the staining waters from which it rose, as did its companions, stretched along the waterfront.

These homes were a far cry from the crowded hovels and decaying properties of the Arsenale, or the newly aspiring modest places built where the metal foundry used to be in the Cannaregio.

Light spilled out from the windows above me and the noise from the crowd inside could be heard even from the street below. We moved through the *loggia* and climbed the stairs to the *sala* eagerly, except for me. Beads of sweat gathered as I mounted each step. I passed the luxurious tapestries, paintings, rugs and ornaments without a second glance.

Inside the *sala*, the heat was stifling from the press of too many bodies dressed in figured silks, every finger, ear and neck draped in jewels. Another rich gathering, like the last time I'd been here. When I'd first met Alessandra. And Tomaso.

I glanced to the side of the large room and saw, as before, a table where a few were playing cards, onlookers gathered around them. Women with daring necklines and peeping nipples leaned over several of the men playing.

I noted the players, picked up a glass of wine and made my way to the windows, desperate for a bit of air before I began my queries. The windows were flung open to catch a breeze from the night air, discounting any hazard to health or the stench of the nearby canal. There was no need, since perfume had been liberally applied to most of the attendees to combat the stench and artfully placed pomanders were wielded against the threat of any dangerous humours from the canal.

After the dry air of the desert lands I'd recently inhabited, I found the humidity oppressive. Or perhaps it was because of the wound. Either way, I knew I must conclude my enquiries as quickly as possible.

"*Amico*, it is some time since we've had your company," came a voice.

I turned to see Pietro's uncle approach. I bowed, struggling to remember his name. "Signor Voltini, a pleasure."

Voltini smiled and returned the bow. "No, no. It's my pleasure that you should grace my home again. Last time it was, let us say, vastly entertaining."

"Ah, much has happened since."

"Fortunes won and lost?"

I laughed, noting the edge to his voice. "Not yours, I hope?"

Voltini gave me a mocking look. "Tsk, tsk. How could you suggest it? With all this wine and food? And these treasured beauties ready to entertain us?"

I laughed and shook my head. "Merely a jest. You are too wise a merchant to be anything other than prosperous."

"Ah, I come from a family of wise men, if you base all wisdom on prosperity. But you have not been so wise, I hear."

"Fortunes come and fortunes go," I said waving a hand in dismissal. "But then they come again."

Voltini raised his brows and studied me. "They come again, do they? How interesting. And fortunate for you."

"With fortunes no longer tied to Alessandra, I had more freedom to take risks. She wasn't able to recognise the opportunities I did."

"I'd heard that you and Alessandra were sharing some trading ventures and they foundered. I believe she discovered some other opportunities to explore," he said with a shrug.

I looked at his face, waiting for some tell-tale sign or indication he knew more. There was only a flicker, but it was enough.

"A pity she felt she had to betray me," I said boldly. "If she'd only been a little more patient she could have had all the fortune she desired."

"You have found a new market for yourself? Where, the Indies? You must have a care for that kind of trade. It is indeed risky. And dangerous as well. You could lose your traders as well as your goods."

"No, I went east, along the trading roads to Samarkand."

Voltini gave me an incredulous look. "I fear you're not a wise merchant at all. And fortunate not to be dead."

"It was a calculated risk."

He glanced down at the rings adorning my fingers. I'd ensured that every one of them were rubies or emeralds. It was garish and tasteless, but the point was made. At my throat was the large ruby Ulugh Beg had given to me, now surrounded by a gold filigree setting.

"It appears you are good at making calculations."

"I am indeed. My calculations in this case included the influence I would gain. Have gained." I patted his arm. "But I'm not here to discuss business. I am here to enjoy myself. To play cards. Is Tomaso here? I would savour the opportunity to match my wits against his."

Voltini gave me a surprised look. "You think Tomaso is here? But you know he left Venice with Alessandra some time ago."

"But I hear they've returned," I said blandly. I glanced around. "Though I see Tomaso has decided not to put in an appearance here tonight. Or perhaps he wasn't invited?"

"*Amico*, I'm not certain what you heard, or who said it to you, but Alessandra isn't in Venice. She may have been here briefly, but she's long gone. As is Tomaso."

"Ah, *sfortunatamente*. He is the best challenge at cards."

"Only at cards?" said Voltini.

I shrugged. "We have a rivalry."

Voltini laughed. "Try his home, then. I'm certain he would be pleased to see you."

"His home?"

"Mantua. He would welcome a chance to win back money. It seems he's had to return home when his own fortunes took a downturn."

"Fortunes come and they go."

"*Si*. For some who aren't wise."

"Let's hope we can both retain our wisdom."

Voltini raised his glass in acknowledgement. I met it with my own and we exchanged long, sizing glances. He gave a hint of a nod. A wish for luck.

I glanced around for Niccolo or one of the others. They were all gathered around the gaming table, except for Pietro who'd found a place among the card players. For a moment I toyed with the idea of joining them, but the pain in my side reminded me how foolish such a move would be. I'd delayed long enough.

With a small bow I moved away from Voltini and meandered through the crowd, not wanting to seem in any sort of hurry. I made my way to the door and out, chatting to a few familiar faces, all of them surprised to see me. So much so, I began to wonder what exactly the rumours were of my situation. And who had spread them. I had my suspicions that it was either one of two people. One of them was in Mantua and I would soon know.

Once in Mantua, I found the heat oppressive, but less so to me than Venice. Something in the air in Venice stole my breath, pressed on my chest, so that despite the need to rest my wound after the physician chided me, I left with as much haste as possible. It may have been the stench, or the miasma that rose up in the night as a dark mist, or it could have been that my life had been stolen once again in Venice and I found the city too much of a taskmaster. The air of prosperity and power no longer attracted me. I saw behind the mask of its glittering rooms, paintings and tapestries.

In Mantua even my wound seemed to have improved. So I faced this city without the wariness that Venice invoked in me, but with a mild interest and a little intrigued as to how Tomaso would greet me.

I walked by the market of Mantua in the Piazza Erbe, where the newly restored Palazzo del Podestà stood next to the ancient church, the Rotunda di San Lorenzo. The bell in the tall tower up ahead tolled evensong. The sound was sweet and reminded me once again that I was back in Christendom, that the call to prayer I'd grown familiar with in recent months was no longer dictating the daily life of those around me.

I moved over to the arched walkway that provided cover from the strong late afternoon sun. I had taken rooms nearby and I decided to head towards the lake and the trees that shaded it along the bank via the market. Others seemed to have the same idea. Young noblemen strolled in their finery, passing carters and servants carrying baskets filled with goods, as well as sombrely dressed men intent on their business. In the market at the Piazza Erbe, hawkers shouted their wares as people milled around, picking out items.

I scanned the group of young noblemen, wondering if I'd spot Tomaso among them, leading them to merriment at some inn or tavern, or enticing them to some place to game. I'd made a few inquiries about the location of Tomaso's family home and would go there the next day after I'd had some time to assess Mantua and the manner of people who were here.

I had heard Tomaso's family were prominent enough that they kept company with Lord Gonzaga's family, but I knew little else about them. Would approaching Tomaso directly gain me what I wanted? It was too important not to handle discreetly. Perhaps it was best if I found out where the gaming took place and looked for him there. Gamble for the information.

I paused, staring at, but not really seeing the rows of ceramic pots lined up on the table outside the shop's entrance, musing on my next steps. I felt a hand grip my shoulder and whirl me around.

"It is you," said Tomaso, grinning.

He stood there in his fine silk doublet and hose, his hair curling at his shoulders and an arrogant expression on his face. Beside him were three young men, equally well dressed and wearing expressions ranging from surly to bored. I struggled to compose my features, confused a moment by his appearance and afraid of its meaning.

I bowed lightly and forced a smile. "Tomaso. Well met."

Tomaso raised his brows. "Well met?" He threw back his head and laughed. "And just how is it well met? It seems to me that 'ill met' would be more appropriate."

I shrugged. "Let us hope not."

"Yes, you would hope not."

Tomaso turned to his friends, who'd circled him.

"This upstart is a man who contrives sleights of hand in both cards and in business."

I narrowed my eyes. "No," I said softly. "It is others who are more skilled at both. I have a talent for cards and numbers, no more than that."

"A defence of innocence," said Tomaso in a sarcastic tone, nodding to his companions.

"He doesn't look very innocent to me," said the one with the surly expression.

"No, but we only have his word that he is innocent," said Tomaso. "And I'm afraid I don't trust that word."

The youth with a bored expression gave me a sizing look. "His clothes are fine enough. Maybe he bought his innocence."

"Tomaso," I said calmly. "Though I welcome the company of any of your companions at any time, is it possible that I might speak to you on your own now?"

Tomas gave me a considering look. "Is that a begging tone I detect?"

I sighed inwardly. He had to play his games. "No, merely a request."

"Ah, *lo sono deloroso*, but I am engaged at the moment. But tomorrow perhaps? A little card game?"

"I'm happy just to have a few moments, no need for a card game."

"But I insist, *amico*. Please give me the opportunity to face you once more at cards. You see I've learned much since we've last played."

I raised a brow. "As I have I."

"Yes, but perhaps you might be eager for me to teach you what I've learned."

"You think it would be beneficial to me, then?"

"Most certainly. And, besides, you will also be able to see one of your former close companions."

I studied him closely. "Antonio is here? Niccolo? I just left them and they made no mention of travelling here to see you."

"Did you see them indeed? But of course you did." He gave a little snort. "No, it isn't either of them. It's someone you put much greater store in. Or at least you did, until you cruelly decided to abandon all your companions."

I suppressed an intake of breath. "You have Maria staying with you? Why would she go to you?"

"Tsk, tsk. That would ruin the surprise. You'll just have to come tomorrow to my home and see."

I fought the urge to strangle him, so strong was my anger. I was certain he could see the rage in my eyes, so I looked over at the market, studying the people and goods. Anything to dampen the fury.

"I confess, my curiosity is greater than my desire to avoid card playing. Tomorrow it is."

"You know my direction, I take it?"

I bowed. "Yes. What time?"

"Let's make it in the evening, say sometime after ten?

I nodded and took my leave as quickly as possible, not able to trust myself in his company a moment longer.

CHAPTER TWENTY-ONE
MANTUA, LATE SUMMER, 1448
BARNABAS

I stood outside Tomaso's home and made an effort to calm myself. I needed my wits about me – and for that to happen I knew it was important that I remain as passive as possible to Tomaso's jibes. That he might be in the company of Alys for whatever reason, I mustn't let cloud my judgement. My best hope was that Alys was there of her own free will, seeking information just as I was. How she'd come to know he was there could be simply explained. She had as many acquaintances in Venice as I did and there seemed no doubt she could have found out Tomaso's location from one of them.

That she might be there under duress didn't make sense, but rationalising it, somehow didn't stop the swirl of fears and anxieties from crowding my mind or repress the urge to kill Tomaso.

I steadied myself, raised my hand to the large, imposing door and pulled the bell. I heard its ring echo inside and stood waiting, willing the door to open quickly.

A few moments later a servant appeared and I introduced myself. He ushered me into the *sala* and bid me wait.

The marbled floored *sala* was spacious enough to hold several carved tables and chests as well as benches and chairs. Tapestries, depicting scenes from myths and battles fought long ago, were colourful against the white walls and illuminated by candlelight. Sitting in the centre of one of the benches was Tomaso, his right arm draped across its back. Across from him was the surly one of his companions from yesterday. I scanned the room but there was no one else present. I gave them both a cursory bow and greeted them.

"I'm glad to see you couldn't resist my invitation," said Tomaso.

"You made it impossible to resist," I said. "I believe you mentioned the presence of an additional person?"

"I don't think I introduced my friend yesterday," said Tomaso, ignoring my question. "This is Francesco, a friend from my youth."

Francesco nodded his acknowledgement. His broad, flat face was more pleasant today, except for the slight sneer.

"I'm glad to see that you can manage to find someone who still would call himself your friend. I didn't think that was possible. He must not play cards with you then."

Anger flashed in Tomaso's eyes for a moment and was swiftly replaced by a studied blandness.

"It is perhaps because of your own trouble at keeping friends that you might think it the case with me. But it is not." He rose and Francesco did as well. "Come, shall we start our little game of cards? I assure you that Francesco will give you good play."

I smiled apologetically. "Perhaps you've forgotten, but that is no matter, I will tell you again. I won't play cards with you."

Tomaso frowned. "But that is such a shame. My little companion that you desire so much to see won't appear unless you comply."

I gave him a direct look. "Why does it matter so much? Can't we talk instead? There's a proposal I would put before you."

"A proposal? I am intrigued. But surely we can talk as we play cards."

"I think you might want to give all your attention to my words."

Tomaso paused and considered. A moment later he looked at Francesco. "Perhaps you would be good enough to return tomorrow. I promise I will have what you want then."

Francesco nodded. "A promise I will hold you to." There was a hint of menace behind the words.

I eyed Francesco with interest. His flat face betrayed little, but there was a swagger to his gait as he made his way to the door in his finely cut doublet and hose. Was he less a friend than Tomaso had painted him?

"A little strain on the friendship?"

Tomaso opened his mouth to say something but a loud screeching filled the house. The screeching continued and was soon joined by shouts and cursing. I walked to the door but Tomaso got there before me.

"Nothing to concern you," he said.

"Oh, but I would like to help. It could be something serious."

"There is no need, I say. The servants will resolve any problem that might arise."

"No, I think you do need my help."

I pushed him out of the way and opened the door. A figure came flying down the passageway, a flash of tail and fur, and a moment later two servants followed, their hands outstretched, hurling curses. The screeching began again and continued as the figure scampered onto a ledge above our heads. I looked up into the eyes of a monkey. Tomaso.

I grinned and turned to Tomaso who stood behind me. "My former companion giving you a little trouble?"

Tomaso shrugged. "The servants. You know what they are like. Excitable."

I looked back up at the monkey and gave a soft croon. "Come, now little one. Come down from there." I reached out my hand.

Tomaso, alert and his tail twitching, made a cautious leap into my arms. He was trembling his back rigid, eyes wide. I frowned inwardly, knowing what kind of treatment had brought that reaction.

"Still a companion, it seems," I said, my tone amused. "How is it he came to be here?"

"In my possession? For he is my possession, I assure you, though you are free to have a little visit with him."

"Yours? I'm not certain he agrees, albeit that he might be your namesake."

"He is called Piccolo."

I raised my brow. "Little. How imaginative. But I'm afraid he will always be Tomaso to me."

Tomaso bristled and made an effort to smile. "That's your choice. But Piccolo remains here, with me." He paused, licking his lips. "Unless of course you want to make an offer for him."

"Tell me first how he came to be here."

A nonchalant shrug. "He was a gift."

"A gift?" I tried to conceal my surprise. Surely Alys wouldn't have gifted it to him.

"From a friend whom I delighted as much as she delighted me. She thought it would be amusing to send Piccolo to me."

"And is it she gave him the name Piccolo?"

Tomaso's face darkened. "No."

"This 'friend' then isn't here. Do I know her?"

Tomaso shook his head slowly. "No. She is a woman of many talents. I'm not certain you would suit."

I decided not to rise to the bait. "How much then?"

Tomaso gave me a hard stare. "A hundred ducats."

I paused, looking at him in surprise. So little. I'd expected more. "Fine, seventy-five ducats," he said flatly.

I sighed. Looked down at the monkey, still in my arms, still trembling a little. "Fifty?"

Tomaso shook his head. "Seventy. I can't take lower than that."

"Some pressing gaming debts?"

A barely detectable flinch escaped him. "Let's just say that though I find his company growing tiresome, his value hasn't escaped me. And after all, it was a present."

"Would you be interested in increasing your...funds for some information?"

Tomaso narrowed his eyes. "What information?"

"On another one of your female companions," I said carefully.

"Alessandra." He snorted.

I indicated the *sala*. "Shall we resume our seats?"

Tomaso eyed me and then the monkey who remained quiet in my arms, his trembling soothed enough that he chattered a little. Tomaso gave a curt nod and I followed him into the *sala* and took a seat on one of the benches. Tomaso sat opposite.

"How much are you willing to pay?" he said.

I gave him a considering look. "It depends on the information. I want to know where Alessandra is. Where did you go? What did you do? Where did you part company?"

"I want another hundred ducats."

I made a play of sucking in my breath. "So much? Is this for your debt or for some other plan?"

"It's of no concern of yours," he said coolly.

"Ah, but it gives me an indication of your sincerity and perhaps even the truth of your words."

"You think I would play you false?" His tone had turned coy.

I laughed. "I'm not going to even answer that."

"You'll just have to take the risk, then. But the price remains the same."

"I shall give you fifty ducats now, as part payment for little Tomaso and to show my good faith. And in return, you shall give me a few particulars. As a show of your good faith."

"I shall give you nothing. You already have the monkey. Pay me one hundred ducats now, the price for the monkey and a part payment for the information."

I shook my head slowly. "I'm beginning to think that you put too high a price on your information. In fact, I wonder if you know anything at all. Did you even make it outside of the Grand Canal in Venice before she tossed you off the ship?"

His face reddened. "You know nothing," he said with a sneer. "It was I who left. A choice I made. I no longer wanted to be part of her schemes."

I nodded. "So, you were no longer useful to her then."

He stiffened. "If you want to know more, you must pay the stated sum."

I shifted the monkey to the side of me and reached for my purse and untied it. I tossed it in my hand once then threw it over to him.

"There's eighty ducats in that pouch. It's all yours."

"I said one hundred."

I shrugged. "Eighty is all I have with me now. If you want that amount then you must wait a few days until I can see a banker."

Tomaso scowled and opened the purse. Carefully he counted out the amount and when he finished he looked up, frowning. "You must pay me all of the rest as soon as possible. That's ninety ducats." He looked over at the monkey. "I'll take back the monkey on account."

"Until I hear the worth of your information, little Tomaso will stay here with me."

He stared at me, his eyes filled with anger. "It's almost worth it to tell you just so she can wreak her revenge on you. My hesitation is because I'm trying to think of who I hate more. You or her."

"You don't have to decide. Just tell me what you know and leave us to our fates."

Tomaso laughed. "It is tempting. Very tempting. She is someone who would get the best of you again, I have no doubt. She's determined to keep that brat, too. As I told your little concubine."

"Maria was here?" I tried to keep the tone casual. So Alys had passed this way, I thought.

He laughed again, and I detected a small note of triumph present. "Oho, as I thought. Things aren't going well for you, are they? She left you, did she? Well, who can blame her? You have managed to lose her everything, including the precious child of hers."

"When was Maria here?" I said patiently.

He shrugged. "A while ago. Before the monkey arrived."

I sighed. "And how long has he been here?"

"Well, if you ask the servants they would say too long. A fortnight perhaps."

I tried to keep the hope from my face. Alys. Her trail wasn't that old. She was safe and well until that point, of that much I could be certain. "And what did you tell Maria?

"What I just mentioned. Alessandra won't give up the child, no matter what price you name. She's not seeking payment."

"What is it she's seeking?"

"Revenge. Against you. Maria, it seems is just a victim, a tool."

I frowned. "A tool?"

He smiled again, slowly delighting in his words. "Against you. The child. She planned it all, you know."

"She knows the child is mine?"

"Didn't I just say that she planned all of it?"

"To revenge herself on me," I said flatly. "For the fire."

"Oh, you have finally worked it out. It took you a while, and everyone always says how clever you are. Well it seems you're not."

"What does she intend to do with the child?"

"You must ask her. But at a guess, as I told Maria, she wants to mould her, create a formidable beauty who can enter any court and do Alessandra's bidding there." He tilted his head. "She thought you two were handsome enough to make a beautiful child. You should be flattered."

"Forgive me if I'm not." I toyed idly with the little collar around the monkey's neck, the only sign of agitation that I permitted. Inside, I raged.

"Where then, sir, is Alessandra now?" There was a definite edge to my voice.

Tomaso leaned forward. "Of that, I can't be certain. What I can tell you is what I said to Maria. She mentioned she would be heading to her sister, in Paris.

"The sister's name?" I could hardly contain my impatience. It was all I could do to resist taking a knife to his throat.

"Hmmm," he said, clearly enjoying the moment. "What was it now?"

I rose quickly and grabbed Tomaso by his doublet and twisted the cloth until it was choking him. "No games. Tell me the name."

"Julia," he said sputtering. "She's married to a merchant. His name is Antonio Barberigo."

I threw him back against the bench and nodded. With a quick stride I scooped up the monkey and made for the door.

"The monkey is to stay here until you give me the money," said Tomaso loudly.

"You'll have your money," I said. "Tomorrow."

With the monkey still in my arms I walked out of the *sala* and made my way to the street outside, barely able to contain my fury. Once on the street I took deep breaths. The evening air was still thick with summer heat and did nothing to cool my temper. I looked down at the monkey who, sensing my anger, started to chitter.

"You're missing her too, little one. I know. But hopefully it won't be long before we can both see her again and be reunited." And hopefully, I thought, she won't banish me for leaving her, for not trusting in her instinct – and for most of all, causing this mess to begin with.

CHAPTER TWENTY-TWO
BRUGES, LATE SUMMER 1448
ALYS

The canals that weaved in and around the city carried boats, providing transport for goods and people. Buildings rose tall above the water, capped with tiled roofs that gleamed red in the summer sun. But that's where any similarities to Venice ended. There was nothing of the sensuous, almost lazy quality that permeated Venice like an undercurrent that flowed beneath the dignity of the Council and the Doge. Even the pageantry of Venice, most evident in the ceremony in spring where the Doge symbolically weds the sea, had an otherworldly sense that could never be found in Bruges.

Bruges was prosperous. Bruges was bustling, filled with people intent on commerce. Even the language suggested something earthbound, something commercial, though Alys couldn't understand it. She found she had to resort to English or Latin to make herself understood. Hal recalled a few phrases from his sailing days years ago, when he served on ships crossing the North Sea to bring wool from London to be turned into cloth.

Hal had adapted quite well, Alys noticed. As if the day's sailing had brought back a swagger and assertiveness he'd not had in Venice or Paris. No stutter required here, thought Alys as she watched her brother approach a market stall ahead of her. The weather was damp and humid and her hair was sticking to the back of her neck, underneath the kerchief she wore. Joanie picked up the basket she'd set down for a moment and gestured to a stone wall by the canal.

"Come, we might find a breeze over there while Meister Swagger makes his enquiries," she said.

Alys stifled a giggle and made her way to the wall. Joanie and Hal had grown both closer and with it more quarrelsome since their arrival. Perhaps it was because they were nearer to home. Home? Had she really thought that? Was London, the docks of Queenhithe, her home still? She didn't know. Her life, her thoughts and her experiences were so different from when she left, it was hard to imagine the young girl who had gone stumbling into service for the Duchess of Gloucester.

"Well, what are your thoughts, Joanie? Shall I approach the bishop with my letter of recommendation or one of the burghers of the cloth merchant's guild?"

"Why not the guild itself?"

I smiled. "Yes, that's true. Perhaps that would be best. Something for their guild hall. We should look there before we make a decision."

"But 'ow will you do it? You can't ask them. Will you get Hal to?"

Alys sighed. "I'm not sure. I thought perhaps I might try a disguise."

Joanie turned to look at her. "A disguise? As a man? Don't be foolish, Alys."

Alys bit her lip. "To be truthful, I'm not certain that Hal could be convincing enough. I mean, what if they ask him questions about his work? How he selects his colours, or anything else specific or technical? He's hardly likely to be able to reply."

Joanie frowned. "That may be so, but you can't expect them not to see that you're a woman. And then what? If you're lucky they'll just throw you out, or banish you from the city. But they could put you in prison at worst."

"I think it's the only way. I'll borrow some of Hal's clothes. Have you take them in. Or perhaps we should hire some."

"No, the fashions are different 'ere. You can see that. No, you want to appear to be from Venice, if that's what you're saying your story is."

"Yes, of course. We'll just have to cut one of Hal's doublets to fit. And the rest."

Alys sighed. She knew it would be difficult, but she was finding it expensive here in Bruges and they were going through the money she had from Paris faster than she'd anticipated. They'd been here ten days now searching and inquiring after Alessandra, but they'd had no luck. No hint of Alessandra's presence and Alys was beginning to think that her carefully made decision to come here might have been wrong. But she was willing to try longer here. She had to try longer; there was nowhere else she could think to go, except back to Venice. And that seemed defeatist. As if she was giving up entirely. That would never happen. No, she would remain here until she knew for certain that Alessandra had never travelled here. She just needed to think. Figure out Alessandra's reasoning behind the decision to come to Bruges.

"We'll go to the guild. I'll approach them about a commission and ask about Alessandra at the same time."

Joanie snorted and began to wave a hand in front of her face against the heat. "You'd be better off asking the burghers' wives if they know anything of her."

Alys laughed. "You mean because they would more likely know if any one of the burghers was warming her bed?"

"No, of course not. I know she's not for that anymore. Not with 'er scars."

"You know I saw her once without her veil. It was awful. I can understand why she might become bitter." Alys frowned. "But I won't forgive her for what she's done. Never."

Joanie patted her hand. "Don't worry. You'll 'ave the chance to tell 'er so directly. And I'll get my bit in too, mark my words. She'll feel more than my 'and across her face if I have anything to say about it."

"I hope so." Alys sighed. "So why do you think the wives would know?"

Joanie shrugged. "They'll know what goes on. Newcomers and that sort of thing." She pointed to a sturdy young woman, the train of her rich green gown draped across her arm, a female servant at her side. "See, they go about. And the serving women too. They meet others, they talk and gossip. I've seen it."

"Yes, it's true.

"And look over there." Joanie pointed again. "See that stout servant holding the hand of the young lad? That's not 'er lad, you can tell by the clothes. That's her master's lad. She's taking 'im out and about. So there you go. Any new child might be noticed."

Alys nodded slowly. "You're right. Very observant. But the fact remains that Hal's inquiries have turned up nothing about Alessandra."

"Cause you have 'im asking. And 'e's asking in the wrong place. It's the burghers' wives you should be asking. And the servants. The woman servants. They're the ones that would notice a child more than any man."

Alys brightened and squeezed Joanie's arm. "I could kiss you, Joanie."

Joanie patted her arm and smiled broadly. "There. That's better now."

"What?" Alys said, a puzzled look on her face.

"The light is back in your eyes. It's been gone these last few days and I didn't like it. You 'ave 'ope again"

Hope. Joanie was right. She actually felt a bit of hope rising inside of her. And with some luck and determination she would make that hope into a certainty.

Alys pulled at her doublet, trying to improve the fit. Her hair, tucked inside her cap, kept coming loose and falling in long tendrils down her back and shoulders. She sighed and glanced out of the window. The noise and bustle of the street below filtered its way through to her chamber at the inn where she'd managed to find rooms for the three of them. She shared with Joanie, but Hal had his own room down the hall. It was a respectable enough inn, housing travellers and merchants here to trade and do business. The linen and room itself was clean enough, if not luxurious.

"You'll never manage," said Joanie, studying her from her seat on the bed. "Not with this, this and that." She touched Alys's hair, breasts and hips.

"I can strap my chest and cut my hair," she said tentatively.

Joanie snorted. "It's no use, my sweeting, you're just too much of a woman to carry this off."

Alys stared down at her figure. Even with the hose adjusted and padded, the doublet lengthened to cover her to her thighs, there was no disguising she was a woman.

"I suppose I'll have to send Hal then," she said. "Or write to them. Perhaps I can do all my necessary negotiation by letter."

"That might be best," said Joanie.

There was a knock on the door and Hal entered a moment later. He paused, stared at Alys and began to laugh.

"I hope you can make that doublet fit me again," he said. "Because I don't think it will be of any use to you. Or the hose."

"I just told 'er that," said Joanie.

Alys looked at her figure again and sighed. "You're right. I won't convince them. Perhaps I'll write."

"Visit the wives," said Joanie.

"Yes," she said frowning. "Perhaps." She thought a moment and looked over at her brother. "The members of the English Merchant House." Many of the important regions that traded here in Bruges had Houses, designated places for them to trade on specified days. England was one of them. "Can you find me their names?"

Hal nodded. "You might need to tell them you 'ave a relation here. Someone in trade."

Alys beamed at him suddenly. "I have you. You're in the spice trade.Or maybe the cloth trade. Recently arrived from Venice. Awaiting the ship to come. They're due around now, aren't they?"

Hal nodded slightly "I'm in the spice trade?" He said doubtfully.

"You are," said Alys. "Our cousin has recently expanded his business and wants to trade here in Bruges."

"But we haven't any spices to trade," said Joanie. She shook her head in disapproval

Alys gave an impatient shrug. "It doesn't matter. We'll just say that the ship was lost at sea, or something of that nature." She gave Hal a thoughtful look. "You'll be the cousin's representative, Hal Goodkin. I'll write the necessary letters."

"Goodkin?" A slow smile crept across his face. "You know, I like it."

☙

Outside, the work bell went off and Alys noted it from her seat where she mixed her paints. Already so much time had passed. Time in this day, and time also in the weeks that they had been here and not one thing had come of it. No sightings of Alessandra or Eleanor, not even a hint. And now, after waiting days for this meeting with the head of the English Merchants' House, she'd still heard nothing from them either.

She dabbed a little paint on the small canvas in front of her, trying to concentrate. She was painting this small work of Mary and Joseph on the way to Bethlehem in the hopes that the guild would consider her to paint a commission for them at the merchants' house in St John's Place. This work would prove she had the necessary skill and talent. Or rather A.R. Gregis did. She'd decided to continue using the name she'd adopted for those paintings back in Venice and then used in Paris if only to give some credibility should anyone care to check.

But after all her work and plans it might prove a fruitless exercise. She'd written the letters, dispatched them with Hal. He had met with the merchant house members, gradually making their acquaintance and establishing his credentials. On one such meeting at the English Merchants' House he'd mentioned his friend, the painter A.R. Gregis, who'd travelled with him to Bruges and suggested they might consider him for a work on their walls. The head of the merchant house, the self-styled burgomeester, said he would consider the idea and perhaps put it before the others. Then it became a question of waiting. She'd waited days now, and still no reply. She knew it took time for men like that to make decisions, but she wasn't certain how long her nerves or her purse could support the wait.

The door opened and Joanie entered, her basket loaded. She deposited bread, cheese and some wrapped pies on the table. Alys raised her brow in the daily silent question and was met with a shake of the head. No sign of Alessandra or Eleanor. Alys blinked back the tears that came.

"I managed to get this much," said Joanie, her tone brisk. "But you'll 'ave to forget wine and settle for a jug of ale." She unloaded the bottle from the basket.

Alys nodded, mentally counting how many groats they'd just spent on food. "You always do well, Joanie. Even though the language is different, you manage to find a way to get the best value."

Joanie laughed. "Well, don't praise me too much. I did find a man who spoke English."

The door opened again and Hal entered, frowning. "You found a man?"

"Good day to you, too, big ears," said Joanie. "A stall holder, in the market. 'e speaks English."

Hal's expression eased. "Oh, good." He eyed the food. "That's what you got, is it?"

"And for what money she had, she did well," said Alys.

Hal looked up at Alys and sighed. "She did. Yes. She did well."

He blinked a moment, still staring at Alys and reached in his doublet and withdrew a letter. He handed it to her, fixing his gaze on it grimly.

"A letter? From the burgomeester?"

"I met the messenger at the door. 'e recognised me and said what it was. They expect an answer within the next day."

Alys eagerly broke the seal of the letter and unfolded it, scanning the contents almost before it was open. When she'd done she looked up at them joy on her face.

"They're offering a commission. For the hall."

Joanie clapped her hands. "What's the painting then?"

"They want me to paint something that symbolises the importance of the ties the English merchants have with Bruges and the Duke of Burgundy."

"How are you to do that?" said Hal and laughed. "Paint a bunch of sheep circling the Duke?"

Alys looked at him and smiled weakly. "Not quite. They want me to paint the Duke of Burgundy being presented with a chest of wool. By the members of English Merchants' House."

"Oh," said Joanie. "Well at least it isn't sheep."

"No," said Alys. "The chest of wool will be no problem to paint."

"What about the Duke of Burgundy?" said Hal. "How are you going to paint him? Have you ever seen him, or a picture of him?"

Alys held out the letter to him. "Apparently they have a portrait I can use to create the likeness. No, it's the others."

Hal started to nod slowly. "You 'ave to paint their likeness without actually meeting them."

"Yes," said Alys. "Exactly."

❦

Before her was a large board that would be her work, the under painting already begun. Preliminary sketches were on a table beside it. She had the Duke of Burgundy on the left, prominent and richly dressed, facing a group of men, with the burgomeester kneeling and offering a richly adorned chest with wool spilling out from it. It was to be set in the guild hall itself, its lush tapestries and expensive marble floors denoting the guild's wealth and prominence.

The time had come to begin detailed sketches of the guild members. The painting of the Duke of Burgundy was in the burgomeester's home and it was there she was to go this morning, and after that to the merchants' house in St John's Place, not far from the Beursplein.

To circumvent the problem of her ruse, she'd informed the guildhall members that A.R. Gregis's assistant was his daughter. She, being an only child of a widow and a faithful and obedient daughter, had helped him mix his paints and do some of his sketches since his infirmity made it impossible to venture out. She hoped the ruse would work. Today was her first real time to test it.

She turned from the easel and put the dark veil over her head, draping it over her shoulders. She'd braided her hair and coiled it at the back of her head, with only a few curls on either side of her face. The gown was a plain brown, belted just above the waist, but the cloth was good. Under Joanie's deft fingers, it had been made over from one of her old ones. She wanted to look the part of a Venetian daughter, whose father might be originally from England, but whose own birth and ensuing years were definitely spent in Venice.

Joanie tugged lightly at the back of the dress, to improve its fall. It just touched the floor, no train at all, for she wanted to convey practicality.

"You're ready now, sweeting," said Joanie. "You look fine."

Hal grunted his approval and held out his arm to her. "Well my lady of Venice, are you ready?"

Alys nodded. "Remember, call me Carlotta."

"Carlotta," said Hal. "I won't forget."

The three of them made their way to the street in silence. Alys was reviewing the possible questions she might have to answer, her eyes barely on the cobbled street as Hall steered her out of range of puddles, muck and other potential hazards. The journey wasn't too far but it took them through a small market place and past the docks where crowds bustled noisily in the sultry weather.

Alys wiped a bead of sweat from her forehead, the gesture hidden under the veil. Despite the sheerness of the headcovering, it still stopped the air from moving through. She was tempted to remove it, but resisted, and resigned herself to dabbing periodically at her forehead and chin. She would just have to look wilted when she met the burgomeester.

At the market square, Joanie drew them over to a shaded stall where small pots of ale were being sold from a large cask with a wet cloth draped over it. Alys took a pot gratefully and drank deeply. On the other side of the stall, a woman with a young child in her arms passed by just as Alys turned to look at her. The child stared at her with large, wide eyes. Something tugged at Alys. A group of men passed between them, cutting off Alys's view. She blinked and gripped Joanie's arm, splashing Joanie's pot of ale in the process.

"Careful, now," said Joanie. She turned to Alys. "What's amiss?"

Alys paled, disbelieving. "Eleanor."

Joanie looked at her. "What?"

Alys drew away, plunging into the market crowd, searching for the woman and child. The woman had been dressed in grey, a servant's garb, she was certain of it. She scanned the crowd, shoving her way through in the direction she thought the woman had gone.

Joanie and Hal caught up with her. "What is it? Did you see Eleanor?" asked Joanie.

"Yes, she was with a woman. A servant." said Alys, still working her way through the crowd and cursing the limp that hindered her progress.

"Are you certain?" asked Hal. "I know she's your child, but it has been some time…"

Alys shot him a look so murderous he halted his words. "She is my child. I would know her eyes, her face anywhere."

"What's the woman wearing?" asked Joanie, ever practical.

"A grey dress."

Joanie frowned, searching the crowd with her as the three pushed their way through. Alys caught a flash of grey at the edge of the market, heading down a street.

Alys pointed. "There!"

She didn't think twice, just rushed forward, ignoring the shooting pain in her leg, Joanie and Hal trailing in her wake. She shoved and pushed harder, determined to get to her quarry, disregarding the curses and protests hurled at her as she fought her way to the other side of the square. She tried to keep the woman in her sight, but the flash of grey and Eleanor's golden head soon vanished.

She walked down the street, but it was long and filled with people. There was no sign of the woman or Eleanor.

Nevertheless she hurried on, disregarding her throbbing leg, checking each person she passed just in case, looking in doorways and alleys, anywhere that might have swallowed the woman in grey and Eleanor. She looked down every crossroads for signs, but she could see none. She came to the end of the street and stopped, undecided, tears gathering in her eyes. Hal and Joanie caught up to her.

"Did you see anything?" asked Hal.

Miserably she shook her head, too overcome to speak. Eleanor and the woman in grey had disappeared. Suddenly, her leg screamed with pain and gave out from under her.

CHAPTER TWENTY-THREE
BRUGES, LATE SUMMER, 1448
ALYS

Alys stared at the small painting of the Duke of Burgundy, but saw nothing of his features. She saw only an image of the woman in the grey dress clutching Eleanor and heading down the street. Alys hadn't really seen her features, but she strained to recall them nonetheless.

"The Duke is a tall man, long of limb," said John Cardingham.

A small cough to draw her attention came from Hal, seated in a chair by the door. He'd taken the seat when they entered, content to let her play out her role with little assistance from him beyond an introduction to John Cardingham. When they'd been introduced Cardingham had told her he preferred "Johann", since that was what he'd grown accustomed to here in the years he'd been in Bruges, trading. She'd settled on mynheere, and he had beamed at her.

Hal coughed again. Alys turned to look at Cardingham.

"I'd heard that he was tall," she murmured.

They spoke in English, his own accent marking him as a Londoner, except for the small trace of something foreign. His years here were evident in that quality alone. Alys gave her own speech a slight inflection, one that spoke of foreign ports, of Venice.

"He has a noble carriage, and as you see here, a fine profile."

"You've met him?"

"Once. During Eastertide. He graced our House with his presence for a few moments." He paused and admired the Duke's portrait once more. "It is through him that this House has been able to contribute to the wealth and profit of our own kingdom."

There was a strong note of pride in his voice. Alys forced a smile. "Then I can rely on you for a faithful description, mynheere."

He gave her a slight bow. "Of course. I am most happy to help your father in any way I can."

"Thank you."

Alys sighed inwardly, opened the stiff leather case that held the paper for her sketches, and withdrew some sheets. She opened the small pouch at her side, withdrew some charcoal and began sketching while Cardingham looked on. The Duke wasn't particularly handsome, though his features were distinctive overall. His nose was long and his face seemed inclined to be jowly, a characteristic she would downplay in the painting.

"Your father's infirmity, has he had it long?" asked Cardingham.

She waited a moment before answering, intent on her sketching. "He has, mynheere."

"Is it so very debilitating that he cannot come here himself? Surely that would be simpler. More reliable."

She tried not to frown. She would have preferred to sketch in silence, but she knew he must have his answers. She composed a pleasant expression for her face and looked over at him.

"I'm afraid my father was injured in a serious fire. His hands are still good, but he is scarred badly on his face and his legs are of little use. He prefers to remain indoors. Especially in this weather. The heat makes him uncomfortable, as do the stares of others."

Cardingham looked immediately apologetic. "I do beg your pardon. I didn't mean to pry."

Yes you did, thought Alys impatiently. She took a deep breath. She knew her impatience with this man lay only in the fact that she wanted more than anything to be out there searching for any trace of the woman in the grey gown. As it was, she'd sent Joanie to do her utmost to find the woman again while she and Hal continued on their way to John Cardingham's house. She must have faith and trust in Joanie to do all that could be done. In the meantime, she would sketch the Duke and then sketch this man who hovered above her.

She worked away in silence for a while, Cardingham not stirring from her side. She managed to ignore him after a while and lost herself in the features of the man she was drawing. Eventually, she stopped, satisfied that she'd captured the important elements of the Duke, at least enough that she could confidently paint him in her own work.

"You're very good," said Cardingham, his tone full of surprise.

She made herself look down modestly. "Thank you. You're very kind."

He patted Alys's arm. "The praise is well deserved, my dear."

She looked away, keeping up the appearance of meekness and slipped her drawings inside the case.

"Now, if you are able, I would like to begin sketching you as we agreed."

"Of course, of course." He gestured to the room. "Is there anywhere you would like me to stand?"

Alys indicated the window. "Over there, if you are willing. The light is best there."

Cardingham walked to the spot she'd designated and adopted a pose with his hand on his sleeveless jacket that hung past his knees, over his long skirted doublet. He was dressed for the heat in silk, but still his large size made the long cloak, however impressive and richly made, an extra burden for him. Large rings of sweat circled his arm, now visible with his pose. She could also detect a band of sweat at his throat where the lace edge of his shirt peeked out. These observations were added to all the things to omit or soften in her sketches and the final painting.

She wouldn't ask him to kneel and pretend to offer the chest of wool. She would leave that to Hal, who would be much more able to endure the time necessary to capture the elements of that pose. She would work with what was before her because it took little time and then she could be off.

Alys's charcoal flew over the pages and somehow with necessity came skill and she was able to capture the man before her in fewer strokes than the Duke. Perhaps because her model was live and she could see the essence of the man freely, not filtered through some other artist's eyes. Or it was the pressure to be gone. Or both those reasons. But finished she was after a short time and when she declared herself so, Cardingham looked disappointed.

"You took more time over the Duke's painting," he said in a plaintive voice.

"The Duke's face isn't given over to artistry the way your own is," she said.

He nodded and seemed placated. "You'll want to go to the Merchants' House next?"

"Would you be offended if I returned to our rooms? I would like to check on my father. He wasn't particularly well today."

"Of course," he said.

Hal gave her a questioning look but she ignored it. Alys could see Cardingham was disappointed again. Well there was little help for it. She was in no mood to visit the Merchants' House today. She was tired now and out of sorts. Her back ached from standing and concentrating on her sketching and the strapping on her leg that had become a regular feature since it had given way, was too tight. More than anything, though, she wanted to find Joanie and hear what she had to say.

Joanie was waiting for them when they returned. Alys knew the moment she saw her face that she'd not been able to find any trace of the woman in grey or Eleanor.

"Nothing?" she asked, even though she knew the answer.

Joanie just shook her head.

"I'll go look," said Hal.

"No," said Alys. "We've looked enough for today. She probably won't be outside. Not now. But maybe tomorrow." She tried to glean some hope from her statement.

"I'll go there each day at the same time that we saw her today, until I see her. She's bound to be back at some point. Even without Eleanor."

"You think you would recognise her again?" Alys asked.

Joanie frowned. "I think so. Maybe."

Alys heard the doubt in her voice. Her own image of the woman was vague. She'd caught a glimpse only, but that glimpse haunted her.

"I'll ask around in the market," said Hal. "See if anyone knows her."

"A woman in a grey dress?" Alys said sceptically, sudden giving into despair. "How will you ever find her with that description?"

Hal put his arm around her. "We know more than that. She had child with her that wasn't her own. We can describe Eleanor. And together we'll piece together as much as we can about what she looks like."

Alys turned her face into Hal's shoulder and fought the sob that rose. "We seem so close, but in some ways it's as though we're just as far as when we were in Venice."

He tightened his hold on her, giving her the only comfort he knew how, and she was grateful.

And so it continued. Days of Joanie quitting the rooms at the appointed time, making her way to the market square and scanning the crowds, her eye always on the street, hoping the woman in the grey dress would emerge once again with Eleanor in her arms.

Hal had made his inquiries the best he could, given that there were few enough who had sufficient English to understand what he was asking. The answers were usually in the negative, or responses so vague that they were rendered useless.

Now Alys sat in the room, wearing a loose gown and apron, attempting to paint by the open window. The paints weren't behaving well in the heat and humidity and she was of little mind to manage it. She put down her brush and looked out towards Silver Straete to see if there was any sign of Hal or Joanie. A *houdeslager* patrolled the streets looking for stray dogs. He strode confidently in his wooden shoes, pole in hand, weaving among the carters, servants, tradesmen and strolling men and women.

In the distance she could hear the clacking of looms from the open windows of the houses a few streets over. So much industry, so many people, and among them was her daughter.

She turned back to her work and picked up the brush. The painting was progressing well. She'd sketched the hall of the Merchants' House and the other men in one day, after asking them to gather at the hall, so that she might do it all together. They'd obliged happily as it made good sense to them. She had been amused to note a very dubious painting of King Henry hanging in the hall, along with a dark and unremarkable painting of a man posing with two questionable looking sheep.

With those drawings in hand, she quickly built up her background and, sketching out the men, found some contentment in the splashes of colour in the foreground detail and then working on their robes and head coverings. She'd started on the faces now, the Duke's nose giving her a little trouble as she tried to soften out its heaviness to a more refined and noble quality.

The door opened with a slam. Joanie stood there, her eyes wild. "I found 'er."

"It's too risky. She won't give 'er up," said Joanie.

"Joanie's right. You can't just knock on the door and demand she hand 'er over. She won't do it."

"What do you suggest?" Alys demanded. "I want my daughter back. She has no right to her."

"Stop and think," said Hal. "We need to plan it. Otherwise she could whip her away before you can get 'er and we'll be back to where we started."

Alys bit her lip. She knew Hal was right. They were both right. She couldn't demand Alessandra hand Eleanor to her. Alessandra would never do it. She must be stealthy about it. But since Joanie had returned a few hours before she'd been frantic, fighting the urge to rush over to the house where Joanie had discovered Eleanor was being kept and retrieve her. It was a modest house, down a quiet street of respectable traders and merchants. Unassuming. And behind its façade was a woman Alys hated and her beloved daughter.

"We'll steal her back," said Alys.

"How?" said Joanie. Her tone was cautious. "And then what?"

"We'll leave Bruges."

"But your painting?" asked Hal.

She glanced over at it and thought. "I'll finish it. But in the meantime, we'll plan this carefully. I'll get the money for the commission and when we have Eleanor we'll leave Bruges right away. Go somewhere Alessandra won't find us."

"Where?"

"London. To Queenhithe. Back to where we know. I will be Alys again."

"Alys?" Hal said tentatively.

She looked at him, her expression determined. "Barnabas will find us there."

Hal nodded slowly. "Alys and her brother Hal Goodkin." He looked at Joanie. "And their beloved Joanie."

It was a question. He looked at Joanie for an answer.

"Alys and Hal Goodkin. And their beloved Joanie." She smiled. "I like the sound of that."

〜

They waited patiently in the square. Alys was poised at the edge of the market, a shawl around her arms, ready, while Hal milled about in the crowd that was growing around the small troupe of jugglers who were tossing balls up in the air and performing acrobatics to the amazement of the onlookers. It had taken Hal some time to locate the troupe and engage them for this distraction at a time when it was likely the woman would be out with Eleanor. The troupe had come twice a week for the past fortnight, enough that their appearance took on some semblance of regularity and every servant within the area would have heard of it.

Alys only hoped that today would reap some kind of result. She wasn't certain she'd be able to face one more day here with no sign of her daughter, with no possibility that she would hold her in her arms by nightfall. The painting was finished and delivered, the money now in hand, so there were no other distractions for her to focus on.

And the ship they'd been promised passage on left tonight. There would be another one, but not for a few weeks. At the moment everyone was waiting for the ships from Venice to appear, filled with treasures from the East. Some of those treasures would find their way across the sea to London. So the English ships would wait. The ship that left on the morning's tide which had agreed to give them places was filled with cloth and some perishable fruits that couldn't wait. It was a fortunate turn of events, but only if they had Eleanor.

On the far side of the square, Alys saw Joanie move towards the crowd, glancing back to a figure that followed a short distance behind. The woman, still in the grey dress, a kerchief over her head, clutching a child. Eleanor. Alys's heart quickened.

The woman made her way to the gathered people circling the performers, chatting to Eleanor and pointing. Joanie slowed, allowing the woman to pass, too caught up in her conversation with Eleanor to notice Joanie. The woman pushed her way forward, closer to the performers. Alys watched, her heart in her throat as Eleanor wriggled in the woman's arms, chattering and pointing. The woman laughed and set Eleanor down on the ground, her hands placed protectively in front of the child. Hal worked his way through the crowd until he came to stand behind her. Joanie came up alongside him and gave a nod to the performers.

A ball flew up and out, a hoop circled and rolled towards the crowd and people surged forward, eager to catch a hoop, a ball, laughing at the merry antics. They swarmed past the woman in grey and she tried to grab Eleanor, but the child had gone after the ball, along with the other children and adults intent on the entertainment. Hal blocked her movements and her view, an unintentional move by all appearances, while Joanie glided quickly along to snatch up Eleanor. The little girl squealed in delight, but so many other children were laughing and squealing that it became just another sound added to all the others.

Joanie emerged from the crowd and Alys was there, her arms outstretched. She hugged Eleanor in close to her and quickly covered her daughter's head with the shawl and hastened away, down the street. Searing pain shot down her leg, even with the strapping she'd carefully applied before she'd set out. She hugged her daughter tighter, determined not to fall. She thought of Barnabas, willing him to feel this victory, this joy, wherever he might be. He would find her. Find them. He must.

CHAPTER TWENTY-FOUR
PARIS, EARLY AUTUMN, 1448
BARNABAS

I stared at Hal. There was no mistaking it. It was definitely Hal, his face peering up at me, his figure curved over the lute he held. I could even detect a glint of mischief in his eyes. I looked at the signature and could barely suppress a laugh.

"A fine painting indeed," I said, turning to Julia Barberigo.

From the moment I entered this chamber and saw the painting in its pride of place I had to suppress the great bubble of laughter that welled up in me.

I had found Alessandra's sister to be a meek woman, much put upon by her husband. When I arrived at her home, asking after Alessandra, she'd been tentative at first, though thankfully her husband wasn't at home, so I was able to convince her that I was of no threat to her or her sister. It was then that she'd allowed me to enter the receiving room where she took a seat and I encountered the painting of Hal.

A mixture of relief, joy and admiration flooded me on its sight. Relief and joy that Alys was still alive and well and admiration that she had pieced together Alessandra's trail and had carved out a way to support herself while she followed it. And in such style, too. A painter no less. One A.R. Gregis. I fought another urge to laugh. Who could fail to love such a woman as that? I gave a thought to what her daughter, our daughter, would be like when she was older. Another gem, I didn't doubt. But I must find her first, before Alys, if possible. I must be the one to deal with Alessandra. She was too dangerous for anyone else, and my greatest fear now was that Alys, having found Eleanor, would be harmed or killed trying to get her back. I forced those thoughts out of my mind.

"Yes, we're very happy to have it," said Julia from her seat. "Sadly, the painter is no longer here. He went to Bruges."

"Did he?" I said. My spirits sank for a moment. I reminded myself that at least I knew where she'd gone. Or at least where she'd told Julia Barberigo she'd gone.

"He was called there for a commission. It was something that arose quite suddenly."

"A pity," I said. "I would have liked to meet him."

"That's him in the painting," she said, looking up at it.

"Oh, then you met him. An interesting looking man."

"He was. His speech, unfortunately, was affected by a severe stutter. His sister was there to speak for him on most occasions. A lovely woman. Very pleasant company. And, like you, she knew my sister."

I raised a brow. "That's remarkable. But of course I haven't been in Venice for some time, so it's possible that she met your sister after I left."

"But you heard that she was here?" Julia's expression was puzzled, curious.

"I did. It was Tomaso Cortini who said I might find her here. They were...close friends. Did your sister mention him?"

Julia flushed and looked down at her hands. "No. That is my sister isn't here. But she never mentioned him in her letters, either, so I think your friend is misinformed."

"Oh, a pity. I looked forward to reacquainting myself with Alessandra."

Julia raised her eyes briefly then cast them down again. "Were – were you one of her...close friends too?"

I look at her, pitying her embarrassment at what she clearly knew was her sister's profession. I smiled kindly.

"A long time ago," I said mildly. "There was a fire, you see. Did she mention the fire? She was injured badly. The scars are quite severe. But a remarkable woman. She was able to move on to other avenues. We had an enterprise together. It went well. But then we each pursued other things."

Julia lifted her face and gave a tentative smile. "I'm glad to hear it. I had a letter from her recently, but she mentioned little about Venice."

"But she is well?" I asked, my tone casual.

"She is well," said Julia. "She mentioned something about a venture. She had thought to come here, but she told me in this letter that circumstances prevented her."

"I'm glad to hear she's well. And that she is embarking on another enterprise. I had wished to consult her, to see if she would be interested in working with me on my next project."

Julia gave a hopeful smile. "Perhaps she will. Maybe you can entice her back here. She's in Bruges now."

"Ah, how fortunate! My own plans take me to Bruges. Can you give me her direction? I would like to renew our acquaintance."

"Of course," said Julia.

I smiled widely as she sent for ink, paper, quill as well as refreshments. I was anxious to get back to my rooms to check on Tomaso. He'd been out of sorts since I'd rescued him. I'd tried to get him to eat, but there was little he found interest in. It was a worry, but one that I hope would be solved soon, when he would be reunited with his mistress, Alys. If all went well.

Bruges seemed unchanged. The bustling streets, the energy and the dank smell of the docks. A cooling breeze blew off the canal, signalling that summer was becoming a memory. I had taken a little longer than I'd hoped to get to Bruges, but I was here now, contemplating my next move. But had Alys come here too? It was a question that had dogged me from the time I'd arrived. I'd made a few inquiries already to determine Alessandra's location, but had discovered nothing of use so far. As a consequence, I'd decided to make my way to the English Merchants' House to arrange for some trading and make a few more discreet inquiries in the process.

I arrived at St John's Place and was pleased to see signs of life even at this early in the day. I entered the house, nodding at the two middle-aged men who passed me on their way out. Their hats and light-weight cloaks were dark and conservatively cut in a manner that labelled them English. Probably wool merchants.

In the reception area a man approached, looking at me quizzically. He was a dark-haired, bulky man, but his clothes were finely cut and the cloth expensive. He bowed.

"I am the burgomeester of this merchant house," he said in Flemish. "Can I help you with anything?"

I bowed. "Yes, thank you," I replied in English, smiling pleasantly. "I would like to arrange to trade here. Would it be possible to join the list of English traders?"

"You are new?" He looked me over. "English, but not lately from England?"

"As you say. I am English but I have been abroad for a number of years. I traded here briefly some time ago, but perhaps you don't remember me. My business was small at the time. Since then I've built it to something more substantial from my travels east."

The man smiled and bowed again. "Forgive me, I am John Cardingham. I am pleased to welcome you to the House. You have your credentials with you?"

I returned his bow, withdrew folded parchments from inside my doublet and presented them to him.

Cardingham went over to a table by the light, murmuring briefly to the two men he passed who were consulting a few sheets of paper. I followed quietly and gave the men a nod. Cardingham carefully unfolded the documents and read each one in turn.

While he was reading I studied the room. It was a fair size, the furniture well made, if not graceful or in any way remarkable. The paintings were of uneven quality but one at the far end of the room seemed superior to the others. I went to inspect it closer and eventually came to a halt, staring. There was no need to go any closer to tell me who'd painted the picture. The style, so familiar, so distinct, was enough. Alys. I grinned. I was happy that at least I could mark her progress this far. And it appeared to be fairly recent. With luck she might still be here and Cardingham would know where she'd gone.

"A remarkable painting," I said. "The painter has captured your likeness well."

Cardingham gave me a pleased look. "Thank you. Yes the painter is talented. We were all pleased with the result."

"Is he doing another painting for you?"

Cardingham shook his head. "Sadly, no. Though it was a bit awkward to deal with the man, since he wasn't available to consult in person. He sent his daughter instead, but mark you, she was very talented herself. She did the sketches for him."

I laughed inwardly. "The man's name? It might be that I would know someone who would have a commission for him."

"Gregis," said Cardingham. "Though I understand he is no longer here. He suffers from a severe affliction that leaves him unable to go anywhere. Severe burns, or something of that nature."

"Such a pity for someone so obviously talented. Do you know where he went?"

"No, I don't. But I made no enquiries. Perhaps one of the others here may have had it from the daughter when we were sitting for her." He gestured to the painting. "She had us all assembled in here, as you can see. And she made sketches. They were very good. Good enough to get a very good likeness, as you mentioned."

I nodded at his words. I hid my disappointment at the news that Alys had left, but I wondered if that really was the case. Had she just decided to limit the commissions here to the sole painting in front of me and pursue her search for Alessandra without the need to complete another work? I could only hope so. Tomaso wasn't the only one missing her. Her absence was beginning to tell on my humour and nerves. I was determined to find her.

"Well," said Cardingham. "I've looked through your credentials and I see that they are more than adequate."

He put a hand on my shoulder. "I see no reason why you shouldn't join us as one of our merchants here in Bruges. Welcome to the English Merchants' House, Barnabas Thomason."

I bowed my head and grinned. What would my old Bruges friends, Luigi and Paolo, employees of the Portinari Genoese merchants think? "I'm very appreciative of this opportunity."

~

There was buzz in the air. The ships from Venice were in, bearing all manner of goods from the East, and crowds moved closer to observe the crates, sacks, kegs and other items as they were unloaded. Some ships had already rid themselves of their cargo and were preparing to leave. The docks were alive. Bustling and chaotic, the air was filled with shouts and cries, the creak, clank and groan of winches, straining ropes and the occasional sailor's curse. I walked by the docks, idly scanning the ships in port and looking for an opportunity to question a merchant about Alys or Alessandra, under the guise of having newly joined the English Merchants' House.

I thought it was possible I might see Luigi or Paolo, though it would be better if I didn't. I wouldn't approach them because they knew me by a different identity to the one I had presented to Cardingham and the English Merchants' House. It was a decision I hadn't taken lightly. It was an opportunity to present my real self, to establish me, Barnabas, as a merchant and give up the identity of Giacomo Bonavillagio. That identity carried more risk with it than my true one. The danger that might arise as Barnabas should be long past. It had been seven years and more since the burning of my former mistress Margery Jourdemayne and the witchcraft conviction of the Duchess of Gloucester. Who would remember the little imp, Barnabas, here in Bruges? Or anywhere else? It was time. I was going to set out on a different course. I had taken the first step. The next step would be to find Eleanor and Alys. And then convince Alys we could begin a new life together. If only she would have me.

I rubbed the short trimmed beard I'd kept since returning from Samarkand. It was doubtful that Luigi or Paolo would even remember me, the cheeky lad they shared drinks and gamed with, among other things, years before. But keeping the beard wouldn't hurt. And my manner and dress were so different now.

I looked over at a man standing near the dock's edge, surveying a ship that was being unloaded onto couple of boats. I recognised him from the English Merchants' House, I thought, and decided to take the risk.

"Mynheere?" I said.

The man, dark and thin as the staff he held, turned to me. His eyes were slate coloured and they surveyed me coolly.

"Yes?" he said in heavily accented Flemish.

"I am sorry to trouble you," I said English. "But I saw you recently in the English Merchants' House. I was presenting my credentials to Mynheere Cardingham. I am Barnabas Thomson. English, but newly arrived from Venice."

The man's expression warmed a little. "Of course. George Wallingford. You have a ship arriving?"

"No. My own goods are already in hand. I was hoping to locate a friend that I heard was newly arrived here too. He was accompanying a Venetian woman. Alessandra Cardina. It is with her I wish to speak. Have you heard tell of them?"

Wallingford shook his head. "No one of that name."

I shrugged. "It was worth a try. But it's nothing urgent. I'm certain I will see her and my friend at some stage."

"Is your friend a merchant?"

"No. But Alessandra's husband was. That's why I thought you might know of her, if she's arrived, yet."

"I'm sorry I couldn't be of more help," said Wallingford. "You might ask at the Venetian House."

I nodded and after a few more exchanges of pleasantries we parted.

I continued on, not quite ready to give up. I didn't really want to go asking around the Venetian merchants. I stood idly looking through the various clusters of people on shore and then switching my eyes to the passengers disembarking from the ship nearest me. Something caught my eye in a boat beyond, rowing out to a ship anchored a short ways out. I wasn't certain if it was the dark veil that flapped in the wind that I'd noticed, or the whole manner and stance of the woman who stood on deck. The figure was ramrod stiff, the anger present even at this distance. I stared at the figure, unbelieving. Alessandra.

Her arms were empty. Beside her was another figure, a woman standing close by. Her servant, I imagined, but her arms were empty too. I looked around her, hoping to see some sign of my daughter, but there was nothing. The boat had halted by a ship and the passengers were slowly boarding with the help of the sailors. I squinted, trying to see the name of the vessel. It was a single-masted crayer commonly used to cross the Channel. It couldn't be going far. Not to Venice, in any case.

I turned and scanned the people around me, searching out a sailor, or anyone who might be able to tell me something more. I spied a young man standing there, a small notebook in his hand, scribbling something inside it. I approached him quickly.

"Excuse me, young mynheere," I said in Flemish. I pointed to the ship. "Would you know anything about that ship?"

The young lad looked up at me and followed the direction of my finger. He studied the ship, frowned and shook his head. He glanced over to his right, called out rapidly to a man bending over a pile of coiled ropes some distance away. The man hesitated by his ropes and looked where the young clerk had indicated. A moment later he shouted back. His words were just as rapid and I struggled to understand. The young clerk, seeing my struggle obligingly repeated the words.

"The ship is the *Mary Louise*," he said. "It's English, bound for London at the next tide."

The next tide. By my estimation that would be in about an hour's time.

"Would your friend know if there is any space on that ship?" I asked, daring to hope.

The young clerk shouted to the rope coiler again. I needed no translation for his answer. The shake of his head told me everything. I would have to wait until the next ship to get passage to London. I only prayed that it would be soon and there would be space for me.

CHAPTER TWENTY-FIVE
LONDON, LATE AUTUMN 1448
ALYS

Alys smoothed her hand over the golden head that lay against her chest. It didn't worry her that she'd been seated here for two hours, her child cradled in her arms, sound asleep. Even her leg felt good. Eleanor still had fits of bad dreams, waking up, crying and fearful. Alys could only imagine what troubled her daughter, because she could get few words from her as young as she was. All she knew was that despite Eleanor's seeming good physical health, her mind was sometimes troubled.

The bubbly, bright young baby Alys remembered was now replaced by a solemn little girl, whose large eyes, so like Barnabas's, stared out at her with traces of caution and hesitation. It was an improvement on the terrified and unresponsive child that she'd taken from Alessandra's servant over a month ago. Alys knew it was risky to snatch Eleanor from the servant she'd come to know and feel secure with, but there'd been no choice. It had been difficult, especially at first, to get Eleanor to trust her, to allow her to even touch her without pulling away. Joanie had helped, soothing and clucking over Eleanor so carefully.

It had taken some time before Eleanor would allow Alys to hold her and then it had only been for a brief embrace, after time spent with Alys sitting next to her. Only then would she allow Alys to slide her arm around her shoulder. Then, early this morning, when Alys had rushed to her screaming daughter's beside after she'd awakened from a bad dream, Eleanor had crept onto her lap and snuggled in, resting her head on Alys's shoulder.

She was still a little wary of Hal, but Alys believed that was because Eleanor wasn't familiar with him in the way she was with Joanie or herself. Over the days it was as though Eleanor started to remember her mother, her real mother, whether it was her voice, her scent or something more intangible, but it warmed Alys to see it grow.

They still needed to be careful how they behaved towards the child, keeping even voices, a reassuring manner and slow movements. The reasons why her own daughter would require such an approach she put out of her mind as much as possible.

Eleanor stirred and Alys eased her neck and shoulders. She felt a contentment she hadn't felt in a long time. Not since she'd been a young girl in Queenhithe, her mother well, Hal teasing her and her father earning a wage. How old had she been then? Very young.

The bed, so comfortable with its feather tick and mounds of cushions, seemed hard as a bare wooden board now. The room was still warm enough, though. She'd ensured there was a brazier available for the rooms when she'd rented them after they first arrived in London. Though she'd been tempted to go to the familiar quarters of Queenhithe, she'd decided to try somewhere else, felt it might be safer, though the name she gave to the owner of the large, respectable inn was her own.

The door opened and Joanie peeked around. She smiled at the sight of the two of them.

"Little duckling still asleep?" she asked in a whisper.

Alys nodded. "She's hardly stirred."

"Poor little lamb." She moved quietly over to her and softly patted the child's cheek. "I've been out to the market. I've some fresh made bread, some ale and pies."

"Where's Hal?" asked Alys.

Joanie pressed her lips together. "Gone to ask around for some work."

"No," said Alys, hoarsely. "I told him not to."

"Still, needs must. We can't live on that money forever."

"We won't have to. I'm certain of that. Besides, I have other plans. Hal doesn't have to labour on the docks anymore."

Joanie raised her brow. "You intend to keep us all with your painting?"

"And why not?"

"It's fine for a little while, but you can't be doing it forever. People will find out, and then what will you do? What will they do to you? To Eleanor? No, you can't."

"I'm not saying it would be forever."

Joanie shook her head. "I'll say no more on it. But you'll have to take it up with your brother. 'e won't be so easy to overrule."

She'd told the innkeeper her husband was a merchant and due to return from Venice at some point in the near future. She'd explained that they had been abroad for a number of years and were now returning to London, where he would run his affairs from now on.

Joanie and Hal had frowned at these statements and hardly softened when she'd presented Joanie as her dear friend and Hal as her brother. When Joanie questioned the wisdom of it, Alys had told her it was the perfect disguise, since Alessandra had no idea what her real name was, or that Hal was her brother and Joanie her friend. "Especially when the two of you finally get married. That would be an even better disguise," she'd said. That had only brought embarrassed and reddened faces from the two of them and a sigh from her. Someday they would have to settle this.

"More to the point," said Joanie after a moment. "You can't be going around creating paintings if you don't want that woman to find you. She'll know it's you who's painted them. And then where will you be? She'll find out where you are, that's what, no matter that you're using what she thinks is a false name."

Alys bit her lip. "I can try a different name and a different approach. And she would only know if she discovered that I've come here with Eleanor."

Joanie sighed again and shook her head. The door in the outside room opened.

"That'll be Hal. I'll just tell him to be quiet," said Joanie.

She disappeared into the other room. The murmurs from their conversation drifted to her ears. She laid her head back against the wall, thinking about Joanie's words again. She would try for commissions, despite Joanie's concerns. She wanted to paint. And with some effort she could try different subject matters, a new style. She'd study the paintings in the churches and get acquainted with the clergy who might give her a commission using the same ruse she had in Bruges. She knew she couldn't do it forever, but she would make it work until Barnabas arrived.

She had toyed with the idea of writing a letter to Barnabas, care of one of his old friends in Venice, but she wasn't certain it was the best course. Now, she decided she must try. Carefully, she lay Eleanor aside and put her gently on the bed, pulled the coverlet up and tucked her in. She stretched, easing the ache in her back and the rest of her body. Out in the other room she could hear angry whispers exchanged between Hal and Joanie. With a sigh, she dragged on a simple gown over her shift and pulled at the laces the best she could. Joanie would have to finish them off.

She opened the door and went into the room. The anger was written clearly on Hal and Joanie's faces.

"What is it? Why are you two arguing?"

"You're up," said Joanie. "What about Eleanor?"

"It's fine. She's still sleeping. I just came out to get you to lace me up. I have a few things I need to do, but I'll still keep an eye on her if she wakes up."

Joanie glanced at Hal. She sighed. "Go on then. You may as well give it to 'er now."

"Give me what?"

Hal handed a folded note. It was sealed with wax but there was writing on the outside. "It's addressed to you. I thought you should 'ave it now, but Joanie said to wait. That you should 'ave a few more moments of joy."

Alys grew cold when she heard his words. Silently, growing numbness spreading throughout her, she reached for the note. The familiar writing blurred. She blinked, forcing her eyes to focus. She broke the seal, unfolded the paper and began to scan its contents.

"What does Alessandra say?" Hal said, his anger barely contained.

Alys looked up and stared into space. "She says she's coming here today. She says I will give her back Eleanor when I hear what she has to say. That I must not try to evade this meeting, or take Eleanor away, because the consequences to us will be too dire to contemplate."

"What!" Hal said. "She's bluffing."

"You can't do what she says," said Joanie. She began to pace. "What can she mean by it, though? What could she possibly do that would make us give over our little darling?"

Alys shook her head slowly, too numb to respond.

"What if it's Jacko, I mean Barnabas?" said Hal, his anger turned cold. "Maybe she 'as 'im captive and she'll kill 'im if we don't give 'er Eleanor."

"No, she couldn't 'ave," said Joanie. "Could she? Surely Barnabas is too wily for that. Besides, where would she 'ave got 'im? He's probably somewhere beyond Samarkand now, still thinking Alessandra's there."

Alys heard this discussion as if at a distance, the words swirling around her until finally, they settled. And her mind became clear. Her actions became clear.

"Joanie, get Eleanor dressed. Hal, I want you to take her somewhere safe. The church in Queenhithe. Stay there with her until we send word. I'll meet with Alessandra and see what she says."

She would hear out Alessandra, weigh the threat, but under no circumstances would she give her daughter back to that woman.

~~~

Alys stiffened on the small cushioned bench where she was sitting when she heard the knock. Beside her Joanie squeezed her hand and then rose to answer it. They'd been waiting for hours, Alys's mind conjuring all sorts of possibilities. But now the moment was here. She would discover exactly how Alessandra meant to manipulate her into surrendering her daughter.

Joanie opened the door and Alessandra stood there, paused on the threshold for a moment. She wore the familiar dark veil that fell past her shoulders, and her gown was of a rich velvet madder red, under a dark cloak edged with fur. She wore matching leather gloves that she now held clasped in front of her. Alessandra entered the room, brushing past Joanie without a glance and gave Alys a regal nod. She crossed the room and took a seat next to Alys.

"Maria, *cara*," she said in Italian. "So good of you to see me. As a newcomer to London, I find it reassuring to see a familiar face."

"Please, Alessandra, dispense with the pretence. Just state what you have to say and take your leave."

"Very well. Should I perhaps call you Alys, then? And then all pretence can be swept away?"

Alys's eyes darkened. "You know my real name."

"Of course *cara*, did you think I wouldn't find out? That's the problem. You've always underestimated me."

"It wasn't a question of underestimation. It was a question of limited choices and trust. Though perhaps not so much trust." Alys recalled the time she'd seen Alessandra holding the newborn Eleanor in an unguarded moment, her veil off, her scarred face showing visible tenderness. "I thought I could trust you with Eleanor. Keep her safe until my return."

"But did I not do that? She came to no harm under my care. She was fed, clothed and guarded like any dear child would be." Her voice was nearly a purr. "She wanted for nothing," she added with an edge to her voice.

"She didn't have her mother. No matter what you gave to her physically, you couldn't give her that."

Alessandra stiffened. "She didn't need you. She had me. I was as much a mother to her as you could ever be."

"I doubt that. Even if she wasn't suffering from nightmares, I will always wonder exactly what you did to her under your care."

"I did nothing," she said, her voice soft and silky again. "She loved the journeys, the various animals. Did you know she laughed when she first saw a camel?"

"You took her east?" Alys could barely control her rage. "You went on the trading route?"

"I did. And what a merry time we had. Such exotic places. The landscape, so dry at times, the sun so strong, I had to be certain Eleanor's fair skin was completely covered. She would keep removing the head cover. In the end I had to get a servant to mind her in a litter."

"How could you put Eleanor in danger like that?" said Joanie in Italian, visibly shaken. "She could have been struck down by some foreign illness, or killed in an attack. That just proves you're no mother. No mother would do that."

Alessandra turned to Joanie. "Be quiet, woman. No one asked for your comments."

"Nevertheless, every word she spoke is true," said Alys.

"I took all necessary precautions. She was never in danger. And Samarkand is much more cultured than any place that you could imagine. Especially this filthy damp hole you call London."

Samarkand. So Barnabas had been right. Tears pricked Alys's eyes. She had doubted him. Doubted his gifts, or at least his ability to understand what he'd seen. Or thought it might have been some leftover imagining from his former opium use. She put these thoughts aside and frowned at Alessandra.

"However risky and foolish the decisions you made were, they are in the past. What we need to address is now. And that you are in no measure going to have Eleanor."

"Ah, but I think you may find yourself changing your mind."

"I doubt that. There's nothing you can say that will bring that about."

"Oh, but I beg to differ. As I stated before, you underestimate me. I know all about you, Alys. And I have it at my disposal to make it impossible for you to support yourself and your child in London. I could also, for example, explain to anyone who cared to listen that you were a glorified whore in Venice, no matter what you might say about being a merchant's wife."

Alys strove for calm. "You may say what you choose. You have no proof of these statements."

"Ah but I do. I have your contracts, for one. And I have other proofs. Letters, notes, poems."

Alys paled. "That's of no account. They are for a woman named Maria. Not Alys."

"Ah, but then the paintings. Hmm. Did I not send one to my sister for safekeeping? Perhaps you saw it?"

"That means nothing," said Alys. "Only that I posed for a painter."

"Oh, but surely a letter from said painter explaining that the woman in the painting is the one and same whore named Maria, whose virtue was purchased at a very high price?"

Alys pursed her lips together. She had nothing to say to that and she knew it.

"Now, where is the child?"

"She's not here. She's out. With my brother."

"Your brother? Would that be the man who was Giacomo's companion?"

Alys looked up sharply. Another part of her life that Alessandra had discovered.

Alessandra laughed. "You still think I was lying when I said I knew all about you. Is that not enough proof? Or should I say more? Should I tell you about your lover, Giacomo? Giacomo who has bedded every whore and woman I threw at him from here to Samarkand."

"He wouldn't do that," Alys said firmly.

"Of course he would. He's Giacomo. Did I not throw him in your path and, despite his better judgement he succumbed? Though I know he prefers them dark haired, as he once told me, he knew I had groomed you. That, I was sure, would make you irresistible to him."

Alys rose stiffly. "I think it's time you left."

"But I am waiting for Eleanor."

"You won't have her, not today. I must prepare her. Tomorrow. You can come for her tomorrow."

Alessandra stood gracefully and lightly placed her hand on Alys's shoulder. "Tomorrow, then. Out of the kindness of my heart, I will wait until then. But no tricks or games. I have no patience for that, and you can be certain that if you try, you will suffer the consequences greatly."

Without any further word Alessandra drew her cloak around her and left.

When she'd gone Joanie crossed the room and drew Alys back down beside her, taking her hand. "Surely you're not going to give her Eleanor?"

Alys shook her head. "No. I'm going to kill her instead."

Joanie looked dumbfounded for a moment and then she smiled. "I'll help you in any way I can."

Alys stood and went to the window. Outside, in the street below, she watched Alessandra's retreating figure, a servant woman following in her wake. She would find a way. She would talk to Hal. He would know someone who would help, she was certain.

As if she had summoned him, Hal appeared, threading his way hurriedly through the people in the street. She watched him enter and heard his footsteps as he took the stairs at a bound. He burst through the door.

"She's taken her. That bitch of a woman has taken Eleanor."

Alys and Joanie stared at Hal, unable to comprehend his words.

"What 'appened?"

"How?" said Alys faintly.

"Two men." His voice went hoarse, the distress clear in his tone. "They attacked me from the back, took Eleanor. It wasn't that far from 'ere. I went after them, but I didn't catch them. They disappeared for a moment, and then the next thing I saw them on 'orses. That bastard woman."

"It was all a ruse," said Alys in a whisper. "She came here as a distraction, when really all along she planned to snatch Eleanor back." She looked at Hal. "She knew I wouldn't allow Eleanor to be in the same rooms while she was here. And if Eleanor had been here, she would have taken her. Either way, she knew she would win.".

CHAPTER TWENTY-SIX
LONDON, LATE AUTUMN 1448
BARNABAS

I stared at the outside of the Turk's Head. Its sign was perhaps a little more weather-beaten, the door bearing more gouges and chips, and the shutters more adrift, but largely it remained unchanged. That surprised and comforted me in equal measure. So much had happened in the intervening years since I'd been here, that it was unnerving to see some part of my old life still so unchanged, but it also gave me hope that my old contacts would be here to help me.

I entered the tavern and blinked at the darkness. Thick smoke from the fire wafted towards me from the draught of the door opening. I glanced around as my vision adjusted and noted the familiar stools and the ale kegs balanced on a long bench, and the line of tankards and cups. I weaved my way through the seated men and occasional drab, perched on a knee or rubbing the arm of a blurry eyed drinker, and found a corner from which I could observe the room. I didn't want to make myself known to my old friend the tavern owner, Jack

Hodgekiss, immediately. It seemed best to assess the situation first, ensure that he still owned it, for one, and that he hadn't changed in any significant manner that would make identifying myself to him dangerous.

It was my old sense of self preservation, so necessary as an orphan growing up in Queenhithe and Eye by Westminster, come to life again. Though if I admitted it to myself, it had never deserted me. I'd used it all these years, albeit in different guises, and it had kept me whole and alive so far.

I spied Jack talking to some sailors in the far end of the room. He was a little stooped, his great mane of black hair was threaded with grey, but other than that he seemed much the same. There was no sign of his wife. She was most likely out, because he'd pulled up a stool and was having a cosy chat. I decided to watch for a while and then wait for an opportunity to catch his attention, rather than approach him directly.

It took a while, but eventually he looked up, scanned the room quickly and then saw me, a new customer. He slapped one of the men on the back and with a few parting words made his way to me.

"A pot of ale, my fine fella?" he said to me in his best voice.

I stifled a laugh and grinned at him. "That's very proper speech for you, Jack."

Jack stared at me uneasily. "Do I know you?"

I laughed. "Well it has been a few years," I said and fell into my old accent. "But back along we was partners. Business partners. We did a bit of this, a bit of that."

He looked at me in disbelief. "Barney?" he said softly. "Can it be?"

"The very same."

Jack shook his head. "No. It can't be."

I nodded to the stool beside me. "Sit. We can catch up. But bring two pots of ale before you do. And don't worry, I'll pay for both of them."

Jack gave a hearty laugh. "Either you've changed or you ain't Barney."

"Come and find out," I said genially.

It wasn't long before he was seated beside me and each of us was sipping a pot of ale. I drank deep, savouring the flavour. Jack always did brew a good ale and this time he hadn't weakened it for my benefit.

He saw my approval. "I didn't water it down, Figured you're a man, now. No need."

"Yes. It's been many years since I was here, drinking watered ale. Though I don't think you watered it for my benefit."

"Maybe not," he said, a twinkle in his eye. He gave me a direct look. "But lad, where've you been? You disappeared without a trace all them years ago." He tugged my fine doublet. "And you're dressed like nobility and you talk like it too."

The light banter had helped me to judge what I might say to him next. I took a deep breath. "I left because of what was going on at the time. Because of the woman I worked for. And others who were connected to me. I went abroad. I've done well out of it, as it happened."

That woman I'd worked for was Margery Jourdemayne. She'd been a wise woman, who some called a witch. She'd helped the Duchess of Gloucester to conceive a child, and used my abilities with the showstone. The Duchess's political rivals had Margery and the Duchess arrested for treason and witchcraft. Margery was eventually burned as a witch. It was all seven years ago, but I needed to know if there was any lingering sentiment or interest in pursuing her associates. I hadn't mentioned her name because I wasn't going to take any risks, but I thought Jack would remember. At least I hoped so.

"Oh, aye," he said eventually. "I 'eard tell of that, now that I think on it. It set London all acluck at the time. I forgot you worked for 'er. But lad, that was a long time ago. Things have moved on. The Duchess is dead and so is the Duke. No one is worried about that anymore."

I sighed with relief, not realising how anxious I had been. Though my rational mind told me it was unlikely that anyone would be looking for me, the years al Qali spent ingraining the worry in me were hard to shake. But I could trust Jack on this.

"Well that's welcome news," I said. "One less thing to worry about."

"You got troubles?"

"Of a sort. I'll tell you all in a moment. But first I need to ask you if you've heard anything about a woman I know that has newly arrived—"

Jack put his hand up to cut me off. "Before you say more, let me just tell you that some fella has been coming every few days asking after you. I should have said earlier but, well, I wanted to hear what 'appened to you."

"Someone has been asking for me?" I said incredulously. My mind spun wildly to consider the possibilities. "What did he look like? Did he say who he was?"

"Let me think, now. He were stocky and fair-haired. I think 'e said he were called Hal. I seem to remember he said he drank in here on occasion some years back before 'e went to sea. His speech weren't quite Queenhithe, but I suppose that changed from being away."

My spirits rose so much at his words that I had to resist the urge to embrace him. As it is I clapped him on the back.

"Truly? That's marvellous news. Did he say where he was staying?"

"Now that 'e didn't. But I do suppose 'e'll be back one day soon and I can tell 'im where you are."

I put aside my disappointment that I couldn't go there now, at this moment and tried assure myself that the solution Jack proposed was good enough. I opened my mouth to give him the name of the inn where I'd secured rooms on my arrival when the door opened. I looked over and saw Hal, standing there blinking, scanning the room. It took a few moments, but he found me, surprise on his face that was quickly replaced by a thunderous expression. He strode over and hauled me up from the stool. I was too stunned to react.

"You!" he shouted. "This is all your fault. If you hadn't pursued some hare-brained idea of your own, instead of staying with us, then she would never have been taken again."

I stared at him a moment, trying to make sense of his words. "What? What's happened, Hal. Who was taken – Alys? Is Alys all right?"

"Besides being upset beyond words that her daughter is gone, she's fine."

"Wait. Eleanor was taken again? Do you mean you got her back from Alessandra?"

Hal frowned. "Just come with me. You can talk to Alys yourself. Though she's not best pleased with you, if you ask me. You've lot to explain for yourself."

I nodded and took my leave of Jack, who sat bewildered on his stool. I followed Hal out of the *Turk's Head*, trying to make sense of the conversation and fighting the guilt that I'd suppressed for so long over parting with Alys in Tyre. I'd gone over and over the reasons in my mind so often and carried on, determined to prove I was right. But what had it gained me in the end?

✺

I entered the room tentatively. I'd opted to go first, to see Alys's reaction to my appearance as soon as she saw me, so that I might judge what I should say. But it all flew from my head when I saw her standing by the window, a letter in her hand, surprise written all over her face.

We stood staring at each other for a moment, Joanie and Hal forgotten.

"I found 'im in the *Turk's 'ead*, as luck would have it," Hal said with a growl.

"The *Turk's 'ead*?" said Joanie darkly. She was seated on a bench, mending in her hand. "What were you doing there, if you please?"

Hal gave her an amused look. "Nothing you wouldn't like. I've been going there sometimes to see if anyone 'eard if Barnabas was about. It's where 'e used to go when he was young, or so 'e told me. Figured it was worth a try."

"Aren't you the clever one," said Joanie, trying to suppress a grin. She looked at me. "And what 'ave you got to say for yourself?"

I drew my eyes away from Alys and looked at Joanie, trying to collect my thoughts. "Hal said Eleanor's been taken again. She was here with you?"

"She was, you clod. I told you that already," said Hal.

"Quiet there, Hal," said Joanie. "We took her in Bruges, came here, but she found us. And yesterday she tricked us. Came here to see Alys, she said, because she said she would tell us something that would make us give her Eleanor. So Hal took Eleanor to the church in Queenhithe, meanwhile while she was here, she sent men to snatch Eleanor back."

"I saw her leave Bruges," I said. "She was boarding a ship and I was on the dock. I looked but couldn't see Eleanor." I turned back to Alys, grief, remorse, frustration and a hint of melancholy warring inside me. "But you had her. How was she? Had she been harmed?" I looked at Alys appealingly.

Sorrow filled Alys's face and she bit her lip. "Oh, Barnabas. I'm so sorry you missed it. You missed her."

She turned away and I went to her, folded her in my arms and pressed a kiss on her head. "My darling, darling Alys. It's I who should be sorry."

Alys collected herself and pulled away. She searched my face. "She said you have been whoring your way to Samarkand. I believe her exact words were that you have 'bedded every whore and woman I threw at him from here to Samarkand'."

"Who? Do you mean Alessandra?"

"Who else?" demanded Joanie. "And don't pretend it's a surprise. I know your past, remember. You were warming Alessandra's bed and plenty others, I'll be bound."

"Alys, listen to me. She was telling lies." I looked at Hal. "Have I ever had a woman in all the time I was in your company?"

Hal looked uncomfortable. "Well, no. But ...there were reasons for some of it."

I sighed and put a hand under Alys's chin. "I swear to you on our daughter's life, Alessandra is full of lies. I love you Alys, you know that. I wouldn't do that, not when I was searching for our daughter."

She searched my eyes. "Find her, Barnabas. Find our daughter. We can't let that woman have her any longer."

I kissed her. "I will do everything in my power to get Eleanor back. I promise you that."

"If you get her back, I can bear anything you might have to tell me Barnabas," she said softly.

"There's nothing to tell," I whispered in her ear. "Except to say how much I love you and that I am so desperately sorry I left you in Tyre."

"But you were right," she murmured. "Your vision was true. I shouldn't have doubted you."

"You were right to doubt and I can only wish that we had made the journey back together. So much wasted time."

"You will get her back." It was half question, half statement. And it pained me to hear it put in that manner.

"I will," I said firmly. "If I have to expend my last breath doing so."

I held her tightly and she slowly relaxed in my arms. We stood like that in silence for a few moments, my thoughts slowly turning to how I was to fulfil the promise I had just made.

CHAPTER TWENTY-SEVEN
LONDON, LATE AUTUMN, 1448
BARNABAS

"You're certain that's what he said?" I asked Jack.

He nodded. "The woman was foreign, wearing a dark veil like I said already. And she 'ad a child and servant with 'er. Saw 'er going into a building just by *The Barge*. 'e was on 'is way there with two of his mates."

"You don't know which building?"

Jack shrugged. "That's all I got from 'im. Drunk, 'e was. I'd been asking others to keep a look out and someone brought me to 'im, said 'e was talking about some foreign lady with a dark veil. Said the servant gave a right shove as 'e passed 'im, muttering some foreign gibberish."

I clapped Jack on the back, sparing a satisfied glance for Hal. "You've done well, old friend. I won't forget it."

"Imagine that. Barney with a child," Jack said shaking his head. "Good luck with it and I'll let you know if I 'ear anything else."

"Thanks."

I gave him a smile and bid him farewell. I made my way out of the tavern, Hal following.

"What do you want to do now?" asked Hal. He had softened his attitude to me once Alys had explained that Alessandra had gone to Samarkand. There were still traces of enmity, though. It would take time. Until then, I knew I could at least rely on him to help me get Eleanor back.

I looked at him, deciding finally on a plan. "We'll go to *The Barge* and have a look, first."

It didn't take us long to find the place. It was north of the *Turk's Head*, near St Stephen's Wallbrook, as Jack said. My memory of London's streets came flooding back as long-forgotten landmarks appeared, allowing me to make good progress, Hal struggling to keep up with me. The sense of urgency grew as I neared the area, something telling me that time wasn't on my side and Alessandra would soon be gone, vanishing with Eleanor for good.

We drew up beside *The Barge* and I studied the surrounding buildings. One was a shop, with its stall just outside, and on the other side was a small alley with a larger building next to it. It was a two storey wattle and daub building, the cross beams darkened with age. I strained to look through the window facing the street, but I could see little from my vantage point.

"Knock on the door, Hal," I said. "See if anyone is there."

"What should I say?"

"Just ask if there are any rooms available."

Hal nodded and I watched him cross the street and knock on the door. I could feel the tension growing inside me as a woman opened the door and conversed with Hal. She shook her head after a little while and I tried to decide whether that was a good sign or not.

Finally, unable to contain myself, I crossed the street, weaving through a group of children running down towards the church and reached Hal's side.

"Sorry that I was delayed," I said to Hal. I turned to the woman. "I don't know if my friend has explained the situation."

"He said he was looking for rooms. I tell you what I told him. There aren't any available at the moment, but there might be in a few days. The lady said she was leaving soon."

I kept my expression neutral. "Oh, really? Is the lady here at the moment? Perhaps I could ask her directly when she plans to depart. It's only that I have some cargo arriving and I want to ensure I can put one of the chests in my room."

The woman's interest was piqued, I could tell, but she shook her head. "I'm sorry, but she's not here right now. She went out with the child some time ago and I haven't seen her since."

"You wouldn't happen to know where she went? Or when she might return?"

Again the shake of the head. I fought the disappointment. I wanted Eleanor now. I'd had an idea of forcing my way into Alessandra's rooms and seizing my daughter. But that idea was thwarted.

Resigned to delaying any action, I gave the woman my thanks and promised I would return in a few days' time to inquire again.

I walked a short way down the street and turned to Hal. "Stay here and see if she comes back. If she does, grab a lad and send me a message."

Hal nodded. "What will you do?"

"I'll tell Jack what happened and see if he can find out anything more and then let Alys know. I don't like the fact that Alessandra has left and taken Eleanor with her, going who knows where. It certainly wasn't to arrange passage across the Channel. She would send her servant to do that. No, there's something more going on here."

I bid Hal farewell and took off, heading towards Jack's tavern. I arrived there nearly breathless and entered the dark room. I heard Jack's laugh before I saw him. It stopped when he saw me.

He approached me quickly, drew me to the side and asked me in a low voice, "Well? Do you find out anything?"

"She has rooms there, like you said, but she's not there at the moment. Have you heard anything more about her? What ship she came in on, for instance?"

"Nothing, Barney boy, not a thing."

I frowned, thinking furiously. "Can you find out when the next ship to cross the channel is sailing and if there are any passengers of her description going?"

"I'll do my best," he said. He squeezed my arm. "You'll find the little 'un. I feel sure of it."

"I hope you're right, Jack."

I left the tavern and fingered the small mirror that hung on its chain around my neck. It wasn't the first time I'd been tempted to use it since leaving Samarkand. I'd resisted up until now, certain that I was following the right trail. But now, everything seemed urgent, time wasn't to be wasted. I darted into an alley and weaved my way to the church I knew was nearby. It was taking a chance, to use something that could be construed as witchcraft by any curious person, and even blasphemous that I would use it in a church. But it was the quietest place I could think of.

I slipped inside and went to a small side chapel around the back of the altar. There was just enough light to see. I held up the mirror, tried to calm my breath and focus on the image in front of me. I had seen Eleanor in this mirror before, symbolised through a small unicorn surrounded by a wall of flames. I recalled that image, focused again and cast about in the reflection for any hint of a vision.

It was slow in coming, my heartbeat accelerating as I waited for it to form. Please let her be whole, unharmed, I prayed. This time the unicorn was standing beside a tall woman, her hair a nest of snakes swirling around. Around them were chests spilling with jewels and fine cloth of gold. The woman fingered the cloth, smiling slowly. A gold chain hung from the unicorn's throat and its end was fastened around the lady's wrist. I scanned the surroundings, looking for clues, but it was dark, for the most part, the only light coming from a window that was narrow and deep set in a stone wall. I blinked again, but the image disappeared.

"Hello?" called a voice.

I tucked the little mirror back in my doublet and rose. It was the priest. He gave me a puzzled look, taking in my fine clothes and demeanour.

"Sorry, Father. I came into pray and when I knelt, a pin fell from my doublet. I went to retrieve it."

His face cleared. "Of course. I'm sorry to disturb you."

I nodded to him and he left. I removed the little mirror again and tried briefly to recapture the image, even though I knew it was no use. There would be no more visions. I had all the clues I was going to get. Which amounted to very little.

❧

"A unicorn?" said Alys, tears in her eyes. "What does that mean?"

I'd returned to the rooms and given Alys and Joanie a brief explanation of what happened and they were trying to make sense of it all.

"It's Eleanor," I said. "I saw her before, in Samarkand." I held up the small polished mirror. "In this. Ulugh Beg, the Transoxiania ruler gave it to me." I explained about the vision I'd seen there. "I've never seen Eleanor, don't forget," I said softly.

Alys stared at me, stunned. "No. Of course. I keep forgetting that." She frowned. "So you think she is in danger? That Alessandra has something planned for her? But what could it be?"

She began to pace until Joanie stopped her and put her arm around her. "Calm yourself, duckling. We'll think this through." She looked up at me and her expression held command. "Won't we?"

I nodded and went to Alys and pulled her into an embrace.

"We will. I've already thought some of it through. Alessandra has set herself up as a merchant, that much we know. I think the cloth and the jewels tell us that."

"You think she is here as a merchant?" Alys asked doubtfully.

"Alessandra can never resist an opportunity to turn a profit," I said. "I've told Jack to ask around. I also told him to check when the next ships are leaving port to cross the Channel."

Alys pulled back and looked at him. "You think she's leaving. On the next tide?"

I shrugged. "I can't be certain, but it's worth checking." I kissed her head. "I'll leave now and find out what he's discovered, if anything. Failing that, I'll find out myself."

Alys grabbed my hand. "I'm going with you."

I shook my head. "It's better if you stay here. Out of harm's way."

"No. I can't stay here waiting any longer. I want to be there when you find her." She touched the dagger hanging from my side. "Because if you don't succeed in killing that woman, I will."

❧

"A warehouse," I said quietly. "Yes, it makes sense." I looked at Alys and could see she understood.

"That's what Geordo told me," said Jack. "Mind you, it took a little persuasion, since 'e was paid to keep 'is mouth shut. But giving 'im a promise that you'd pay 'im well to boot, kind of opened the dam, if you like. 'e started telling me 'ow the woman had 'im lugging crates and chests from the warehouse onto a cart. Paid him well, but very off hand with 'im. Slapped his head a few times, called 'im imbecile when 'e dropped one chest that was too 'eavy for 'im."

"And where was he taking the chests?" I asked.

"To the dock, he said. To *The Fleur*. She sails tonight. Crossing the channel."

"When did he load the carts?"

"Earlier today. Noontide?"

"Where's the warehouse?"

"At Broken Wharf. You know it?"

I nodded. "Near here. Next to Queenhithe docks."

"That's right," said Jack. He glanced around. "Do you want me to come with you?"

I shook my head. "No, but can you send a lad to Hal and tell him to meet us there?"

Jack glanced at Alys but only nodded. I squeezed his shoulder in thanks and, grabbing Alys's hand, left the tavern.

Alys trailed beside me, struggling to keep up in patens that slid a little on the cobbled streets. I had leather boots on, so had better purchase on the slippery stone, wet with the late Autumn rains and fog that hung on London's riverbanks at this time of year. Our breath formed clouds in the late afternoon as we hurried along, determined to cover the distance as quickly as possible.

We arrived outside the warehouse and I scanned the building quickly. There was nothing to give me any clue as to its contents or if anyone was inside. The double doors were firmly closed and the shutters fixed tight. It seemed deserted.

Alys dragged me up to the door and gave it a good shove. Surprisingly, it was unbolted. I took her hand and pulled her behind me, entering the warehouse cautiously. It was a dark inside, with a shaft of light coming from a narrow window above. Gradually I made out the chests, crates and barrels that were stacked against the wall on the side opposite to the window. Bales of straw were piled on the opposite side, some of them opened and strewn around the floor, a large part of it most likely serving as packing material for the delicate pottery and other fragile goods that came and went in this warehouse.

I made my way forward slowly, my eyes adjusting to the low light. Ahead I could hear voices and realised they were coming from a room at the back of the warehouse, probably for the clerks, or whomever managed the warehouse goods. Alys squeezed my hand to signal that she'd heard them too. We crept our way forward. When I neared the door to the room, I could distinguish the voices enough to realise I recognised one. Alessandra. And she was speaking Italian.

I withdrew the dagger at my side silently and motioned for Alys to remain where she was. I pushed the door a fraction to see inside. Alessandra stood beside a table, wearing a dark travelling cloak and veil. She was talking to a man, counting coins from a bag in her hand.

"It is too much," she said. "We agreed a price and I will go no further."

"But you said that I would sail with you so that I might return to Venice, when we agreed that. Now you say I must remain behind for a month to secure this next shipment of goods and yet you leave me no more to do so. Nor have you given me enough to pay my fare back home."

"Circumstances have changed, as I've told you. But the price was agreed, you signed a document."

The arguing continued and I could hear the impatience in Alessandra's voice. She would dispatch the man soon, one way or another, I thought grimly. Though I could see no other men to guard her, there might be someone inside who was out of my view. I pushed the door a little more, hoping their voices would cover any noise. My breath caught. A small golden-haired child stood a few feet away from Alessandra, her fingers in her mouth, her eyes opened in fear. She clutched a wooden dolly that was half covered by the dark cloak she wore.

Behind me I heard Alys gasp. Hearing the sound, Alessandra turned and upon seeing us, snatched up Eleanor in her arms. The child cried out in alarm.

"Eleanor!" Alys, rushed into the room and I followed close behind her.

"Mama!" said Eleanor.

Straining forward, Eleanor stretched out her arms for Alys but Alessandra held her back. Alessandra reached inside her cloak and pulled out a small dagger.

"Stay where you are," Alessandra said. She pressed the knife against Eleanor's neck. "Or this dagger will find its way across her throat."

I halted a few feet away and pulled Alys behind me.

"Now, Alessandra," I said in Italian. "You don't want to harm the child."

"That's true, but if I must, I must."

"Give the child to me, and I promise that you can do what you will to me. It's me you want to injure, after all."

"Though that offer is tempting, I prefer to leave with my fortune and plans intact."

"We'll let you leave, without any hindrance to do as you wish, if only you give us Eleanor," said Alys.

Alessandra looked at Alys. "Ah, poor Alys. So concerned for her child at last. You didn't care enough when you wanted to go traipsing after your lover. I'm afraid it's too late now. I have my plans. Now, if you'll just let me leave, I promise you no harm will come to the child when she's in my care."

"What do you plan to do with Eleanor?" asked Alys, her eyes blazing.

"Now that would be telling." She looked at the man in front of her. "Come, take your money and we'll leave. You can escort me to the docks." She turned to Barnabas. "An extra bit of insurance that you won't try anything."

I watched as she threw the remainder of the money pouch towards the man. He scooped it up with a nod took up the rush light that sat on the table and held it aloft for her as she led the way, past me and then Alys, through the door and into the warehouse. I followed her, looking for a chance, any chance, that I might safely knock her over. Alys closed in on her, reaching forward to touch Eleanor's fingers which were clutching Alessandra's neck.

Alessandra turned and gave an angry snort. "Stay back," she said to Alys.

"Can I at least kiss my daughter goodbye?"

Alessandra laughed. "Do you think I'm a fool? Stay there, or your daughter will have a cut throat. It would take very little for my hand to slip."

While they spoke I edged toward the man. I swept forward and knocked the rush light from his hand, sending it flying. I hoped at the very least to send us into darkness so that I might have a chance to disarm Alessandra.

For a brief moment the room dimmed and I lurched forward, but Alessandra was quick. She stepped back several paces and the opportunity was lost. Behind her, the straw went up in a blaze of light and the whole warehouse became alive with flames that spread quickly, licking the bare wood, the open half packed chests, while the sacks and barrels provided only more fuel for the fire.

Smoke clouded the room and Alessandra screamed, dropped the knife and froze to the spot. Eleanor joined her cries, wriggling away from Alessandra with all her might. Alys rushed forward, taking advantage of Alessandra's paralysis, and snatched Eleanor from her. A moment later, a burst of flame shot out, catching Alessandra's veil.

I watched a moment in horror as I saw the flames consume Alessandra, the veil melting under the heat to reveal her scarred face, twisted in pain. She screamed and fell, the rest of her clothes alight. Her body burned hotly and the screams stopped. She was dead.

I turned and made my way to Alys, coughing at the thickening smoke. When I reached her I pulled my cloak to cover her and Eleanor against the flying sparks and tried to find a path to the door.

The fire was spreading quickly and I was blind from the burning flames and the smoke stinging my eyes. Coughing, I moved in what I hoped was the right direction, dodging around a cask that had just caught fire, the brandy that was doubtless inside giving a great burst that erupted into a ball of flames. I continued to head blindly, until someone grabbed my hand and I was pulled forward. A few moments later cold air met me and I inhaled deeply. I was outside.

I pulled the cloak from Alys and Eleanor and looked at their soot stained faces. Eleanor whimpered softly while Alys made comforting noises and stroked her head. Suddenly, filled with an overwhelming amount of gratitude, I took the two most important people in my life into an embrace. My family. Something I'd never had before. Something I would treasure as long as I lived.

CHAPTER TWENTY-EIGHT
LONDON, EARLY WINTER, 1448
BARNABAS

I stared at my daughter as she lay asleep on our large bed. She looked dwarfed among the pillows and coverlets. The heavy bed curtains were drawn back just enough that we might check she was content and she could see the room if she should wake. Without the full protection of the curtains to block the draught of the early winter nights in the sizeable room, I had pulled the coverlets high and lit a brazier.

I never tired of looking at her, her sweet golden curls, her long lashes resting against rosy cheeks. I dared not approach closer, for fear of waking her. She was still so anxious and a sudden awakening might frighten her. It was only in the last several days that she'd allowed me to hold her and I didn't want to ruin the slow healing that was taking place in her, in all of us.

Alys came up behind me and rested her head on my shoulder, her arms slipping around my waist.

"She looks so peaceful there," she said.

I nodded and slid an arm around her shoulder. She nestled into me and we stood together in silence for a few moments.

"Your chest is packed," she said softly. "The servants have taken it down to the dock for loading, along with the other items."

I was sailing back to Bruges to arrange for the sale of the goods I'd left there. Since I was now part of the English Merchants' House in Bruges, it made sense to continue my trades from there for the time being.

I kissed her head. "Thank you."

"You will be back for Yuletide, won't you?"

"I will. Didn't I promise you?"

"Yes, but it's important that you be here." She looked up and smiled at me. "I think there might be more to celebrate than just Christmas. Hal has finally asked Joanie to marry him."

"How did that ever happen?" I asked, grinning. "I thought he'd been unable to utter those words ever. Did he get someone else to ask for him?"

Alys gave a soft laugh. "As much as I was tempted to do that, it didn't reach that point. No, I sat him down and told him he must stop being such a fool. That Joanie adored him, but she would never ask him directly."

"So Joanie asked you to get him to offer marriage?"

She tilted her head. "Something like that."

"And she said yes? More fool her."

Alys gave me a light slap on my chest. "Be happy for them."

"I am, of course. You are gaining the sister you always wanted and I am gaining....? Let's see, Hal is already my business partner, my brother-in-law. Joanie is my friend. But now I suppose I'll have a sister-in-law."

"You're gaining a larger family."

I squeezed her. "And someday an even larger family."

"Yes. God willing."

I stroked her chin. "Well, I'm certainly willing to try as often as possible."

Alys blushed becomingly, no doubt recalling our lovemaking just hours earlier when Joanie and Hal were out with Eleanor, and the rest of the household were engaged elsewhere. I blessed my fortune again that the trading and funds I still had from my journey east allowed us to live in this house in Westminster, just a short wherry ride from the docks.

"But Joanie and Hal will still stay here with us. I should hate to part with them."

"Of course," I said. "If that's what they wish. They belong here with us. And, if the time comes that our family should increase, well we'll just get a larger house."

Alys laughed softly and squeezed me. It was a sound I would never stop tiring of. With a woman I would never stop loving. I was content to begin my sojourn back in London. My home. A sojourn I had no intention of ever ending

You can learn more of what's coming next by signing up for my newsletter at www.kristingleeson.com

CHARACTERS

Venice
Barnabas/Giacomo/Jacko
Alys/Maria Barnabas's childhood sweetheart
Joanie-Alys's childhood friend, now servant
Hal- Alys's brother
Alessandra- former courtesan, Alys's sponsor
Tomaso the monkey
Tomaso Cortini- gamester and poet, friend of Alessandra's
Carlo Crivelli- a painter, Alys's mentor and admirer
Cosimo Fabriano- prominent Venetian politician who has bought Alys's courtesan's contract

Silk Route
Shafik ibn Taghri- Tyre harbour official
Abila- servant woman of Taghri
Cyla- Taghri's wife
Caterina/Halifa- Taghri's Italian concubine
Ahmad ibn Allah- merchant former Turkic JanissaryI
Padia – Greek woman who attempts to seduce Barnabas
Abdul Mansur- Tangir scholar on journey with father
Kasim Mansur- Tangir scholar
Usef ibn Battuta- merchant accompanying scholars

Famagusta, Cyprus
Floramundi- mistress off Caesare Ravella
Valentina- Courtesan Flormundi and Tomaso Cortini's friend

Samarkand
Ulugh Beg – Ruler of Transoxania.
Hosan- merchant in Samarkand

Xuan Zang- Chinese merchant
Razim Nezam-al-Molk – scholar at madrassa
Ali Qushji- court astronomer
Paris
Julia Barberigo- Alessandra's sister
Bruges
John Cardingham- head of English Merchant's House

HISTORICAL NOTE

The city of Samarkand was a fabled crossroads of the Silk Route and famed long before Timur for its diverse cultures and craft products. The Tang Chinese who traded with them were charmed by the exotic glamour of the city where they saw flute players, twirling girls, pygmies, leopards and golden peaches. The Arab invasion in the 8th century brought their own religion and culture, erecting mosques and deporting most of the population and eventually in a clash with Chinese, took some prisoners who showed them papermaking and other skills.

In the 9th century under Samanid rule did Samarkand grow anew as new buildings were erected including government offices, mosques, bazaars and warehouses. Walls and four gates were erected around the city and the streets paved with stone. As other groups invaded and took power in the ensuing centuries the population declined and Samarkand suffered. In the 13th century Genghis Khan invaded and plundered the city and slaughtering many of its inhabitants. In 1333 ibn-Battuta, dubbed the greatest traveller of pre-modern times still called it 'one of the largest and most perfectly beautiful cities in the world.'

Once the Turco-Mongol Timur (Tamerlane) achieved supremacy in Transoxania in 1370 and he chose Samarkand as his capital. He began a building campaign that restored the city to its former glory and even exceeded it with its stunning mosques, madrassas (schools) and mausoleums, topped with the fabled turquoise domes. Under his grandson, Ulugh Beg the city continued to blossom and grow.

Ulugh Beg was the grandson of Timur (sometimes known as Tamerlane) who founded the Timurid Empire. Timur recognised his grandson's talents, naming him Ulugh Beg 'grand duke' and took him on campaigns to the Caucasus and India. In 1419 when he was 15, his father made him viceroy of Samarkand and lord of Transoxiana. Ulugh Beg developed a love of mathematics, history, theology, medicine poetry and music and gave the city a reputation for learning and culture that drew many to it, including the Turkish astronomer Qazi Sadeh Rumi, who tutored the young ruler in that subject.

Ulugh Beg was so inspired that he ordered the construction of an observatory without equal on a scale to ensure unprecedented accuracy. He honoured honest debate among his scholars and with a group of scholarly experts Ulugh Beg charted the stars, devised rules for predicting eclipses and measured the stellar year to within one minute of modern calculations.

His knowledge and interests in the sciences did little to help his ability to rule and quell the growing hostility and power of the Sufic dervishes, nor his many sons' plots to overthrow him. In October 1449 one of his sons seized him and a secret court of dervishes dispatched him on a redeeming pilgrimage to Mecca. Enroute, his son arranged to have him killed. Ulugh Beg's trusted astronomer, Ali Kushji fled to Constantinople where he published the star chart to much acclaim in the Muslim world.

In the years following Ulugh Beg's death, factionalism and the city and region declined and the nomadic Uzbeks took control. In 1512 Babur, Timur's great-great-great grandson seized back control, but the Uzbeks chased him out towards India where he would later found the Mogul empire. As the silk route declined in use during the following centuries so did the fortunes of Samarkand, becoming virtually deserted by the 18th century until the Bukharan emir repopulated it in the 1770s.

The Silk Road/Silk Route, one of the world's great highways, acquired its name from a German scholar as recently as the 19th century. The great caravan route crossed not only China, but also Central Asia and the Middle East and consisted of a number of roads carrying a multitude of goods beyond the silk that has made it famous. Advancing year by year as the emperors pushed China's frontiers further westward it was ever at the mercy of marauding Huns, Tibetans and others. Consequently the Chinese policed it with garrisons and watchtowers. As part of this policing they extended the Great Wall.

Along the way the traders stopped at strategically situated oases, and as the trading traffic increased so did the importance of these oases who grew in prosperity, some becoming centres of trade. The journey was made most often by a mixture of donkeys, horses and camels. Camels could cover large distances in shorter times than donkeys or horses and were often used.

AUTHOR'S NOTE

I would like to thank profusely my Alpha Girls: Karen, Jean, Claire, Babs and Jane. Without their help and input this novel would be so much less than it is now.

Originally from Philadelphia, Kristin Gleeson lives in Ireland, in the West Cork Gaeltacht, where she works as a librarian and runs a book club. She holds a Masters in Library Science and a Ph.D. in history and for a time was an administrator of a large archives, library and museum in America. She also served as a public librarian in America.

Kristin Gleeson has also published *The Celtic Knot Series* and *The Highland Ballad Series*. A free novelette prequel, *A Trick of Fate* is available free on Amazon and other retailers. In addition to her novels, she wrote a biography on a First Nations Canadian woman, *Anahareo, A Wilderness Spirit* that is also available.

If you have enjoyed this book please post a review. It helps so much towards getting the book noticed.

If you go to the author website and join the mailing list to receive news of forthcoming releases, special offers and events you'll receive *Along the Far Shores,* and *A Treasure Beyond Worth* a **FREE prequel novelette** to *Along the Far Shores.*

www.kristingleeson.com

www.ingramcontent.com/pod-product-compliance
Lightning Source LLC
Chambersburg PA
CBHW031035120726
47905CB00007B/2195